God has moved mountains to get me here. He's given me people in my life to push and encourage me, a church family that supports me and the right contacts to make this dream a reality.
To God be the glory!

RAINSTORM

CINDY BONDS

Scrivenings
PRESS
Quench your thirst for story.
www.ScriveningsPress.com

Published by Scrivenings Press LLC
15 Lucky Lane
Morrilton, Arkansas 72110
https://ScriveningsPress.com

Printed in the United States of America

Paperback ISBN 978-1-64917-104-7

eBook ISBN 978-1-64917-105-4

Library of Congress Control Number: 2021937279

Cover by Linda Fulkerson, bookmarketinggraphics.com

ACKNOWLEDGMENTS

I have a lot to be thankful for as this book comes to publication. I have a wonderful team of women who have helped me form and shape this book into a suspenseful novel. Big thanks to Linda, Shannon, and Elena!

I also want to thank my current hometown! I've had so much support from family, friends and people I've never even met! Thanks to the local VBC Library that helped to announce my first release as well as this one. Also big thanks to The Pottery Shop for being so willing to sell both of my books locally in their store.

PROLOGUE

A jolt of blinding pain woke her.

"Laurel?"

That voice ... it was familiar.

"Come on. Open those eyes."

Taking a deep breath, she squinted, Uncle Walter's face finally cleared through the blurriness.

"What happened?" she whispered, the pain in her jaw made her moan.

"Now, take it easy. I was going to ask you the same thing."

"Mom ... mom was ..." she closed her eyes, trying to find the memory from the blurred moments of last night.

"Where's your mom?"

Her body ached, her head spun.

"Laurel?"

"I don't remember what happened. Where's my mom?" Her mind eased as darkness sank in once more.

1

15 Years Later

R ain trailed off the brim of Laurel Ashburn's hat as she pushed the release on the jack.

She shook out her freezing hands and shivered at the cool, autumn air hitting her soaked fingers. The breeze shifted, driving the rain onto her skin like icy darts. "The one day I don't pack a rain jacket."

Laurel took in a deep breath, the chilly air stung her throat. Fall had come to Cave Springs, Arkansas, and with it, rain showers and cool evenings.

Lights engulfed her. She heard the sound of a car pulling up from behind and frowned.

"Of course, after I get the tire changed, someone wants to stop and help," she muttered, yanking the jack from under the car.

With a sigh, she stood and turned, raising her hand with a wave. "I'm fine, thanks. Already changed the flat." She motioned to the figure stepping from the car.

Popping the trunk, she dropped the jack inside and slammed the lid down. As she turned, an imposing figure stood only a few feet behind her. She jumped. His face was barely visible in the night and the shadow of headlights.

"Oh, um, like I said, I'm good." She turned to walk away when his hand gripped her left elbow.

She spun, fisting her right hand and yanking her elbow away. Her instincts went on high alert as she pulled the keys from her pocket. Something didn't feel right, and her gut told her to get ready to fight.

"You should come home with me." The ragged voice echoed, the man angled into the light.

Taller than her 5'5" frame by a good six inches, the man was skinny but broad-shouldered. His large, wide-brimmed hat collected rainwater falling in sheets. It rolled off the side as he tilted his head. Dark eyes and a narrow nose disappeared, replaced by a brooding smirk.

"No. I'm going home." She narrowed her gaze, threading the keys between her fingers.

A chuckle echoed over the sound of the rain, then he lunged. Stepping back and out of the way, she jabbed the keys into his arm, then punched his side as she rushed past him.

He straightened, turning with a grunt.

"You're surprising." His murmur barely sounded over the wind.

The man produced a knife from his pocket, and she frowned. It had been years since her training, and after moving back home, she hadn't needed it.

Laurel steadied her breaths and waited for him to attack. Blocking his first punch with the knife, she landed a hit to his chest with the keys. But they fell from her grip as she side-stepped another thrust at her body.

A kick to his leg as she deflected the knife put him on his knees. The glimmer of her keys on the ground took her focus for a second. As she sprinted to pick them up, she heard his breath behind her. Suddenly, heat and pain surged through her back.

With a scream, she turned, landing a punch to his chest. He

reacted with another slice of his knife, catching the back of her arm. Yelling again, she gripped his hand with her right and twisted his wrist until the blade fell.

He yelled, then threw a wild punch. She dodged, pulled his arm behind him, dislocated his elbow, and then his shoulder. A hit to his back, then a sweep of her leg put him to the ground.

Trembling, she hobbled to the front of her car. Using it as a brace, she slid around the side and away from the headlights that lit the road.

2

"Mrs. Beecham, I'll be glad to make a trip out to check." Detective Dev Hollister rolled his eyes as he stood, searching through the paperwork on his desk for his keys.

"I'd rather Walter go and check for her. He knows her." The older woman's voice went stern.

"Like I said, ma'am, Walter went home sick. It's just me here tonight. I'll take a trip around town and then head your way."

"Fine, that's fine." Her sigh echoed.

He smirked. "I'll call if I find her."

Pulling on his rain slicker, he shoved his baseball hat on and headed out to the cruiser. The rain came down in waves, and the radio said the weather would just get worse as the night went on.

He sighed. "God, I know you had a plan bringing me out here, but I'm not so sure."

After two years as a beat cop and then seven years a detective in Little Rock, Dev had grown weary of crime. The constant death, destruction, and lawlessness that affected the innocent ate at him for years. After his injury last year, he was done.

With months of leave time stacking up, he took it all, then handed in his resignation. He figured he'd be able to find another job somewhere. His buddy pushed him into this one, a county detective in rural Arkansas. After lots of prayer and distinct thoughts of running away, he got a call with the job offer and decided to follow God's lead. For about a month now, he'd been here, enjoying the slow pace, the area, and the people. Most of them anyway. He heaved out a sigh.

Mrs. Kendra Beecham. He'd been warned to keep on her good side. Not that she wasn't nice—she just expected things to happen her way and in her timing. And she had connections in town.

Like tonight. Mrs. Beecham wanted someone to check on her girl. She kept repeating that phrase as if her girl didn't have a name. It was Laurel. Laurel apparently got off work at six and hadn't come home yet. Mrs. Beecham said her girl would've made it home by no later than seven, even if she stopped for dinner. So here he was, eight o'clock at night, driving in the rain through town, expecting to discover Laurel out on a date or with friends.

Seeing nothing similar to her car in town, Dev started toward Mrs. Beecham's. On State Road 19, the rough gravel reminded him just how different roads were here than in the city.

His eyes focused on red taillights. A car up ahead fishtailed as the tires spun and sped away. He flipped on his blue lights and pulled up behind another car still parked on the side of the road. The make and model matched Laurel's.

Grabbing his flashlight, he slid down from his truck, unsnapping his sidearm.

"Hello?" He shone the beam around the car and road. The light caught a glint. Striding up to the shimmering object, the long blade of a knife stood out against the dark pavement. Unholstering his sidearm, he called again.

"Hello? Detective Hollister here. Everyone okay?" He eased around the car to the front when something pointed pushed into his side.

"Who are you?" a whispered voice muttered as he raised his hands.

"Mrs. Beecham called. Are you Laurel?"

"Mrs. Beecham?" The voice sighed, and the object moved away from his side.

He turned. A woman with blood covering her shirt stood in the rain, keys threaded between her fingers.

"Are you okay?" He reached out, and she stepped back, holding up her hands.

"Yes. But you let him get away." She motioned down the road.

"We need to get you to the hospital. Come on."

"I—I don't need a hospital." She stepped back farther. "I don't think I need stitches."

"Either you get in the cruiser in the front, or I'll put you in the back for attacking an officer."

She crossed her arms as the rain continued to soak her body. "Fine," she gritted through her teeth.

"Wait in the car. I've got to bag the evidence before we leave."

Dev jogged back to his cruiser and grabbed a bag. After taking pictures of the car and knife with his phone, he pulled on latex gloves and slid the weapon into the bag. He secured it in the cruiser and noticed Laurel staring down the road, blood saturating the back of her shirt, her body completely soaked from the rain.

Grabbing his jacket from the backseat, he made his way behind her. "We need to go." After her backing away twice, he carefully stepped forward and slid the jacket over her shoulders. "Come on."

With a nod, she turned and pulled the jacket tight. He paused at her car and saw a handbag sitting in the seat. Opening the door, he grabbed the bag and phone, then locked the door before he shut it.

"You've got your keys, right?" He slid into the cruiser and looked her over.

She nodded and held up her hand. Taking out another bag,

he had her drop them in, then made a U-turn, he took off toward town.

"You don't have to drive so fast. I told you. I'm fine." Her voice was barely above a whisper.

"You're in shock."

"No. I'm not," she punctuated her words.

"Okay."

As he drove, he caught a glimpse of her face. When Mrs. Beecham said girl, he'd expected a teenager —not a woman closer to his age. Her jaw clenched, but with the ballcap on, he couldn't see her eyes.

"Tell me what happened."

"Don't you need to record it or something?"

He chuckled. "I've got a pretty good memory."

Her huff sounded over the pelting rain.

"I got a flat. There's no cell service on the road, so I changed the tire. A car pulled up as soon as I got done. When I put the jack in the trunk and turned, he was right behind me." She paused.

"And?"

"I told him I was fine." She blew out a haggard breath. "He grabbed my elbow and told me I should go with him."

Dev's jaw tensed. "So, he was trying to kidnap you?"

She gave a slight nod.

Heartbeat pounding, Dev shook his head. He'd been hoping for less crime when he moved out here. Evil seemed to be everywhere these days.

At the hospital, Dev pulled up to the ER and parked. He ran around the front, but Laurel got out without his help, trembling as he escorted her inside.

"We need to see a doctor, now."

The ER liaison stood with wide eyes, then ushered them back to a room.

"Someone will be here soon."

"Thanks."

The woman gave Laurel another glance before she closed the door.

Laurel let out a deep sigh and heaved herself onto the examination table. Hat still pulled low over her face, her dark hair stuck out from the back in a matted mess. Soaking wet and shivering, she was less than fazed. Her hands rubbed together from beneath the sheath of the coat.

A quick rap on the door, and a woman in scrubs stepped inside.

"Laurel? Oh my gosh! Are you okay? What happened?" The woman quickly descended upon Laurel, grabbing paper towels and handing them to her.

"It's fine, Liz. Don't worry," Laurel huffed as Liz pulled armloads of gauze from the cabinet.

"We need to get you cleaned up."

"If you could get her a set of scrubs, I need to get pictures of her injuries and gather her clothes for evidence."

The nurse turned to him with a nod. "Oh, yeah. Okay. I'll be right back."

As the door slammed, Laurel slid from the edge of the table. She took off the coat and her long sleeve flannel to reveal a snug, black tank top underneath. Her arms were toned, her shoulders broad. Dev pulled out his phone as she lifted her left arm. Frowning, he took a picture of the jagged cut.

"Turn around." Refraining from leading her, he snapped a shot of the same cut from the back. "I need to see your back where you were cut."

"No." She turned, crossing her arms as if daring him to try.

"Laurel, we'll need it for the report. To prosecute, we'll need all—"

"You won't catch him."

His jaw clenched. "Do you know who it is?"

She shook her head. "No."

As he started to debate her stance, the nurse returned with a set of scrubs.

"I'll be right outside." Dev left, closing the door behind him.

He pulled off his rain gear, piled it in the chair in the hallway, and leaned against the wall. Laurel acted odd for a woman who was just attacked. Shock would be the norm for any assault victim. But after talking with her in the truck and her calm demeanor in the exam room, she appeared more than centered. Maybe he needed to dig into her past.

The door opened, and he straightened.

"She needed some privacy." The nurse nodded and rushed away.

He needed a picture of her back, but based on her reaction, that wasn't going to happen.

Dev blew out a deep breath, grabbed his phone, and called Mrs. Beecham.

"Mrs. Beecham?"

"I'm on my way."

"What? I mean, how did you—"

"Word travels fast."

He sighed. "She's fine, ma'am. After she gets cleaned up, I'll take her to the station for her report, then I'll bring her right home. No need getting out in this weather."

"Well, I think I should be there."

"Um, ma'am? She seems to be just fine."

"Yes. Yes she would," the woman muttered. "Fine then. I guess I'll stay here."

"I'll get her home safe."

"Thank you, Detective. I appreciate all you've done."

"You're welcome, ma'am. That's what I'm here for." He slipped his phone into his pocket.

"You must be Detective Hollister." A sweet, southern accent made him turn.

Dev straightened as a woman made her way in front of him.

"Yes, and you are?" He smiled at the pretty redhead.

"Doctor Carrington, Lacy Carrington." She grinned big and offered her hand.

He shook it with a nod. "Nice to meet you."

"I'm so sorry to have to meet you over something like this." She tilted her head to the side, her lips parting with a smile.

"Yes, well, I'll need to get the information about her injuries for the report."

"Oh, of course. I hate that something like this happened to a woman like her." She frowned.

"What does that mean?" Dev crossed his arms.

She shrugged. "I mean, it's terrible for anyone, but for her." The doctor sighed. "She's been through so much, and she's, well ..." the woman leaned forward. "She's just a little different is all." The doctor winked and straightened.

Clenching his jaw, he tried to offer a smile, irritated that the doctor seemed so judgmental about an assault victim.

"Well, I need to get to work. Hope I'll see you around." She smiled and headed into the room without knocking.

Huh? Now he really needed to get some background on Laurel.

3

Gritting her teeth, Laurel tried to ease her breathing as the doctor pushed into her personal space.

Lizzy came back into the room, her arms full of equipment. She stacked it to the side, rushed over, and held up Laurel's arm. "She mentioned the cut to her back being pretty deep."

"I haven't gotten to it. I'll look at it in a minute." The doctor's harsh voice echoed in the small room.

Shivering, Laurel tried to relax her muscles as they pulled and ached from the cold.

"Okay, let me see your back."

She frowned and lifted her shirt slightly.

The doctor's mouth dropped for a moment and she glared. "What is that?"

"Previous injury."

"I don't have that in your medical history."

"You don't have my medical history," Laurel murmured, barely holding in her irritation.

"Dr. Carrington, I've known Laurel all my life—"

"When I need your opinion, Liz—" the doctor huffed and pushed at the cut, the rough gauze wiping across her skin. "It's not deep, just a rip through the skin and fatty tissue. We'll need to stitch it up, if the skin will hold."

"Can you let Lizzy do that?"

Dr. Carrington stepped back with a frown. "Why?"

"I want my arm taken care of first. It'll scar, and I want to make sure you'll take care of it properly." Laurel glanced at Lizzy, who frowned.

"Fine. We don't get much of these kind of injuries around here. She could use the experience."

Lizzy grabbed the syringe.

"No. No shots." Laurel groaned.

"You need the local before we take care of this."

With a sigh, Laurel nodded as the sting of the needle burned into her back, then her arm.

Closing her eyes and taking a deep breath, Laurel worked to hold off the uneasiness of having both women up in her space. The prodding and burning of the staples and glue was nothing compared to dealing with everyone pushing too close.

Numbness set in, and her jaw clenched as memories surfaced. Her scarred skin, the shouts of her shipmates, the smell of fire … Flexing her injured hand, she winced. Her mind jumped back to reality.

After the doctor left, Lizzy cleaned up the mess.

"You know why I did that, right?"

Lizzy's chuckle echoed. "Of course, Laur. I've known you too long. I'm surprised you held it together with both of us working on you at once. I'm sorry about Dr. Carrington. She can be … frustrating."

"That's an understatement," Laurel murmured. "Why're you still here? You could get paid better in a big city like Fayetteville. Then you wouldn't have to drive so far for class."

"I know. But I wouldn't have the help I do now," Lizzy mumbled.

She nodded and leaned against the edge of the table, exhaustion weighing her down.

"You have a ride?"

"I'm sure I have to go to the police station," she muttered.

As the memories piled up, Laurel did her best to push them back. There was no way she could get out of going to the police station. The detective needed to take her statement.

Laurel's worry amplified as she watched Lizzy clean up. Her attacker's strange voice echoed in her head. "Lizzy, be more careful. Okay?"

"You're the injured one." Lizzy frowned.

"I mean it. No being out by yourself at night. Promise me." A lump welled in her throat as she wondered if Tara had fallen into the same situation and was unable to escape.

Lizzy nodded. "Let's get you out of here."

Laurel straightened from the bed with a groan and paused to get her equilibrium. Still shivering, she followed Lizzy out to the nurses' station, rubbing her bare arms. The detective stood by the wall, speaking with Dr. Carrington. His eyes cut to hers a moment, and Laurel looked away.

"You working tomorrow?"

She nodded. "Of course."

"You need some rest." Lizzy sighed. "Here. Sign this."

Laurel filled out the form and signed at the bottom.

"We need to get to the station and get your statement."

She turned to the detective, then slowly to the outer doors. The detective paused, pulled on his rain gear, and handed her the jacket.

"It's still wet, but better than the alternative." He flashed a smile.

She pulled it on, shivering underneath the damp cloth. Once in the car, he turned the heat up, aiming the vents at her.

"You said we wouldn't catch him. Why not?"

Here we go again.

"I'm sure you've heard—"

"I've only been here a few months, and I'm not as interested in listening to gossip as you might think." He glanced her way.

She focused on the road. Maybe he didn't know, but the last thing she wanted to do was explain.

She sighed. "Never mind. I don't want to talk about it."

"If you know who he is, I need to know."

"I told you I don't." She clenched her jaw, pulling the jacket tighter as she stifled a shiver.

"Why don't I take you home? You can get dried and warm, then we can go over what happened." His soft voice was kind, unassuming.

How long had it been since someone spoke to her that way?

"No, I ... Mrs. Beecham, she'll be around. I don't want her to hear."

Silence lingered as her body trembled. She put her head in her hands and before she realized it, the detective stood outside her door, gently tapping her shoulder.

"Let's get inside."

Laurel unbuckled and slid from the vehicle. She gripped the door a moment, letting her body catch up. As he ushered her up the stairs to the office, the detective's arm gently settled around her shoulders, and she paused.

"I'm—I'm fine." She kept her gaze down and pulled away, uncomfortable with him being so close.

Once at the landing, he held the door open. She hesitated a moment.

"Something wrong?"

She sighed. "Not anymore I guess," she whispered.

Stepping inside, she swallowed the bile working up her throat. Being here, where her father worked, with the men who refused to protect her and her mother ... the memories overwhelmed her already exhausted body.

But there was no reason to be concerned tonight or any night, for that matter. The police department was no longer a danger to her, even if everyone who worked here thought she was a killer.

"Laurel?" The detective motioned to a desk in the corner.

The room was empty. No one else was around. A shudder ran down her spine as she walked to the desk and sat in the chair he offered.

"Take that jacket off." The detective pulled off his raingear and disappeared for a moment, returning with a sweatshirt and a blanket.

She pulled the soggy coat off her shoulders and handed it to him, accepting the dry offerings.

"You need help?"

"No," she muttered and slipped it on, groaning at the pull of her stitches. "I'll—I'll pay to get your jacket cleaned."

"No need."

He sat across from her as she wrapped up in the blanket. When he took off his ballcap, she finally got a good look at the newcomer. Her small town of Cave Springs had few people who moved in and hung around. Most residents drove to the city to work, thirty minutes away, if they lived here. Several got better jobs and moved out.

But she'd heard that Detective Hollister had moved here from Little Rock, looking for a slower pace. Well, besides tonight, he'd probably get his wish.

The detective let out a breath, slamming drawers and shuffling papers. He stood at least six-feet. He drug his fingers through his sandy brown hair a couple of times, and water drops flung around him. His square jaw sported a shadow, and his big, green eyes drooped when he looked at her, making him look sad.

"Tell me about the man. Can you describe him?"

"Six two, at least. He was skinny and lanky." She cleared her throat. "He had on a large hat, with a wide brim."

"Okay." He nodded as he wrote. "What else?"

She sighed. "His voice was strange, a higher-pitched sound. He'll have a dislocated elbow and shoulder, left side. He's a lefty." Pulling her hat down, a wave of exhaustion fell over her again.

"Left-handed? He attacked you with the knife in his left hand?"

"Yes." Her irritation burning through, she nodded. *How was that hard to understand?*

"Ms ..."

She looked up and found him waiting, pen in hand. "Ashburn, Laurel Ashburn."

"Just out of curiosity," he continued to write, "how did you defend yourself against a man much bigger than you, who had a knife?"

"Practice," she muttered. Laurel focused on her lap. Her hands ached, and her body eased.

The silence lingered.

"You ended your story with him lunging for you?"

"Yeah. He wanted me on the ground. After that didn't work, he pulled that knife. He wasn't all that strong. I just didn't ... I saw my keys on the ground, and for some reason, I went for them."

"You wanted to get away."

"No." She shook her head. "That's not usually my first thought," she mumbled, her voice growing soft and raspy.

The sound of movement drew her attention. The detective stood and walked around the desk to sit next to her.

"Let me see your hand."

"No. It's fine."

"You didn't have them check it out." He held out his, and she sighed.

Pulling the sweatshirt cuff from over her right hand, she lifted it. With a frown, he gently turned her hand palm up, then back around. Why was this strange detective taking such an interest? Fingers moved over her knuckles, down the back of her hand. He reached to the desk, pulled some tissues, and pressed them gently into the bloody cuts from the keys.

"You've definitely broken something. You need an X-ray," he murmured.

"It's fine. Wouldn't do any good anyway." She'd busted that hand so many times ... Shuddering, she pulled back and slid the sleeve back down. "After he hit me with that knife, I grabbed his arm and disabled him, then moved in front of my car to get out of the light."

He sat and watched her a moment, his sad eyes searching. *What did he hope to find?*

With a huff, he stood, walking back around to sit in his chair. "What kind of car?"

"Twenty ten or eleven Nissan Altima. I think it was navy, but it was hard to tell in the dark."

"That's pretty specific."

She nodded, rubbing her fingers over her pained hand.

"You don't miss much, do you, Ms. Ashburn?"

"No, I don't. Is there anything else?" She gave him a glare. It was getting late, and the question session needed to end.

Besides, as soon as Officer Lester informed the detective of who she was, her report would be disregarded as if she had made it all up. And once the new detective learned from everyone else about her troubled past, he'd also think she'd lied. It's as if the whole town were against her. Why did she even move back here?

Where would you go? The thought pushed through her mind once more.

"I just need you to sign this." He handed her a statement and a pen.

She stepped to the desk and signed the bottom of the page with a wince.

"I'll get you home." He slipped on his rain gear again.

After pushing away from his steadying grip, she slid into the front seat and buckled up, relieved to be out of the office and heading home.

She sighed. Between the attack and the memories of the station flooding her mind, there would be little sleep tonight.

4

"So, what is it you're not telling me?"

Laurel pulled the blanket tighter, ignoring the scenery as Detective Hollister drove. "I'm sure you'll be told," she muttered.

"I want to hear it from you."

Glancing over, she watched him a moment. What was his play here?

"Something you're looking for, Ms. Ashburn?" He gave her a smirk.

"Why do you want me to tell you?"

"I get the feeling whatever it is, you don't think I'll believe you."

"You already know I'm *different*," she air quoted with her fingers. "I just figured you already had your radar on."

That doctor better not step foot in her shop.

He chuckled, his deep voice echoing in the car. "Look, I don't know anyone or their backstory. It's easier that way. I'd much rather find out what's going on from the specific person instead of hearing the rumors that flow through a town like this."

"You'll get the speculation either way, Detective." She let out a huff.

"Dev. Just call me Dev."

She shook her head. That wasn't happening.

"Come on. What could it hurt?"

Biting the inside of her cheek, she let out a sigh. If she told him, and he didn't believe her ... Well, it's not like that would be new.

"One of my best friends disappeared right after graduation, twelve years ago. I left after my last day of high school, and when I came home six months later, I learned she was missing. The police couldn't do anything because she was eighteen. They kept telling me she must've run off with someone."

"And you don't think she did?"

"No. She's an amazing artist and got into some big, fancy art school up north. It was her dream, and she never made it there. I searched whenever I was home, which wasn't all that often. When I moved back a few months ago, I noticed ..." She shook her head. There was no way he'd believe her.

"Noticed what?"

She frowned and glanced up.

"Look, *different* or not, I want to hear what you have to say." He returned her frown.

"I looked into it, and there are almost twenty women missing from this county and neighboring counties since the year I graduated. In twelve years, that's a lot of women."

He nodded. "It is a lot."

"I recognized a few names, people from other schools, several from my graduating class. All the reports, which are public record, by the way, state there didn't appear to be any reason for those women to just disappear. All had reasons to be home or at their jobs or schools. No drug history, domestic charges, anything. It all seems ... strange."

He sighed. "I agree. I'm guessing the sheriff doesn't?"

"Not really. He said he'd look into it, and that it really wasn't my job to be so concerned." She let out a sigh. "I think that man, the one who attacked me, I think it's him."

"Who?"

"Whoever it is that's kidnapping girls."

Silence met her for a moment.

"Not that I doubt your instincts, but usually those kidnapped are right out of high school, young women who don't know any better. Why come after you? Especially so close to home?"

She faced him. His jaw clenched as he focused on the road, his fingers gripping the wheel.

"He's not from here, and there's no reason for him to be on my road. I know everyone on my road and their families very well. It's a dead-end road, and he doesn't belong. He said I was surprising. As if he knew me."

"The fact that he attacked you could be because he happened to be there. Right place, right time. It's not a well-lit area, and no one else was around. Sometimes it's the easiest explanation."

"But you don't believe that."

His jaw jumped. "I didn't say that."

"You don't have to." Sitting back in the seat, she stared out the window.

"I'll get your report filed tomorrow. If you want, I'll look into the others—"

"No. Don't do that."

"Why not?" He pulled into the large yard in front of Mrs. Beecham's, and put the car in park. "I thought you were concerned. Between the comments and all the digging you did—"

"It's not that. You have no idea what you'll be getting yourself into." She unbuckled. "If you start looking, people will think you're buying what I'm telling you. That won't bode well for you. Keep your distance, Detective. Being around me won't help your rep around here."

Without looking up, she pushed out of the truck and ran

into the house, regretting the decision, as the cuts burned. She shook the rain from the blanket and slammed the door shut.

"Laurel?" A familiar voice called out.

"Yes ma'am?" She stood in the foyer.

"I was so worried." Mrs. Beecham stepped in front of her, her eyes wide as she grabbed Laurel's hands.

"I'm sorry I worried you."

"Laurel, you know I care about you, right?"

"Yes ma'am."

"Sit, we need to talk." Mrs. Beecham huffed and pulled her to the couch.

Laurel sat down, wrapping the blanket around her shivering legs.

"First, are you alright?"

Laurel nodded.

"I'm not sure I believe you."

"I'm fine, really. Just cold."

Mrs. Beecham sighed. "You've been with me for how long now?"

"Almost fifteen years."

"Then it's time you started acting like my family instead of a hired hand. Laurel, I'm sorry about your background and that I wasn't able to give you a better life."

Her eyes went wide as she stared at the woman. "How can you say that?" she stammered. Her jaw dropped, and she willed her emotions to stay back. "You—You saved me."

"It doesn't feel like it. You're the same terrified 14-year-old girl who won't let anyone get close." Mrs. Beecham sat down next to her. "When you went into the Navy, I was so proud. But part of me worried. You've already given up so much of yourself, I was terrified you'd give up the rest. I think you came back worse off than when you left. That worries me."

"I didn't ... I mean, I think I'm fine. Better than I was." She bit her lip and pulled the blanket tighter.

"No, I'm not so sure, honey."

She sighed. "Is this about me dating?"

Mrs. Beecham chuckled and shook her head. "I'd never push you into that dear, never. But I do want to see you happy. There were so many times you were happy here, almost like you belonged. Then something would come and take it away."

It had happened like that so much in her life. That's why all the prayers and church talk felt empty. Nothing changed—no one was better off. She still struggled with her past and felt as if her small life mattered to no one, except maybe Mrs. Beecham.

Back in school, her two best friends had been a light, had given her hope and laughter. Then, it would all be taken away. A comment about her father, an attack on her character—it drowned out everything else.

"This life is a gift, dear. We've all been given something so rare and wonderful. You have talents, more so than I ever imagined. If you'd use those talents, serve with those talents, I have no doubt your life would be filled. God can use you, Laurel."

"God has had many chances to use me." Laurel sighed and sat back in the couch, her body finally easing. "If He had been so inclined, I'm certain my life would be different today."

"Don't give up on Him."

She looked into the kind woman's face. Those blue eyes from her childhood, the only adult who seemed the slightest bit interested in her future.

"I can't give up on something I never had." Laurel stood and trudged through the room to the kitchen. "I need to get cleaned up and to bed, I have work in the morning."

Pulling the blanket over her head, she took off through the back door to the guest quarters behind the old elm tree. Once inside, she threw the blanket in the laundry room, pulled off her soaked shoes and socks, and headed to her bathroom.

After stripping her wet clothes, she piled her laundry. The now soaked sweatshirt from the detective caught her attention, and she smiled. After tonight, he'd be told how crazy she was, a vet with PTSD who'd rather knock your head off than speak to you.

But tonight, he was kind, unassuming. Something new, since getting out of the service and returning to this town. Taking a few calming breaths, she started the shower and stepped into the warm stream. Working to keep her stitches dry, she washed quickly.

After talking about Tara's disappearance, Laurel's sadness intensified. Visions of Tara bounced through her mind, and the deep ache of worry and hurt pushed into her chest. Besides Lizzy, Tara had been her only true friend.

Slamming off the faucet, she stepped out of the shower and dried, then dressed. In the bedroom, she paused at the tattered paper drawing pinned for the umpteenth time to the wall.

Yellowed edges, rips along the corners, but the picture was clear as a bell.

Tara was an amazing artist. The sketch was of Laurel, of her profile, a hat sitting on her head, her messy hair hanging down around it. For some reason, of all the pictures Tara had given her, that one always stayed with her.

It reminded her of a different time. A younger version of herself—angry, hurt, and defenseless. Her burning cuts made her sigh. No longer defenseless, too tired to be angry, but she was sad, and she missed her friend.

"Tara, where did you go?" she whispered as she fingered the worn edges.

5

Dev strode through the office with a yawn.

The morning was slow—a wonderful change of pace from Dev's busy city days.

Leaning against the doorway of Sheriff McGehee's office, he let out a chuckle. "Where on earth did you get those cowboy boots? They can't be comfortable. Did you kill the alligator yourself?"

Walter McGehee let out a huff. "They're just fine. Work like a charm." He winked.

"I guess you're feeling better today?"

Walter sat at his desk. "Sure do. Just a cold, I guess. Did you take care of Mrs. Beecham last night?"

Dev frowned. "Yeah, her ... Well, Laurel was attacked. Here's the report."

"Attacked? What in the world?" Walter grabbed the folder and sifted through the pages. "We don't have much of that around here. What happened?"

"She had a flat and changed it. Then, someone stopped, attacked her, and drove off. I saw the car leave, got out, and found her. Good thing I did. Don't think she would've voluntarily gone to the ER."

"No, she's a bit stubborn."

"What does that mean?"

Walter looked up at him and sighed. "She's got a past. Lots of rumors flying around about her ... situation. Poor girl has some issues ..." He trailed off as he went back to the file.

"I looked her up and found nothing on file for her—no complaints, fights, or calls made against her. So, why do I get the feeling there's a lot going on?"

Walter shrugged. "Most people around her don't trust her, and others, well, I think they're afraid of her."

Dev huffed. "Afraid? Of her?"

"Let's just say, you should keep your distance. For your own good." Walter winked.

With a clenched jaw, Dev frowned and headed back to his desk.

Leaning on the desktop, his mind wandered to Laurel. What was everyone hiding about her? She seemed lucid and in control last night, and that was after someone attacked and tried to abduct her. Even she told him to keep his distance—for his own sake.

He shook his head and pulled up the town directory on the computer. Her car needed to be towed and searched for any evidence the rain hadn't washed away. And he wanted a look at her tire, maybe the flat wasn't an accident.

Both tow company lines were busy, so he grabbed his keys, shoved on his ballcap, and headed out to his car.

The afternoon sun was high, and Dev let out a yawn. After dropping off Laurel, he'd transferred the office phones over to his cell and went to his small house to get some sleep. Eight o'clock came early, and he regretted his decision to cut down on the coffee.

He pulled into the small mechanic shop to see if they towed cars. After almost five weeks, he figured he'd visited most of the local businesses. In the small town, there were only a handful of restaurants, gas stations, and some local shops.

The place sat empty—only one truck in the parking lot. The front door was unlocked, so he stepped inside. The smell of oil and gas filled his senses, but no one was behind the counter.

Walking back outside, he turned the corner into the service area. A car sat in the bay, the hood up.

"Hello?" His mouth dropped as Laurel came around the car, hat on her head and wiping the oil off her hands.

"What do you need now?"

Taking a quick perusal, he smirked at her rugged demeanor as if nothing at all happened last night.

"Detective?"

Dev forced his eyes up. "Why are you here?"

She shrugged. "I work here."

"No. I mean, I didn't know that." He shook his head. "But you should be resting."

"Why?" She dropped the rag, and he noticed her right hand heavily wrapped and taped.

"That, for one reason." He pointed to the hand, and she shrugged.

"Hey, Laurel!"

As Dev turned toward the voice, a low groan emanated from Laurel. A large, heavily muscled man walked in, a smile on his face. The man's gaze hit his, and the smile vanished.

"What're you doing here? Whatever you think she did, it wasn't her. She was with me last night." The man glared at the badge on Dev's belt.

"Oh really? That's interesting." Dev chuckled as he crossed his arms, but the man wasn't amused.

The man mirrored him, crossing his arms, and flexed his muscles. Taking some quick steps, he placed himself between Dev and Laurel. "What do you want?"

"No respect for the police, huh?" Dev frowned. His gaze drifted up as Laurel came back from around the car.

"Cut it out, Mitch. Here, take your car and go." She tossed the keys before Mitch could even turn all the way around.

Mitch slapped at the keys, barely catching them. "What's goin' on Laur? You need help?"

"Nope. Not at all. You can pay Chuck tomorrow. When I'm not here." She turned to leave, but Mitch practically jumped on top of her, grabbing her arm.

Laurel muffled a yell and maneuvered to bend back Mitch's hand. He yelped and released her. Dev took a step, pausing as Mitch reeled back, rubbing his pained wrist.

"Hey, easy! Just wanted to check on you."

"Back off. I'm not interested. I've told you several times. You grab me like that again, you'll find yourself hurting in more ways than one."

Dev stifled his grin, covering his mouth to stop the building chuckle.

"Fine." Mitch's face went red. "One day Laurel, you'll be asking for a date, begging. Don't come crawling back." Mitch stomped away.

Dev's chuckle came out, and he dropped his hand as Mitch left the building.

"Something funny?"

Turning, Laurel set a glare on him, her arms crossed and a red flush across her cheeks.

"Just, um … amused at how you handled that."

"It won't last. By next week, he'll be back." She huffed, leaning back under the hood of the car.

He followed, keeping his distance as she removed the air filter.

"How long have you worked here?"

"Long enough."

"Are you always back here or—"

She sighed. "No. I'm usually out front. But Chuck is sick, and I can do some of his work without his supervision." As she straightened and turned, red seeped through her sleeve.

"You're bleeding." He stepped closer, tugging on her shirt sleeve.

"I'm fine. Mitch just got a little rough."

He frowned. "You should've taken him down a notch."

This time she chuckled, and he saw the sliver of a smile. Nice.

"He's too big. It would take much more effort than I'm willing to dish out in order to bring him down." She pulled off her flannel and raised her arm to inspect the wound.

Taking hold of her elbow, Dev turned her arm and shook his head at the blood seeping through. "You have a med kit?"

"It's—it's fine," she murmured and stepped back, pulling her arm away.

"I should've arrested him when I had a chance." Dev reached for her elbow again, but she stopped him.

"I'll have Lizzy take a look later."

"I've got a kit in my car. Let me change out the dressing, and—"

"Why?"

He furrowed his brows. "What? What do you mean why? You're bleeding." He ignored her brooding stare. "Let me get the kit."

Hustling to the car, he pulled out the med kit and hurried back to the bay to see her flannel back on, tied around her waist.

"Come on, let me see." He sat down the kit, opened it, and pulled out some new gauze and a sterile pad. "I'm not leaving until we clean it up."

"Look, I can manage." She dropped her shoulders with a groan. "It's fine."

Waiting with gauze in hand, he frowned at the standoff. Why was this such a big deal?

The bill of her hat sat high enough he caught a glimpse of her eyes. Big and staring, he saw some of that fire from last night. Her jaw tensed.

"I'm just here to help. I feel bad enough that I let Mitch off. I should've stopped him myself." He waited.

Her body shifted from leg to leg. With a loud huff, she

slammed down the rag.

"Fine." She untied the ends of the flannel and pulled it off.

Laurel quickly unraveled the tape and gauze. He gently turned her to look at her wound.

"It's still together, but barely," he mumbled.

The angry red skin puckered, a few of the stitches pulled taught as blood seeped from under them.

With a sigh, he cleaned the area, then set the clean pad over the top. As he wrapped the gauze, he noticed the red tint creeping up her neck. That hat blocked a lot of her face, but he could see her jaw clenched, her bright pink lips pursing.

Taping off the injury, he cleared his throat. "Next time he shows up, call me, and I'll arrest him."

"Yeah, right," she muttered, stepping back and taking a deep breath.

Even now, the tank top clung to her curves, making him take a quick perusal before turning and zipping up the med kit. He sat on the barstool and watched wihle she eased the flannel back on.

"He shouldn't manhandle anyone, Laurel."

Her gaze flew to his, a clench of her jaw proved she wasn't interested in making friends. "Don't you have better things to do than sit here while I work?"

Car, right. Dev grinned as she stood with her hands on her hips. He was here about her car.

"I need to get your car towed. I want to take a look at the tire, and—"

"He didn't do anything to the tire."

"How do you know?"

"It was a screw. I found it after I changed the flat." She turned her attention to the air filter. "Besides, I kinda need my keys in order to get inside to get to the tire. Any idea when I can get those back? I had to go by and borrow Chuck's set to get in here this morning."

"I swabbed them and took some pictures. I'll let you know as soon as they can be released."

She nodded.

"Look, it's lunch time. Let's go grab a bite, and you can tell me why everyone here has such an interesting opinion of you." The words fell out before he could stop himself.

Normally that didn't happen, and he felt his face heat as she paused her work to glance up. That hat. He could barely see her eyes under that hat.

"I ... no, that's okay. Besides, I already told you. No sense in making things bad for you." She turned back to the car.

"I'm not asking for a date here, just a conversation." He frowned, the date thought now planted in his mind, and he wasn't sure what to do with it.

Something about Laurel Ashburn made him curious. Mystery surrounded her, and admittedly, that just made her more attractive. Although, her toned and tanned body was more than enough to amp up the attraction. She was tough, overtly independent, and he found all of it more than a little appealing.

"Detective, I can clearly see the difference, but most people will not. Now, I do have some work to do." She completely ignored him as she continued working on the car.

He stood with a sigh. "Take it easy, Laurel. Wouldn't want you back in the hospital because you got an infection, or your body just gave up from exhaustion."

"I'll be careful," she muttered.

Dev grabbed the kit and strode back to his car. He looked around the opposite side of the bay, but Mitch was gone. He'd have to look into that guy. Attitude and anger issues—Mitch was bad news.

After circling the block, Dev parked to the side of the station where he wouldn't be seen, and waited. Unless she brought her own lunch, she'd have to go eat soon.

While holding her elbow and wrapping her arm, he felt her shaking. Although, it could've just been him.

He let out smile at the thought.

6

"What happened?" He fumed.

"She's tougher than she looks."

He frowned at the incompetency of his hired hands. "I expect more from you. If you had done your job fifteen years ago, this wouldn't be an issue."

"I could say the same about you."

His jaw clenched. "I'd watch your words, Tobias. You're not as untouchable as you think you are."

"Look, I'm gonna need help if you want her gone."

Staring at the clock, he snarled, "Fine. But it comes from your cut. Don't screw it up again."

He slammed the cell phone on the desk, his head shaking. If he didn't get her out now, the whole thing would be blown. Not just the business, but his life as well.

And there was no way he'd let that happen. He'd come too far to be done in by some do-gooder.

"Your time has come, Laurel Ashburn."

7

After sitting in the cruiser for about twenty minutes, Dev watched the same pickup truck he'd seen in the front of the mechanic shop leave, heading down the old highway through town. Following, he kept his distance as Laurel made it to the outskirts and pulled into a small diner. He passed it by, then turned around, and parked beside her at the restaurant.

Peering through the diner's window, he found the top of her head in the back corner. With a grin, he strode inside.

"Hi, hun. Take a seat wherever."

"Thanks," he grinned and sauntered to the back corner. Laurel's eyes glared up at him from under her hat.

"Well, seems we both chose the same place for lunch. How about I join you?"

She leaned back and crossed her arms as he sat down. With the diner's bright lights, he finally got a better glimpse of her face. Bright blue eyes shown from under the hat's bill, making him smile that much more.

"Um, everything okay, Laurel?" A large man stood over them, his gaze on Laurel.

"Of course." She cleared her throat. "Darrell, this is the new detective in town."

Standing from the booth, Dev offered his hand to the large man. "Dev Hollister. Nice to meet you."

Darrell nodded as they shook hands, but his gaze went back to Laurel. "You okay after last night?"

"I'm good. Thanks."

"Don't drive home alone again. One of us will drive behind you."

Dev took in a breath at her smile, genuine and big. It lit her face. As Darrell left, he slid into the booth, trying to cover his shock.

"So, I guess not everyone shares the same sentiment about you."

Her grin disappeared, and she leaned back, crossing her arms again. "Why are you here?"

"I wanted to talk. Told you that."

"Are you ready to order?" The waitress from earlier appeared, and he grabbed a menu.

"Sweet tea, chicken fried steak, mashed potatoes with gravy, and fried okra."

The woman nodded and left.

"Aren't you going to order?"

"Already did." She sipped at her water.

The waitress returned with his drink, buying him a little time to figure out how to start this conversation.

"So, I'm guessing you grew up around here if you know so many people. What did you do after graduation?"

"Why?"

He shrugged. "Just starting a conversation."

She leaned forward. "Have you turned in the report on my attacker? What did everyone have to say?"

Narrowing his gaze, he frowned. "It's not like we had a morning meeting about it. I turned it into Walter, and we're looking into it."

She huffed. "Sure. That sounds about right." Turning to the

waitress, Laurel got her attention. "Look, I don't know why you seem so determined to get a read on me, Detective—"

"Dev." He interrupted with a frown.

"*Detective.*"

He could clearly see her eyes narrow from beneath the bill.

"But I'm going to warn you again—this is a bad idea. Even though the diner is mostly empty, you'll still get called out for sitting with me. People are watching already." She sighed as the waitress brought her a plastic sack with boxes inside and a to-go cup. "Thanks." Her gaze returned to him.

"If its Mitch you're worried about, I can handle it."

She stilled a moment, then shook her head. "Self-preservation in a small town is important. People around here don't want their beliefs contested. You need to remember that." Standing, Laurel marched toward the door.

As he watched her leave, several heads moved from her, back to him. Guess she was right—people were watching. Taking out his phone, he looked her up online. The database at the station didn't have anything on her, so maybe he could get lucky. Surely there weren't that many women named Laurel Ashburn in the area.

Several hits with the name Ashburn came up. A few newspaper articles included her name, and they were all from this area. The first he read made his jaw clench.

Thursday morning Mr. Baine came out to his field to work and found a teenaged girl. She was unconscious, beaten, and shaking.

"I ran and grabbed her up, brought her inside to Elizabeth, and then called the police." Mr. Baine commented.

The girl was identified as Laurel Ashburn, resident of Cave Springs. After waking, she informed police her father had been drinking, and she had run away, afraid for her life.

He stopped reading and sat back in the booth. A picture formed that made his stomach churn. It was one of the reasons he quit the police business in the first place. The innocent children who always ended up in the middle of heartbreak and chaos gnawed at him for years. Rescuing kids who were beaten on and abused, used as punching bags for parents or boyfriends or girlfriends—it took its toll.

Now, here was Laurel, right in the middle of it all.

"Here you are. Sorry Laurel had to go. She's busy."

A food-filled plate appeared in front of him.

"I imagine she is."

The woman left, and he went back to the search, pulling up each article. Most only used her father's name, no mention of a mother. Her name was listed as daughter of Guy Ashburn, the sheriff from two decades ago. Apparently, the man had died the night Laurel was found, and his wife had disappeared. But the official cause of death wasn't reported.

Setting his phone on the table, he sighed, staring at the plate. It looked and smelled delicious, but his appetite was long gone. As he took a drink of tea, a figure moved into the booth opposite him.

"Hey, man. That looks good."

Dev nodded to Deputy Tim Morris. "Yeah, it does. What're you up to today?"

"Just sitting out, looking for tickets." Morris winked as he called over the waitress and placed his order.

Maybe Morris knew what was going on with Laurel.

"How long have you been in this town, Morris?"

"About three years."

"But you didn't grow up here, right?"

"Nah." Morris shook his head. "About an hour north of here. Why?"

"Just wanted to get some insider information."

Morris chuckled. "This about Laurel?"

"Yeah. Seems the word has spread about last night."

"And today, I'm assuming. She always eats lunch here, sits in this booth usually." Morris winked. "Look, I can tell you what I know, but it's not much."

"Shoot." His appetite picking up, he started in on the potatoes and okra before cutting a big piece of steak.

"When I got here, there's all these small-town dynamics. I was told of a few names that needed to be kept happy, I'm sure you were told about them too."

Dev nodded, Mrs. Beecham being the primary one.

"So, all was going well until a few months ago, when I met this woman named Lizzy Thurstinson."

"The nurse?"

Morris gave a grin. "Yeah. We just talked a little at the diner in town, just friendly. I was warned to keep my distance."

"What does that have to do with Laurel?" Dev took another bite.

"I'm getting there. I asked why the warning. Lizzy's really nice and down to earth. Then I found out she has a kid, and Laurel is her best friend."

"Okay." This information still didn't explain much.

"The kid thing kinda threw me a little, wasn't expecting that. But when I asked about the friend and why that mattered, I got an earful. There's this rumor about Laurel. Her mother disappeared back when she was a teen, and the whole town thinks she had something to do with it. Some people even think she's the one who killed her father."

"What?" Dev dropped the piece of steak to the plate and wiped his mouth. "That can't be true."

Morris shrugged. "Lester filled me in, once I went out a few times with Lizzy. He said it looks bad on the police department if I'm involved with someone who's so close to her. She's a bit of wild card.

"Basically, the night her mother disappeared, Laurel was found way out in the woods somewhere and had no memory of that night. But Walter found her father at their house, blood everywhere, and her father dead on the floor. Lester mentioned that Laurel always had a temper, and she had some blowout fights with her mom."

Dev sat back in the booth with a gaping mouth. "I don't believe it. I mean, that seems thin. Walter didn't find any proof of where the woman ended up or what really happened with her father? There has to be evidence that he was murdered or that he killed himself."

Morris shook his head. "To this day, no one knows. Laurel apparently high-tailed it out of here right out of graduation. Came back to visit Mrs. Beecham every so often."

"Wait—Mrs. Beecham?"

"She's her foster mom. After being released from the hospital, Walter arranged it so she could stay with Mrs. Beecham instead of going into foster care."

Dev couldn't believe the story. "I've asked around about what the deal is, but no one will give me a straight answer. Laurel won't even talk to me."

Morris grinned. "Yeah, I noticed her too, once she moved back. She's hot."

"Not like that." Dev shook his head with a frown. "I just wanted to understand. A few people have warned me, made comments. I just don't get it."

"Well, I'm sure that's not the whole story."

"It's not." The waitress slammed down the plate in front of Morris, making the gravy splash onto the table. "If you want to keep eating here, you keep your rumors to yourself. Neither of you are from here, and you have no idea what you're talking about." She hung her hands on her hips, a frown on her face.

"Sorry, really." Dev sighed. "I'm new around here. Just trying to figure out why I'm getting so much flack just for asking."

"It's small-town business, you wouldn't understand. If you want to come eat here again, talk about someone else." Red faced and huffing, she turned and walked off.

Darrell stepped next to the table with a glare. "Outside."

"Look man, I'm just—"

"Now," Darrell added as he walked down the hallway and out the back door.

Morris waited until the man passed, then focused on Dev with a smirk. "Want me to call in backup?"

"No—just make sure no one messes with my food." Dev slid from the seat and hurried down the hallway.

Outside the back door, Darrell leaned up against a black pickup truck.

"Darrell, right?"

Darrell nodded. "Look, I'm just going to say this, but don't tell Laurel."

"Okay."

"Her father was sheriff, but he was a bad guy. He used to beat on his wife, beat on Laurel. One night, he killed his wife—made her disappear. Then, he turned the gun on himself. "

"Then how—"

Darrell held up his hand, and Dev clamped his mouth shut.

"Her dad had a lot of connections. They let him get away with the drinking and everything. When her mother disappeared and her father was found dead, Laurel moved in with Beecham. All the rumors—people are scared of her, think she was part of it. That's a lie." Darrell wedged his large frame into the truck's cab.

"How do you know ?"

Darrell started the truck and stared ahead for a moment, his beefy elbow hanging out the open window. "Laurel's been my friend all my life. Mostly the only friend I've ever had. She looked out for me. I used to be, smaller." He grinned a crooked grin. "Laurel doesn't deserve this town. I tried to get her to go somewhere else, but she wants to be here for Beecham."

"Still doesn't tell me how you know all this.""

"I know Laurel. She would never do anything to hurt her mom." Darrell shrugged. "Tread lightly, man. You'll be out of a job if you dig too deep. The sheriff's department takes PR seriously. Anything that makes the department look bad will be dealt with." Darrell shook his head and pushed the truck in gear.

The small, black truck disappeared, and Dev frowned. There

was no way a man, a sheriff, could beat his wife and kid like that and not get punished. Right?

Darrell had to be wrong.

Turning back to the diner, Dev sighed. What had he just stepped into the middle of?

8

"You survived." Morris grinned, wiping the gravy from his mouth.

"Yeah, he just wanted to warn me to stay clear." Dev said it loud enough to be heard. The last thing he wanted was for anyone to think Darrell gave out information, even if that information had to be wrong.

"I've got to get back. See ya."

Dev nodded as Morris left. He finished the last remnants of his meal. Leaving a twenty to pay for his meal and a healthy tip, he headed out.

Back at the station, Dev pulled up his email, looking for an answer to the partial print he found on the knife handle. The system was still running from this morning. Maybe the crime lab would have better luck once they received the knife.

Pulling up the initial blood report, he sighed. Type and crossed, the blood came up the same from the clothes, keys, and the knife. That meant it was probably all Laurel's and no one else. The rain had effectively ruined any chance of DNA evidence.

"Hey, Hollister."

Dev glanced up at Officer Lester. "What's up?"

Lester leaned a hip against the edge of the desk. "What's with pursuing Laurel Ashburn?"

He frowned. "What're you talking about?"

"I just heard you're getting pretty cozy with her. Visiting her at the shop and now lunch?" Lester's eyebrow rose.

"First off, I had no idea she even worked there. Secondly, I was on my lunch and drove out to the diner at the edge of town. I saw her there and decided to have a conversation."

"Concerning what?"

Dev leaned back in the chair, contemplating his words. He wasn't interested in making waves after working here only a few months. However, he didn't like the fact he was being questioned. It seemed Darrell and Morris were right.

"She was attacked last night. I wanted to see how she was doing."

"I've read the report. She received minor wounds. The guy she injured is probably much worse off."

"Minor wounds?" Dev's eyes widened. "Stitches and staples don't really scream minor wounds from a one-sided knife fight."

Lester shrugged. "She's got issues in her head. Hears and sees things that aren't there. She attacked her mother as a teen, killed her. Probably killed her dad too."

"So, you're saying she's mentally ill?" That was a lie. There was no way Laurel suffered a mental illness that devastating. Not to mention the malicious comment that she'd killed her parents —without a shred of proof.

Lester nodded.

"I'm sure more people just didn't come forward. They all felt sorry for her, you know." Lester waved his hand, as if that would be enough of an excuse.

Dev's jaw tensed, nodding along to the outrageous story. "And so now, you believe because of her mental illness, she's making up her attack, and that she actually attacked someone else?"

"Probably. I'm guessing a nice man tried to help her, and she flipped out. And now with all her other skills, it wouldn't be a fair fight."

"What other skills?"

"Laurel went into the Navy after high school. Failed out of it too—screwed something up, so they discharged her. From what I heard, she's lucky she didn't get put on trial and thrown into the brig."

"And I'm assuming this is a reliable source, claiming she should've been arrested once discharged from the Navy?"

Lester huffed. "Look, I'm just telling you what I know to be true. I grew up around here before I left for the Army. I've been around her family all my life. Her dad was a good man."

"I've heard mixed reactions about him." Dev clenched his jaw as he returned Lester's glare.

"Tread carefully, Dev. This is a career killer."

"What is? This case where a woman is a victim of a violent crime and attempted kidnapping?"

"*She's* a career killer. As far as my opinion, she's an outright killer. You get involved with her, you lose credibility, and you'll lose your job."

"What?" Dev's mouth dropped at the accusations. "First, you're telling me she's a cold-blooded killer. Then, you assume I'll be involved with her for some reason other than the case. You're pushing awfully hard." He narrowed his eyes.

Lester straightened. "Just trying to give you fair warning."

He walked off, and Dev tapped his fingers on the desktop. Morris wasn't kidding. There was a lot of animosity in this town regarding Laurel.

Turning to his keyboard, he logged into the system. It was time to do a deeper background check on Laurel Ashburn.

9

Pulling up to the diner, Laurel slid sluggishly from the seat. Her back and arm burned—her body, exhausted. It wasn't just her injuries and the attack ruining her sleep. Nightmares flooded her mind as she relived old times from her childhood, living with her father. She shuddered.

Shrugging off the ache, she sighed—four hours left of work. At least Tonya promised a sweet tea and fried pies to get her through.

An older couple exited the diner, and she stepped in to hold open the heavy glass door.

"Oh, thank—" The woman paused mid-sentence with a scowl.

"Let's go, Marsha."

"That poor, poor sheriff."

Her jaw clenched as the husband tried his best to move the older woman along.

"That poor woman, disappearing, and her husband killed. How terrible." The woman called over her shoulder.

Taking a deep breath, Laurel walked inside and noticed her table was taken.

Shoulders slouched, she trudged to the kitchen.

Tonya flitted from the counter to the stove, pencil behind her ear, and a stern expression on her face.

"Hey, Laurel."

She nodded to Casper behind the grill and perched on the wooden stool in the corner.

"Hey, hun. I'll get your order ready in just a bit."

"No rush." Laurel waved off Tonya. "Not hungry anyway," she muttered, hooking her heels on the rung and leaning on her elbows.

"Your booth taken?" Casper gave her a wink, and she huffed.

"It is, but that's not the issue. Besides, I have to take it to go. I work till seven, and Tonya promised me a pick me up."

"Bad day?"

Laurel nodded at Tonya as she pushed past her knees to get to the fridge.

"Then why're you here?" Darrell stood in the doorway, leaning against the frame.

"I always eat here." Laurel shrugged.

"No, why are you *here*, Laurel?"

Laurel rolled her eyes at his question and leaned back with a groan. "Where else would I go, *Darrell?*" She punctuated his name with a frown.

"You had some friends when you served, right?"

"Not really." She edged around the stool and leaned her shoulder against the wall. "It's just been a long, frustrating day."

"Call me when you're ready to leave the station. I don't want you driving home alone."

"That was a fated coincidence." Laurel frowned at Darrell's need to hover. "The flat tire led to wrong place, wrong time." That's how that detective put it anyway. "I've got Mrs. Beecham's truck. It's in great shape—won't be an issue."

Darrell huffed and tossed his work gloves in his toolbox.

"Why are you back here?" Laurel watched Darrell latch up the toolbox.

"Tonya called with a leaky sink and a crack in the molding."

Darrell grasped the toolbox and pushed in front of her. "You should call me. Or that detective guy. He seemed ... competent."

Feeling her face heat, she reigned in her reaction. "I'll be fine."

"Keep your eyes open." Darrell shook his head as he turned. "Let me know if you need anything."

"Thanks," she mumbled as he left.

"He's not wrong."

With a sigh, Laurel looked up to a smiling Tonya. "About what?"

"That detective seemed very competent. He asked questions, didn't seem interested in the rumors, but wanted the truth. I think he was looking you up on his phone. Of course, that was before that other officer came in and told him everything."

Laurel groaned and held her head. Great. Like she needed anyone else poking around into her business and making assumptions.

A bag and cup were thrust into her vision and she took them. "Thanks."

"Get some rest tonight. You need to start taking better care of yourself." Tonya's frown deepened.

"I will," Laurel slid off the stool and headed toward the back door.

A picture sat pinned to the wall and she paused. Her, Lizzy and Tara—their senior year, eating at the bar.

"Tonya, did you ... when Tara disappeared after graduation—"

"Laurel, don't go bringing all that up again."

She turned at Tonya's quiet voice. The woman wiped her eyes.

"I'm sorry. I just, I can't just let it go. Tara deserved much more."

"You all deserve much more." Tonya's heavy sigh echoed in the room. "Tara had that amazing college waiting for her, Lizzy deserved a husband who wanted to be a father," Tonya's jaw clenched as she shook her head. "And you deserved a future. One surrounded by happiness." Tonya took gentle hold of her arm. "Don't give up on it yet."

Staring at the picture on the wall, Laurel realized even then, she never considered a future, peace, happiness. The few smiles she ever shared were with these two girls. Now, one of them was missing, and she was doing nothing to help.

"Laurel?"

"Hmm?" She turned to see Tonya with tears in her eyes. "Now, don't go getting all upset. I'm sorry I brought it up. Besides, Lizzy will find a good guy who wants to be a dad." She winked.

"If I'd known anything about her marrying that loser ... I mean, I'm her sister." Tonya groaned. "She should've told me."

Laurel chuckled and took off out the door. Leaving Tonya irritated was better than leaving her sad.

Edging around the side of the building, Laurel paused. The smell of cigarette smoke filled the air.

"She's here."

Freezing at the man's voice, she silently leaned against the wall.

"Fine," A loud huff sounded. " But any trouble, and I'm out."

She heard the diner's door open and peeked around the corner. A man she didn't recognize sat at the bar. Wearing a blue trucker hat and button-up flannel, he was obviously searching the diner for someone. His head craned this way and that.

He couldn't possibly be looking for her. She didn't even recognize the guy. But still, after last night ...

Rushing to her truck, Laurel started it up and headed back to town. Watching her rearview, the highway stayed empty. A breath escaped her lips.

"Stop being so paranoid," she muttered and pulled back into the station's empty lot.

THE LONG DAY was almost over.

Laurel sat in front of the computer, looking over the statements and invoices. Since everyone knew Chuck was out, no one would want to see her. They'd wait until tomorrow to pick up their cars or equipment, leaving her with little else to do. Her eyes crossed as she stared at the numbers on the screen.

"Good grief," she muttered, sitting back and closing her eyes a moment.

Intense loneliness and sadness pushed the air from her lungs. Darrell was right, she never should've come back here. The memories were bad, a lot of people hated her, and she was miserable. But Mrs. Beecham had been there for her, so she would be here for Mrs. Beecham.

Thinking back to the summer before high school, a shiver shook her body. Clips and pictures flashed in her mind, very few allowed her to actually see what happened that night. Even now, fifteen years later, she had no idea where her mother was, or how she'd ended up in the woods.

The doctor had claimed the concussion was the issue. Laurel's head injuries from being hit repeatedly made her brain swell. Memory was spotty from that night, but only that night. She remembered everything else quite clearly.

It all began when her father started drinking. Then, he'd lash out in his alcohol-infused anger. Her mother hid her bruises and helped Laurel learn how to use makeup on her own.

'We have to protect Daddy's job. He didn't mean to hurt us— he's just ... upset.' Her mother's words echoed in her head, and she swallowed hard at the bile rising in her throat. Snatching the drink from the counter, she sucked the straw until it gurgled.

Although she didn't remember all of that night, she knew her father had finally killed her mother. He'd hit her so hard, it killed her. But with her mom's body gone and only blood remaining, there was no way to prove it. Especially since he decided to kill himself. He would've been the only one to tell the truth, and it died with him.

Without evidence to prove her father's death was a suicide, Walter was forced to enter it as a homicide. Then, Laurel woke up confused and telling Walter that her father had beat her and her mother. The community wondered why she would tell such a lie about the sheriff. After all, he'd saved a family from a burning house and rescued a child from the river, all in one October night. They all thought him a hero.

And now, as an adult, things were worse. No one bothered hiding their stares or attitudes, their contempt for her. The ones who lived there at that time felt for their beloved sheriff. This town blamed Laurel for his death. They said he was so upset about whatever Laurel had done to her mother, that he couldn't go on. Either that, or they really thought she had pulled the trigger.

Sighing, Laurel glanced up. Six o'clock. Just one more hour. Chuck wouldn't care if she left early. But something inside nagged her to hang around, keep the doors unlocked and the lights on.

"Fine, just fine," she muttered to herself as she went back to the computer, working through the numbers.

At seven on the dot, Laurel shut down the computer and locked the bay doors. She came back to the front, and a truck pulled into the parking lot.

"You have got to be kidding me." She continued through the office, turning out lights and gathering her phone.

The truck sat, idling in the darkness. Setting the alarm, Laurel stepped outside and locked the door, then headed to her truck. The truck's headlights were on. The brake lights lit up, but no one came out.

Working to ease her nervousness, Laurel slid behind the wheel, backed up and turned onto the highway. Raindrops pelted her windshield, splattering across the windows and hammering down on the roof.

She blew out a haggard breath. The new detective came to mind. He was working an angle. She just wasn't sure what. He must want something from her—something he wanted her to admit.

The headlights from a truck lit her vision in the rearview mirror. Glancing up, the shape of the grill, the size, it looked remarkably similar to the one from the station. Keeping a steady speed, she took a few deep breaths, the headlights disappearing as the truck inched closer.

"Nothing to worry about, just—" Before she could finish the sentence, her truck was bumped from behind.

Shoving the pedal to the floor, she sped up, trying to keep ahead. Horns blared as they passed, then the truck pulled up next to her on the two-lane highway.

"What are you doing?" she yelled as the truck slammed into the side of her vehicle.

Spinning the wheel to the left, she managed to stay on the road. The truck smashed into her again, and she turned the wheel against it, hoping Mrs. Beecham's larger truck was heavy enough to stay upright against the attack.

Headlights blinded her, and the truck's driver suddenly slammed on the brakes and moved in behind her. A semi passed, blaring his horn, the truck behind her nudging the bumper.

Refraining from slamming on her brakes and causing a wreck, Laurel sped up. Her phone lit and she groaned. The ringtone continued as she pumped her brakes and tried to get the attacker to back off.

The truck appeared to her left again, crashing into the side and sending her tires into the grassy ditch. Swerving, she ended up behind the attacking truck and frowned when she saw the license plate covered.

Laurel's road came up, and she slammed on the brakes, the truck flew down the highway as she fishtailed onto the dirt road. Speeding down the gravel, she pulled into the back driveway. She hit the brakes. The truck slid to a stop in the mud as she jumped out and waited.

As she sat in the rain, the attacking truck roared to life,

flying down the road in front of her. From behind the rose bush, she watched it pass by, not even braking at the drive. Frustrated at her inability to see anything more differentiating than a dark color, she got back in her truck with a groan.

She parked outside her porch, bit her lip, and held her up phone. Her fingers hovered over the keys as her internal debate reasoned out a call to the police. As much as she wanted to report the attack, she had nothing to give them. No make and model or color in the darkness.

"Wouldn't matter anyway," she murmured.

Sliding down from the seat with a groan, she shivered under the stinging raindrops and hustled up the steps.

She snatched the handgun from her desk drawer, rushed back outside, and sloshed through the mud to the edge of the drive. As she knelt down behind the rose bush once again, her body burned and ached. This road was a dead end, the man in the truck would have to turn around and head back this way at some point.

After twenty minutes of waiting in the mud and rain, she gave up, shivering and soaked. It didn't make sense. She knew everyone on this road, each farmhouse and drive. No one around here looked like the man from the diner, and none of them would attack her. Ignore her maybe, glare at her, but not outright attack her.

At least, she thought it could be the man from the diner. In the chaos of trying to keep from crashing, she never really got a good look at the driver.

But where did the truck go?

Rubbing her cold arms, she tromped toward the house. Pausing at Mrs. Beecham's truck, she sighed. The bumper was barely hanging on. The driver's side door was covered in scratches and dents, paint transfer too. But in the dark, it was impossible to determine the color.

Laurel climbed the stairs and looked back to Mrs. Beecham's.

Before going to bed, she'd have to double-check the locks and alarm on the main house.

With a sigh, she stepped inside, and pulled off her muddy boots, then trudged to the kitchen. Groceries. She forgot to get groceries. Opening the fridge, an empty set of racks sat inside— milk, eggs and some lunchmeat looking back at her.

The diner sounded good, but it was too far away, and she was too tried to drive all the way out there and worry about that truck again.

Groaning, she pulled out a can and opened it. As she prepared the soup, the thought struck her that the detective might actually be sincere. After all, Darrell was even better than her at judging character. Maybe she should call in the attack.

Rolling her eyes, she shoved the bowl in the microwave.

"No sense wondering about it. Not with Officer Lester there. He'd set the new detective straight."

Pulling her phone from her back pocket, a missed call registered on her screen. She scrolled to the unknown number and frowned. No one ever called her, except Mrs. Beecham on occasion, maybe Lizzy when she wasn't working.

Who could it possibly be?

10

Laurel settled on the couch with dry clothes and her soup when the doorbell rang. She never had visitors, so she grabbed the handgun, shoving it into the back of her pants. A peek out the window, and she stifled a groan. Officer Miles Lester and Officer Morris stood on her porch. Taking a deep breath, she yanked the door open a crack.

"Yes, what do you need?"

"We need to talk." Officer Lester gave a glare.

"About what?"

"Just let us in."

"No thanks." Stepping out, she slammed the door and pushed past them.

Once she stood on the porch, Mrs. Beecham came running through the yard.

"What's going on? Miles? Is that you?"

Officer Lester pushed out a meager smile, nodding at Mrs. Beecham. "Yes ma'am. How are you, Mrs. Beecham?"

"I guess it depends on what you're doing here." Mrs. Beecham crossed her arms as she stood between Laurel and the officers.

"There's been a complaint, and well, Laurel's gonna have to pay for her actions."

"What actions?" Laurel kept her arms crossed and her back away from them.

The last thing she needed was for them to see the gun and go full tilt. Lester already thought she had killed her parents. If he went off on her tonight, he'd probably say it was self-defense.

"We have you on tape accosting a man."

"What?"

She ignored Mrs. Beecham's gasp.

"Where, when, and who?"

Officer Lester frowned. "You know you did it. Just admit to it, and we'll go easy on you."

"No." She shook her head.

"Miles, I'm her council. Explain these charges." Mrs. Beecham straightened.

"A man called in, claimed he was attacked off the county line road, right past the diner." Lester crossed his arms. "He gave a description that matches Laurel here to a *T*. We're waiting on the warrant for the video."

"A man with a vague description. That's not even enough for a warrant."

"What time?"

Mrs. Beecham turned to her and frowned.

"It was around six thirty tonight."

Laurel smirked. "I was at work."

Officer Lester shook his head. "No one can confirm that. We all know Chuck is sick."

"His cameras can."

Officer Lester's face turned red.

"Guess you didn't know Chuck put in new security cameras. They'll prove I was at work, sitting at the desk, and working on the computer until seven tonight." Her grin widened as she felt vindicated for the first time in her life.

"You can fake those."

"Miles, we're done here. You need to go." Mrs. Beecham pointed to his vehicle, and Officer Lester's face dropped.

"Look, Mrs. Beecham, I'm just doing my job."

"Lester?" Sheriff Walter McGehee made his way across the yard to the porch. "What's goin' on here?"

"He's trying to arrest Laurel without so much as a warrant." Mrs. Beecham's cheeks reddened.

"I have proof."

"What proof?" Walter leaned against the railing, crossing his arms. "I was just at the station. Didn't hear anything about Laurel acting out."

Officer Lester's face turned bright red. "It's her. We all know she did it. The description the man gave matches her perfectly."

"Where's the video?"

Officer Lester's jaw jumped. "Tonya, from the diner—she's getting it for me."

"Well then, I'll want to take a look. Let's head back to the station."

Officer Lester gave Laurel one more glare before stepping off the porch and high-tailing it to his truck. Officer Morris gave a nod, following suit.

"What're you doing here, Walter?"

Walter gave Mrs. Beecham a quick hug, then stepped in front of Laurel. "I wanted to check on Laurel."

She offered a smile. "I'm fine. Not too bad."

Walter frowned as he looked her over. "I read the report, those stitches—you sure you're all right?"

Laurel pulled her elbow from his grip. "The cuts aren't deep. Did you hear about whatever Lester is talking about?"

Walter shook his head. "No, never heard about any report of an attack. I guess I was out of the office by the time they called."

She huffed. If there even was a phone call.

"Well, I'll be going. Let me know if you need anything." Walter gave her a wink and took Mrs. Beecham's hand.

"I'm going to sit out here with Laurel for a moment."

Walter's eyes cut to her, and he nodded. "I'll speak with you tomorrow." He descended the steps and slid into his truck.

"We need to talk." Mrs. Beecham led her into the house.

Before she sat down, Laurel pulled the revolver and placed it in the drawer of her desk.

"What are you—you had that on you?"

"Yeah, with everything happening, I just—I wasn't expecting company." She shrugged and sat down. "What? I have a license."

Mrs. Beecham blew out a breath.

"What's wrong?"

"Miles."

Laurel clenched her jaw 'til it ached.

"Miles Lester was a troubled boy. He stayed with me for several years."

"Laurel frowned. "I never knew that."

"His mother passed away when he was young, and his father raised him. His father is my late husband's nephew, and since I had no children ... Miles stayed with me for the last few years of high school. He really was a kind child, but he was always so mad."

Kendra sighed. "He got into some trouble, and Guy didn't want to see him go to jail. The judge decided he could go into the military instead. I convinced him to agree, and when he left, he was so angry with me—I never thought he would speak to me again."

"Why did he come back here?"

"I guess to prove to everyone that he'd matured, changed. But I'm afraid he might still be upset with me for making him leave. I'm afraid he might try and take it out on you."

Laurel sat next to her on the couch. "Mrs. Beecham, you need to stop worrying about me. As long as I know one person in this town who won't believe the rumors and the lies, I'll be fine." She offered a smile.

Tears built in Kendra's eyes. "I'm so sorry things have been bad for you, dear. I still don't know why you came back." She took Laurel's hand. "You know, if you would take off that hat and look people in the eye, things might change."

"Looking people in the eye and telling the truth was what got me into this mess." Laurel chuckled. "No one wants to look me in the eye." She shook her head and tried to stand.

Mrs. Beecham held her down. "No, telling the truth is always the right thing to do. Don't ever let anyone tell you different. God has a plan and—"

"Please, just stop." She held up her other hand, working to ease her tone. "I'm not going to ever do better than I am right now. This is my life, and it's better than practically any other time I can remember.

"You gave me a chance, and I hope I haven't made it a complete wreck. I did try, even though I'm pretty certain it didn't always look like it." Laurel frowned. "Look, I won't set myself up for a fall. I've lived most of my life that way. After I left and went into the Navy, I decided I trust who I know and that's all.

"God doesn't know me, and I sure wouldn't recognize Him if I saw Him. I'm sorry if that's not what you want to hear, but I—I can't do it anymore." She squeezed the older woman's hand.

As they sat in silence, Laurel cleared her throat. "By the way, I got rear-ended today on the road. I'll pay for the damage to the truck, it's not that bad—"

"Are you all right?" Mrs. Beecham's worried eyes looked her over.

Laurel smiled. "I'm fine. But I'll have to get Chuck to work on the bumper." Her heart heavy at the lie, she tried to reason it out. Worrying Mrs. Beecham wasn't an option.

She stood, grabbed her soup bowl, and took it to the microwave to heat up.

"No, no more soup. Come with me. I have leftovers in the fridge."

"This is fine—"

Mrs. Beecham yanked Laurel away from the microwave before she could respond.

ON THE COUCH, watching a game show with Mrs. Beecham, Laurel sat her plate on the coffee table. Mrs. Beecham was definitely the best cook she knew, besides Tonya at the diner, of course. It felt good to be here with her again, reminiscent of her teen years.

She stood and took her plate to the kitchen. A knock sounded on the door. The clock on the stove read eight forty-two. "I'll get it."

"Nonsense." Mrs. Beecham waved her off and opened the door.

"Mrs. Beecham, hope I'm not disturbing you." The detective's voice carried from the porch, his figure darkened in the doorway.

"You have got to be kidding me," Laurel mumbled and turned to finish washing her plate and fork.

"Of course. She's in the kitchen."

Dropping the plate in the sink, she spun to see Mrs. Beecham bringing the detective into the kitchen, a smile on his face.

With a huff, she turned back to the sink.

"I hope there are no more problems." Mrs. Beecham's tone was more than icy.

"No, no problem. Why? Was there one earlier?"

"Just checking. I'll head upstairs. Turn off the lights, will you?"

"Yes ma'am," Laurel called over her shoulder, hearing the woman's footsteps on the staircase.

Rinsing off the dishes and grabbing a towel, Laurel dried off her plate and cup. "What are you doing here?"

"First, what problem?"

She sighed. "Nothing worth mentioning." Putting up the dishes, she hung up the towel and turned off the light above the sink. "We can talk outside."

Keeping her focus off him, she walked through the house, turning off the lights. Laurel grabbed her hat from the coffee table. She ushered him out, checked the alarm, then locked the door and pulled it shut behind her.

"Now, why are you here?" She shoved the hat back on, looking up at him. "I figured you got enough commentary earlier."

"What's with the hat?" He leaned against the pillar, crossing his arms.

"It's a hat. You wear one too." She sighed and took off down the steps. "Look, I've had a long day, and I'm going to bed. Either ask your question or leave."

His footsteps followed her from the porch and around the house to the back yard.

"Oh, I had no idea this was where you lived."

"Really? You expect me to believe that?" She shook her head, pausing to watch him a moment. "I figured that officer gave you the rundown of everything."

"What officer? What rundown?" Shoving his hands in his pockets, the detective narrowed his eyes.

"Doesn't matter now. But just so you know, I'll be armed a lot more than normal," she muttered as she turned back to her house.

"What? Hey, hang on." Detective Hollister hurried in front of her, blocking her path. "What's going on, and why will you be armed?"

"I have a permit."

"I know you do, but why would you suddenly need it?"

"After being followed home and almost run off the road, I need something to protect myself with."

His jaw clenched. "You were run off the road?"

"What? You don't believe me?"

"You should've called it in."

"Why would I do that?" She huffed. "No one at that station is going to believe me, much less do anything about it. By now you know all the gossip. Between the rumors and Officer Lester, there's no point in even trying." She pushed past him. "Besides, Officer Lester has this grudge or something. He'll be begging for that man to come back and finish the job, take care of me, so he won't have to deal with me anymore."

Dev grabbed her elbow. Twisting away as she turned, the detective's hand dropped, a solemn expression across his face.

"No one would want that, Laurel. I don't believe that for a second."

"Then you don't know how this town works." She sighed and took off toward her house, his footsteps sounding behind her again.

"Why didn't you tell Walter?"

"He's already done enough for me," she murmured, knowing full well he was already tending to that lie about her beating someone up in the parking lot.

"Hey, I've got something I wanted to talk to you about."

"Not interested."

"Look, I'm trying here—"

She spun and he almost ran into her, gripping her elbows to keep from knocking her over.

"Sorry." He grinned as her hands gripped his arms.

His thumbs moved up and down her already cold skin, making her stifle a shiver.

"Why—why are you trying, and what are you after? I'm not interested in some kind of closed-off relationship, if that's your intent."

"No, not my intent. But what does a closed-off relationship mean?"

She shrugged from his grip and stepped back. "Where we date, but no one knows it but us. It seemed quite popular when I was in school."

Detective Hollister shook his head. The grin fell from his face. "No, not interested in that."

"Then why are you here at night when no one can see you?"

"I'm here at night because I just got off work. I work during the day. I've been sifting through a lot of information this evening. This is the first chance I've had since I got off, so I came here."

"Why?"

He narrowed his eyes and shoved his hands back into his pockets. "There's something going on in this town. I can't explain it—something backward. And from what I've gathered, it revolves around you."

"Okay. But you do realize when Lester finds out you've been snooping, he'll get you fired, right?"

"He can't fire me. He's not my boss."

"Yeah, well, Lester has a lot of friends in high places."

"This job ... it's not ..." He shrugged. "I'm not chained to this job."

"So, you want to be fired?"

"No, not really. I'm good at my job, I enjoy the slower pace here."

"Then?" she shook her head with a huff, took the steps up the porch, and sat down on the swing.

Hollister turned the rocker to face her and sat.

"I'm not following here. Aren't you supposed to be some smart guy from the city?"

"Well, I think that was a compliment." He grinned.

She rolled her eyes. "I mean, I've tried to warn you, and you're not taking it seriously. What about your cop friend? Didn't he explain some of it?"

"So, you have spies too, huh?"

"What do you mean 'too'?"

"Well, after my lunch, Officer Lester already knew all about meeting you at the shop and us eating together at the diner."

She exhaled sharply and crossed her legs. *This should be good.*

"He seemed to think you were dangerous, a trained killer, if you will."

Uninterested in giving him anything, she waited.

"Lester mentioned your experience with the Navy and said you were kicked out."."

She stood and pushed past him to the door. "I'm not interested in going down memory lane, Detective. Find someone else to tell stories with. I'm sure someone like Dr. Carrington would be enthralled with anything you have to say." Stepping into her home, she tried to shut the door. Pressure from the other side stopped it from closing.

"Laurel, I didn't mean to upset you."

His big green eyes stared down at her. Why was he lying straight to her face?

"Of course you did. You want to gauge my reactions, see if there's any shred of proof to what Lester said. The whole purpose of this visit is to see how mad you can make me and see if I act out. Attack you or hit something." She glared as he leaned against the doorframe, his body blocking the door. A hint of a smirk formed on his lips.

"You don't seem as mad as I thought you'd be."

She stilled. For him to admit she was right—that was new.

"Well, you should've mentioned my mother. That's the only thing that gets to me anymore. All the rest is just ... it's old news. The same disasters I've dealt with all my life. Nothing much gets me anymore, Detective. I'm too tired to be mad." She shook her head and tried to shut the door again.

His hand stopped it.

Letting out a breath, she frowned. "What are you doing?"

"I thought we could have that talk. No one's here to see us, to make you so uncomfortable."

"You think I'm uncomfortable?"

He shrugged and gave her a grin. "If no one is around, then why can't we talk?"

"I'm tired. It's been a long day, and—"

"I tried to call and check on you earlier. How are your injuries?"

Pausing, she made herself close her mouth. His big green eyes searched hers once again, that sadness peering through.

"Laurel?"

"I—I'm fine."

"You say that a lot."

The air heated as the silence stretched. With no idea how to counter his comment, she cleared her throat.

"I'm not a charity case. I'm not looking for someone to fix me, Detective. That ship has sailed. I'm just trying to survive. That's where I've lived my whole life. Now, if there's nothing else—"

"Laurel?"

She paused, the gentle sound of his voice, much more pulling than she wanted to admit. He took a small step, closing the gap between them.

"If that truck comes back, call me. I'll earn your trust a little at a time, if that's what it takes. I don't want you thinking you can't call on anyone if you need help."

"I don't need help."

He frowned, looking her over. As his arm went up, she thought for a moment he would reach out to her, but he ran his hand through his sandy hair instead.

"Everyone needs a little help at some point in their life."

"Yeah, well, I've needed a lot in my life, Detective. But when no one shows, you learn to depend on what you can do. Good night." She stepped back to shut the door, locked it, and sucked in a deep breath.

Collapsing on her couch, Laurel tried to ease her breaths and the pounding in her chest as his footsteps sounded on the stairs.

Was he really just trying to push her buttons? Was that it?

With her mind spinning into overdrive, she shook her head, then stood and headed to the bathroom to shower. She needed a distraction, a break, a—

Her phone chirped as a message came through. Furrowing her brow, she pulled the phone from her pocket.

Laurel, it's Dev Hollister. Just wanted to remind you of my name, seems you forget it often.

She wanted to frown that he felt the need to text her, but a smile came out instead. Seemed he did try and call, the number matched the unknown caller during the car incident.

My memory is fine, Detective.

Good. Maybe next time you can determine the make and model of the truck following you.

It was dark.

Then call or text next time. I can follow it, and maybe I'll get a good enough look to figure out who it belongs to.

Swallowing hard against the need to mouth off, she made herself pause. He was trying to help, and besides his job and who he worked with, there was no reason to doubt he wanted something more. Yet.

Good night, Detective.

Night, Laurel.

11

Dev switched from messages to the camera app on his phone and took a few pictures of the truck's damage.

The driver's side was scratched and dented, some paint transfer stood out along the back bumper as well. Even if Laurel didn't want to file a report, he hoped he could get a look at the other truck from some of the traffic cameras in town.

Based on the transfer and the height of the scratch, it was a dark, large pickup.

With a sigh, he climbed into his own truck and headed back to town.

His focus skewed as he balanced his worry about the truck and seeing her so relaxed. It was surprising to see her standing at the sink, washing dishes in those faded jeans, boots, and tight T-shirt. But to see her without the hat hit him hard. Her amber hair and blue eyes stood out in his mind.

Maybe he could set up a deputy on her road. Walter might be okay with that. Maybe.

He gripped the wheel tighter. Laurel's demeanor and attitude struck a nerve. She was calm, down to earth and ... amazing. Admittedly, he'd wondered how well she was really doing. But now, he couldn't deny Laurel was more than competent. Whoever attacked her, picked the wrong woman.

Taking a deep breath, he tried to ease the anger boiling at the thought of someone assaulting her. The wave of emotions hit him, just like when he finally quit the force and moved away from the city with all its chaos and hate.

All the work he did tonight revealed some interesting facts about Laurel and about the missing women she mentioned. On a whim, he sent an email to a buddy at the FBI, curious as to why the cases weren't being worked.

She was right—none of the victims appeared to be runaways, young girls just trying to get away from a family member or a domestic situation. But the high percentage of missing women ages 18 to 23 in this area alone during that time period was alarming. Hopefully, he could get an answer and some info on that case in the morning.

Pulling into his garage, he closed the door and slid out with a sigh. He stepped into the kitchen and flipped on the light. Stopping short, he stared at the wall. In large black letters the words *leave me alone* were scrawled in choppy handwriting. The clutter from his kitchen filled the floors. His jaw dropped.

What was happening?

He pulled out his phone and texted Laurel.

Just out of curiosity, what time did you get off work?

Seven, just like I told Lester. You don't believe me either, huh? Get the video from Chuck.

He dialed her number.

"What?"

He frowned at her clipped answer. "I still don't know what you're talking about. What happened with Lester?"

"Then why are you asking what time I got off? You think I did it?"

"Did what, Laurel?" He tried to ease his tone as he stared at the mess around him, the writing on the wall.

"Lester and Morris came here around 7:30 or so, claiming I beat a man up off County Line Road."

His heart jumped. "What? I didn't hear about that. I was at the office all evening. Why did the man think it was you?"

"Lester said the man called in, reported he was attacked, and gave a description that matched me. Said it happened about 6:30. Made Lester completely nuts when I told him to check out Chuck's new security video. It will show me there all night—'til 7:00." She chuckled.

Did Lester hate her so much he was willing to make up evidence just to get her in trouble?

"You didn't answer my question, *Detective*."

A lump built in his throat. "Someone trashed my house. Wrote *leave me alone* in marker on my wall."

Silence slipped by as he rubbed his hand through his hair.

"So, you think it was me?" her muffled voice sounded.

Nausea flooded his stomach. "No, not for a second—"

"Then why would you ask what time I got off work? Why would you call and try and get information about where I'd been tonight? You're the same as they are Detective."

"Laurel, listen—"

"Don't call me again." She hung up.

Dev groaned and tossed the phone on the table. He understood her anger, but he didn't ask because he thought her guilty. She needed a good alibi, someone who could vouch for her whereabouts. Because if he found any trace evidence here, he assumed it would lead right to her. Someone was trying awfully hard to set her up.

It took most of the night to clean up the mess and paint the wall several times, covering the marker. Dev's head ached from the fumes, and he was exhausted. He found the large, black marker behind his TV stand and wondered if it would be possible to get prints without anyone at the sheriff's office hearing about it.

In-depth conversations with women, other than Laurel, weren't the norm since he got here. Just like with the doctor, they were usually in passing or while waiting on something. He assumed that's why whoever did this tried to set her up.

Besides the deputies and Walter, he hadn't carried on a long conversation with anyone.

Sighing, he bagged the marker and decided to see if his buddy at the state crime lab could get a fingerprint match for him—something unofficial.

He showered and headed for bed. At least he didn't have to work tomorrow, just be on call in case something came up that the deputies couldn't handle. Which, in this small town, was next to nothing.

DEV WOKE to pounding on his door.

Rolling over, he groaned when he looked at the clock. It was a little after seven, and he'd gone to bed around four. Pulling on some sweats and a T-shirt, his head still ached from the paint fumes.

"Hang on!" he called as the pounding sounded again.

Opening the door, his jaw dropped. Laurel stood on his front porch.

"What did you do?" Her body rigid, she pushed into his space.

"What?"

"What did you do? Did you say something to someone? I tried to warn you and you didn't listen."

"Hey, hang on." His head spun between the fumes and her comments. "Come inside."

"No thanks." She held up her hands and stepped back.

He grunted and stepped onto the porch, closing the door behind him. "Just slow down. What happened?"

"Someone set Mrs. Beecham's rose bush on fire early this morning." Her neck and cheeks were red as she paced the porch.

"What? Did you call the station to report it?"

She turned to face him, her jaw clenched and body stiff. "And what do you think will happen if I do? Do you really think Lester or anyone else will care one way or the other? " She sighed and crossed her arms.

Exhaustion weighed on her, her shoulders slumped, and even without really seeing her full face from beneath the hat, he knew she was spent.

"Why didn't you call? You didn't have to come here."

"I did call, a couple of times." She paced a few steps. "Fat lot of good it did me," she muttered.

It was like a shot to the gut. Especially since he already told her he would earn her trust. "I'm sorry, I must've turned it off."

"Whatever you're doing Hollister, just stop."

"Why do you think it's me?"

"I'm sure you turned in a report about your house and how you thought I did it. If not, it's whatever snooping you're doing. Things were fine two days ago, but you're doing something to make this worse."

Before he could respond, she was down the steps and in her truck. As she backed out and left, he felt resigned. Although he didn't report the break-in, it could easily be something he'd done.

Last night, he'd spent all evening at work going through her history and anything that related to her time in the Navy. That included the missing persons files she told him not to bother with.

Groaning, he went back inside and called Morris.

"Hey, aren't you off today?"

"Yeah, I am." Dev yawned. "Have you received a call this morning? Something going on at Mrs. Beecham's house?"

"No. What's going on?"

Dev sighed heavily. "Meet me there in thirty, will ya?"

"Um, okay."

"Look, if Deputy Lester says anything, just tell him I asked you. If you can't, then fine."

"Okay, sounds good." Morris ended the call.

As Dev dressed, he couldn't help but think about Laurel—fuming and pacing his porch. She mentioned nothing else gets her worked up anymore except the topic of her mother. But her anger was clear this morning.

Then there were the missed phone calls. Yanking the phone from the charger, he groaned at the sight of the red light on the front. He had turned off the sound.

With a sigh, he grabbed his evidence kit and truck keys. The one thing that stuck out from this morning's interaction, she'd called him Hollister instead of detective. That was enough to give him a jolt, a burst of energy as he headed out the door.

12

P acing the room, he rotated his neck until a pop sounded.

What was it going to take to get rid of Laurel Ashburn?

He hadn't risked everything just to lose it because of her. Taking out every single person who interfered, meticulously keeping plans intact and cleaning up loose ends—he had done everything to keep his name clean.

"This has got to end," he mumbled.

Looking over his shoulder all the time, stressed that she would figure it out, remember everything that happened that night ...

Snatching his phone from the desk, he placed a call.

"What?"

"Why is she still alive?"

A tense silence lingered.

"I told you to take care of her."

"We tried. I've already talked to a friend. He's going to help me next time."

"This better be the last time. You got it?"

"Relax. I can take care of it."

He slammed down the phone. Relax—that's not something he could do. Not until she was gone.

13

Pulling up to Mrs. Beecham's home, Dev found an extra car in the driveway. He strolled across the lawn and rang the front doorbell.

"No, I'll get it, you stay there." Laurel's voice carried through the door. Once the door swung open, a frown appeared on her face. "Why are you here?"

"You reported a case of arson. I'm here to investigate."

Her jaw clenched. "I didn't report it."

"No, but I'm a detective, I'm sworn to help protect everyone. I can see you're upset—"

She slammed the door, and he heard the distinct click of the deadbolt.

"Well, that went just great." He stepped off the porch and headed to the still-smoldering rose bush on the far side of the property.

The road wrapped around this part of the yard. It wouldn't be hard for someone to stand here and not be seen from the house. He taped off the area and took pictures. After a few minutes, the eerie feeling of being watched pricked his neck.

As he turned, Laurel stood a few feet from him, staring intently at him. She sure was sneaky.

"Anything you want to add about what happened?"

She shoved her hands in her back pockets. "It was around 6:00 this morning. I slept in, since I don't jog on Wednesdays. Mrs. Beecham started screaming, and I ran out of the house. Once I smelled the smoke, I turned on the water and grabbed the hose." She nodded to the long green garden hose that snaked around the yard.

He eyed the hose, then took more pictures and studied the charred branches.

"It started from that side." She motioned to the darkest part of the bush. "Where's all your help, *Detective*?"

Back to detective. Great.

"I—he should be here shortly." He hoped.

"Yeah, sure." She grunted and headed back to the house.

Sifting through the grass outside the burned area, he found a cigarette butt.

"It can't be this easy," he mumbled.

Pulling out a bag, he used tweezers, picked it up, and sealed it in the bag. The sound of the screen door slamming caught his attention. Laurel and the nurse from the ER stepped off the porch and walked to the driveway.

"I'll just stay here with Mrs. Beecham today. Thanks for coming over early with him to check on her."

The nurse shifted the bag on her arm. "It's no problem really. Just make sure she gets some rest today and no more excitement. Her blood pressure can't take it. Are you sure you want to keep Johnny today? I can always find someone else."

"Not a chance."

He grinned as Laurel let out a smile, a real smile. A patrol car pulled in behind the sedan in the driveway. Morris got out and walked up to the two women.

"Hey, Lizzy. Everything okay?"

"Um, yeah. I just—I'm here to drop off Johnny." Lizzy grinned at Morris, who wore a stupid smile on his face.

Laurel, however, was done smiling and looked rather upset, standing with her arms crossed, focused on the two.

"Let me move my car." Morris rushed to the driver's side and slid in.

"It's fine, Laurel. Honest. He's a friend." Lizzy bit her lip as she stood in front of Laurel.

Laurel said something Dev couldn't hear then glanced at him for a moment before heading back in the house. Once Morris moved his car, he stopped and talked to Lizzy a moment before heading toward the scene.

"Have a nice conversation?" Dev grinned as Morris came up to the rose bush.

"Did you?"

Dev narrowed his eyes.

"I'm sure you've had at least a few since you've been here. How did you find all this out anyway?"

"Laurel." Dev frowned as Morris chuckled.

"Interesting. Find any clues?" Morris motioned to the smoldering bush.

"There's a cigarette butt." Dev shrugged. "I have no idea if it's related or not."

"Could be someone just threw it out and it caught fire." Morris shrugged.

"I don't think so. Too wet. It rained again late last night. Plus there's a smell of diesel. It's definitely arson."

They continued their search, finally finding one shoeprint in the mud-soaked ground.

"It looks like a man's shoe. Maybe a boot? See the point and the distance from the arch to the toe?" He knelt next to the print, pointing out the evidence to Morris.

"Yeah. Maybe."

Dev sighed. "Hand me my bag."

As Dev prepped the site for casting, he thought of who might be responsible for setting the bush on fire.

"Laurel reported it?"

"Yep."

"Does she know who it was or why?"

Dev glanced up. "She didn't mention anyone specific. Did you tell Walter?"

Morris nodded. "Yeah, he got on the phone with Mrs. Beecham. I have a feeling those two are more than friends."

"That was my thought too."

He let the mold sit for a moment, going back over the scene to make sure nothing was missed. Once the cast was put away, Morris drenched the last of the embers with the hose while Dev trudged to the house and knocked. He was surprised when Mrs. Beecham answered.

"I'm so grateful to you for coming. I just—I was so startled. I told Laurel it could've been an accident, but she was so upset and is determined to find out who did it." The woman clutched her necklace.

"Mrs. Beecham, do you have any ideas of who could've done this? I mean, if it wasn't an accident."

She shook her head, staring over his shoulder and paling. "Walter asked the same question. But I—I don't know."

Worried she was getting worked up again, he opened the screen door and led her to the couch to sit. "Where's Laurel?"

"Oh, she went to lay Johnny down upstairs. It's his naptime."

"I'm going to go check on her before I leave, okay?"

She nodded and leaned back. He handed her the glass of water on the table, and she offered a small smile.

Climbing the stairs, Dev paused at the sound of hushed singing. Quietly ascending the rest of the steps, he followed the sound to the doorway and found Laurel holding a child in her arms. She stood at the window, singing softly.

No hat on, her toned arms held the baby. A lump formed in his throat. He stared as she swayed back and forth, her beautiful voice humming. The boy's heavy breaths rose and fell. She eased over to the small playpen by the window and lowered him gently inside. Leaning over, a smile formed on her face.

He breathed deeply, and she looked up. Shock spread across her face as she turned and grabbed her hat from the windowsill. Throwing him a glare, she rushed silently through the room, pausing in front of him and shoving the hat on her head.

Pushing at his arm, Laurel moved him enough to shut the door partway. She then proceeded to shove him down the stairs and pull him to the sitting room away from Mrs. Beecham.

"What were you doing spying on me?" she hissed, pushing into his space.

"I came to find you because I was worried about Mrs. Beecham."

She frowned and peered around the staircase. "She looks fine to me."

The image of her holding the little boy and singing repeated over and over again as his mind raced. He stepped forward and tugged at her hat, trying to lift it enough to see her eyes again.

"What?" She shoved his hand away. "What are you doing?"

"Just trying to see your face." He grinned as she stepped back.

"Is this funny to you?" She hung her hands on her hips.

"None of this is funny to me." He sighed heavily, his exhaustion draining his common sense. "The fact that someone would try and scare you and Mrs. Beecham upsets me. The fact that you won't talk to me or look me in the eye frustrates me. And now, all I can think about is you have this whole other side to you, and you refuse to let anyone else see it." Stepping forward, he took a hold of her elbow. "How are you feeling, Laurel?"

She froze in place, her mouth agape as she held a hand to her chest. "I—what?" she whispered.

The heat crept up his face as he chuckled. "Sorry. I—I'm running on a couple of hours' sleep and I'm just, surprised. I do want to know how you're doing. How are your cuts healing?"

"I'm fine," she whispered.

He nodded, happy she wasn't pulling away. "I came to tell

you I finished looking at the rose bush, and I'm heading to the office. Mrs. Beecham answered the door. She looked upset, worried. I helped her sit down. I wanted you to come sit with her." He paused, trying to keep from rambling. "How old is Johnny?"

"Almost a year. I've kept him since I moved back. Lizzy— Lizzy doesn't have much help." She looked away.

"She's lucky she has you." He smiled as her gaze cut back to his.

"I'm not sure lucky is the right word. Apparently because of me, no one stays around very long."

"How do you know it's because of you?" He shrugged.

She shook her head and started to pull away. He gently turned her back, keeping hold of her elbow.

"You seem to take on a lot. What you're doing, why you're here, you have an amazing will to help others."

"What? Hollister, you don't know me well enough to—"

"Laurel, you're here because you want to be here for Mrs. Beecham." He stepped closer and felt her arm tense. "You're putting up with all of this, dealing with all of this, because you care for her. You take care of Darrell, Lizzy, and probably a lot more people, because that's who you are. It's an amazing thing, sacrificing yourself in order to help others."

Her mouth dropped again as she stared, a blush rising on her cheeks. He maneuvered her hat a little, revealing more of those big blue eyes. Refraining from pulling her in for a hug, he settled for wiping her cheeks with his fingers, frowning as a few tears fell. He pushed her mouth closed, holding her chin for a moment before he dropped his hand.

"No need to cry about it. Don't get upset that you couldn't fool everyone," he whispered.

"I—I'm not upset," she muttered under her breath, her eyes finally dropping from his.

"I'm headed to the office to file the complaint and see what we can do." He sighed and squeezed her elbow. "I'll let you know if something comes up." He pulled at her hat again until she looked up, those blue eyes glistening.

"Call me. If something else happens, call me on my cell. Even if you think it's nothing. I want you safe and I'm determined to gain your trust." His voice dropped. Staring into her eyes like this, there was so much pull he wasn't sure he could stop it.

Red lips parted for a moment as if she'd speak, but then closed and she tugged her hat down, shifting her gaze away from his. As she pulled away, he realized he was holding her waist and elbow. He wasn't happy about letting go of either.

He released his breath and allowed her some space, then moved past. Pausing, he clasped her fingers, squeezing them. "Call Laurel. I want you to call."

She nodded. He squeezed her fingers again, then walked to the front door.

"Take care, Mrs. Beecham. Let me know if you need anything."

"I'll be fine. Thank you so much." Mrs. Beecham smiled and returned his wave.

The mid-morning breeze didn't help him enough, not near enough. Being that close, seeing Laurel's walls fall, and finding an even more amazing woman standing in front of him. *Man.*

He blew out a breath and headed to the driveway where Morris leaned against his car.

"What's on your mind?" Dev wasn't really sure he wanted to ask. For all he knew, it was about him and Laurel.

"This is just ... something seems off."

"Okay. What seems off to you?" Dev dropped the evidence kit next to him and leaned against the car.

"I was here last night, with Lester."

Dev straightened. "So, you knew about the call?"

"Nope." Morris shook his head. "Lester did the talking. I was finishing up my shift and going inside to check out. Lester met me at the door and said I needed to come with. I followed him out here and heard what he said. But I just don't get it.

"Once we got back to the office, I asked if he'd seen the video yet, and he said he was waiting on the warrant but knew it was her. I looked up the case, but there was nothing on file, not even a phone number for the complaint."

Dev frowned. "What did Lester say?"

"Just that he hadn't had a chance to put it all in the system." Morris shrugged. "When I asked about the warrant, he said he must've forgot to send it in and said he was tired. This morning, I found the case on the computer, but it was just listed as a complaint by an unknown man. Tonya from the diner called and said she had the video ready if I wanted it, but she didn't understand why."

"So, she got the warrant?"

Morris shook his head. "Said Lester called and wanted it, didn't tell her why. I'm fairly sure she knew he was trying to pin something on Laurel."

Dev huffed. "Did she look at it?"

"Yeah, said there was nothing on it, just the trucks and cars that normally park there on Friday night. They were all guests, and she could tell us who each car belonged to. She said Laurel's car wasn't there, neither was the truck.

"When I told her what happened, she said there's no way something like that would've happened without someone hearing or seeing it. There's nothing but the call Lester took that can link her in any way to the complaint."

"So, the guy didn't go to the doctor?"

"It's not in the report." Morris shrugged. "Walter showed up right before we left. He said he was in the office, but never heard anything about a report. That's what doesn't make sense."

"I was there last night too. Lester never said a word." He would have to have a talk with Walter about this. Obviously there is no love lost between Laurel and Miles Lester. But why?

"Do you know if Laurel and Lester were ever an item?"

Morris huffed. "All I know about the guy is that's he's some kind of war hero. Went into the Army and when he got out, he came back here. Brags on his time in the service as if he deserves something more than respect. He's a little older than Laurel, not sure if they were close growing up."

Dev sighed, chewing on the inside of his cheek a moment. "What I don't get is why you stopped dating that nurse." He grinned as Morris looked up at him, a red shadow falling on his face.

"Don't start, man."

"Just because she has a kid? Really? I mean, I get that's a little complex, but she seems really nice. And pretty." Dev chuckled as Morris groaned.

"I just, I never saw myself in a relationship with a woman who has a kid. I mean, it's got to be hard."

Dev sat back against the cruiser, barely listening to Morris explain his aversion to kids as he saw Laurel's figure in the window. She was watching.

Something happened between them, something he wasn't quite sure he understood. God sent him here, and he'd been trying to see the reason. But if this case was that reason, it wasn't going to be easy. Even if he did figure it all out, he wouldn't have a job by the time he finished.

Then, there was Laurel. A woman he had a hard time getting out of his head. He smiled at her, and she moved away from the window. He sighed.

Yeah, what was he going to do about Laurel?

14

Taking a few deep breaths, Laurel paced the sitting room, nervously rubbing the back of her neck. Passing the window again, her eyes found Dev Hollister still in her driveway, talking to Officer Morris. Hollister had said way too much. She knew it, and he probably did too. He'd rambled on, and the second he finally took a breath, he must've realized.

No one ever said so many kind things about her. How did he read her so easily? No one else got it. Darrell, Lizzy, Tonya, even Chuck—they all questioned her constantly about why she came back here. They didn't understand—there was nowhere else to go. No other family, just like Mrs. Beecham.

After losing two husbands, Mrs. Beecham said she'd never marry again. With no children, Laurel was fairly certain there would be no one around to take care of her should she ever need it. Since Mrs. Beecham had fostered her at the age of fourteen, Laurel was her only family, and she'd be there for the only adult who ever believed her and gave her a home.

And with Laurel's issues, Mrs. Beecham's law degree came in handy. Going up against the town's beloved sheriff hadn't been easy. Everyone loved him and couldn't believe he'd been ruthless and violent. But he was. He'd been all that—and worse.

Her body shivered at the memory of Hollister moving in much too close and wiping away the tears she didn't realize she'd cried. Yanking her hat down, she rubbed her arms, needing to cling to something before she fell apart.

Romantic notions, although endearing, were nothing more than fantasies. She never witnessed one lasting marriage without at least one of the people involved falling away. Becoming either angry or helpless or alone like Mrs. Beecham.

Mason Dodge, her first real relationship after she joined the Navy, treated her with kindness and respect, something new after leaving her hate-filled town. All the men she worked with treated her with respect. After Mason discovered he'd be transferred, she decided to end things for him. As much as she didn't want to lose him, she couldn't hold him back, either. She told him to go, to move on and forget about her.

It took several years before the overwhelming hurt of losing Mason faded. He was the first man she ever let close, allowed herself to love. But after he left, she decided then, it wasn't worth it. The pain she experienced all her life was too much. Why invite more pain in when she could prevent it from happening?

As Laurel walked through the house, Mrs. Beecham sat on the couch, her eyes closed and the Bible in her lap. Her lips were moving, praying. Probably for Laurel's soul, even though she still didn't quite understand why.

Silently slipping to the kitchen, Laurel took a deep breath. Suddenly, a wave washed over her.

"No, not now, not now!" she whispered as she leaned against the sink, her whole body shaking.

"Laurel? Are you all right?" Mrs. Beecham called from the living room.

"I'm fine." Laurel nodded, the overwhelming sounds of helicopter blades filled her ears as she strained to ignore them. "Can you check on Johnny?"

"Of course."

Nausea built in her stomach, and she took slow breaths like she'd learned in all her hours of therapy. Trying to regain control of her body, she groaned. Memories pushed into her chest as she envisioned the inside of the building, the screams, the gunfire.

Running outside, she barely got off the porch before she collapsed. Her fists gripped the earth, and her whole body shook.

"Just stop, stop," she whispered. Pain surged through her back.

The injury that removed her from the Navy still burned into her memory, burned into her skin.

A hand gently rested on her shoulder, and she flinched, wrapping her left arm around the attacker's, and fisting her right as she straightened. Hollister's face came into view, and she groaned, collapsing back to the ground on her hands and knees.

"What do you need?" His soft voice echoed, amid the chaos and smell of fire.

The fire. That was it. The smell of fire and the memory of her friends and time overseas triggered everything. Digging her fingertips into the muddy ground, she felt her body giving way, shaking as tears rolled from her eyes to the ground.

Hollister's hand went to her back, then both hands as he knelt next to her. His cologne engulfed her, chasing away the smell of the fire, and with it, the wave. Feeling her body ease, she pulled herself back to her knees and closed her eyes as she sat on her heels.

"I'm fine now, you—you can go."

"Come on."

His hands gripped her wrists, and she shook her head. Her body was spent and exhausted.

"Laurel?"

She started to pull but gave up. "I—I can't stand."

Moving his grip from her wrists to her elbows, he lifted her in front of him. She leaned forward and lowered her head; the bill of her cap pushing at his chest.

"Back inside?"

"Yeah, I—I have to watch ... watch Johnny," she mumbled between breaths.

With an arm wrapped around her waist, he guided her up the steps and slowly to the house. She pulled away and leaned against the sink as she turned on the faucet. The warm water flowed over her hands. Dark mud swirled around the bright white basin before finally going down the drain.

"Laurel, sit."

She sat at the small kitchen table, her hands in her lap, still wet. Lethargy took over as she struggled to keep her eyes open. Looking down, she watched Hollister dry her hands with a towel. His fingers quickly unwound the bandage, then cleaned the cuts gently with the towel.

"You should've gotten your hand X-rayed." His gentle voice sounded in the empty room.

"It's been done four or five times, doesn't really matter now," she muttered.

"Laurel? How often do you have flashbacks?" he whispered, and she shook her head.

"Not flashbacks. I know where I am."

"You can still know where you are, I—I know what I saw. This isn't a panic attack. What happened? What triggered it?"

The sound of his chair against the floor made her open her eyes fully, finding him in front of her, his hands holding hers, and those sad eyes watching.

"The ... the fire. The smell of the fire," she muttered and pulled her hands from his.

Resting her elbow on the table, she held her head in her hands. "You—you can go. I'm fine, I ..." Trailing off, she didn't know what to say or even how to say it. Being helped wasn't the norm in this town. "Thanks," she whispered, forcing her eyes open to see his.

He pulled her right hand back to his, looking down and rubbing a finger across her knuckles. "How often?"

"Haven't had one since July." She sighed, narrowed her eyes, trying to remember. "Last Fourth of July, I—I wasn't even home yet, and there were fireworks in town." She swallowed, remembering the loud noises and the smell of the sulfur in the air. "That one was ...." she shook her head. "It was bad."

"Then, you don't have them often?"

She shook her head again and her brain kicked in gear. Yanking her hand from his, she straightened. "Trying to find some detail that you can use, Detective?"

"Don't do that." He frowned, his deep voice rising. "I wouldn't do that. I'm trying to figure out how to help you."

"Of course, why wouldn't I need help? I'm sure you believe the story about me getting kicked out of the Navy, and now I'm a danger to everyone because I'm—I'm crazy." She started to stand, but collapsed, her legs not quite ready.

"Hey." Hollister took her wrist and leaned in, pushing into her focus. "I don't believe any of it. I didn't when Lester said it, and I don't now. I know for a fact you're not crazy, you're not out of control, and you don't have a mental disorder. He said all those things, but I've never believed him. Not even for a second."

"Then why the call last night? Why the constant prodding?"

He sighed and shook his head. "Last night was because I knew it wasn't you. But when I go to run the prints on the marker left on the floor, I'm expecting the prints to be yours. Someone is trying hard to set you up.

"As far as the prodding, I'm just trying to learn about you. You don't seem interested in talking." His jaw clenched and those green eyes burned into her. "Maybe if I can actually sit down and have a conversation with you—"

"About what? You have access to whatever you want to look up. You don't need to have a conversation to find what you're looking for."

"I want to hear it from you."

She stilled a moment, working to fix her gaze elsewhere, making him push in that much more.

"Yeah, I have dug. But I'm sure you're aware, there's no police file about you or anything that happened when you were growing up. I dug around on your family but got nothing there either. As far as your service goes, there's nothing there I can access except the fact you were honorably discharged and awarded a bronze star and a purple heart. Which is surprising since I don't think anyone knows about that."

"No one does, and you need to keep it to yourself." She rubbed her temples and closed her eyes, her headache coming on.

"I don't understand, why don't you tell people? It will—"

"It will what?" She paused and glared up at him. "You think it will change anyone's mind around here? No one will care, nor would they believe it, no matter who told them. I didn't go into the Navy to change people's minds about who I am, so it doesn't matter."

"Look who woke up."

They both turned to see Mrs. Beecham holding an incredibly happy Johnny.

"Oh, I'm sorry. You two look like you're talking. I didn't mean to interrupt." Mrs. Beecham grinned.

"No, you're not interrupting anything." She started to stand but sat back down as dizziness overwhelmed her. "I just ... can you give me a minute?"

"Laurel?"

"I'm okay, just a headache. Could you watch him for just another minute?"

Mrs. Beecham nodded and left the room.

"Laurel—"

"Just, don't. I—I need you to keep your snooping to yourself, Hollister." She looked up to see a grin on his face. "What?"

He only shook his head as he scooted forward.

"I—I need some medicine." She started to stand when he

held her arm steady.

"I can get it."

"You don't even know where it is."

"You can tell me." He grinned again.

"Third drawer." She pointed and took off her hat, throwing it on the table and rubbing her temples. Shucking off her muddy boots, she pulled her legs up, crossing them in front of her on the seat. She untied her hair from the twisted bun, then massaged her head and closed her eyes.

"Here." Hollister's soft voice made her pause.

Keeping her focus from those green eyes of his, she took the pills with the glass of water on the table. Setting the glass back down, she leaned her elbows on her knees, and closed her eyes, holding her aching head.

"You should lie down." The sound of his voice clearing made her glance up.

He was sitting in front of her again, pushing into her space.

"Look, I'm fine, okay? Can you just ... I think it's time for you to go." She bit her bottom lip and stood slowly, knowing he would too. "I have to look after Johnny and make Mrs. Beecham lie down later, and—"

"You need rest too."

"I don't work tomorrow. I can rest then." She walked around the table on her side, avoiding passing him as she stepped into the living room.

Unlocking the door, she held it open as he came up behind her, his black backpack now on his back.

"Remember what I said. Call me."

"I won't need to." She swallowed and pulled the door in front of her, gripping the edge and hoping it would shield her from another close encounter.

"See you tomorrow then."

"Why? Why would you see me tomorrow?"

He shrugged. "I just have a feeling I will." He grinned big as he stepped through the screen door, letting it slam behind him.

15

S liding behind the wheel of his truck, Dev refrained from starting it as he mulled the situation and the vision of Laurel with her hair down. It was longer than he thought it would be—auburn with blonde streaks highlighting her face. He blew out a deep breath, thinking just how amazing Laurel really was. Not just attractive, but amazing.

As he headed back to the station, the car's Bluetooth went off.

"Hollister."

"Hey man! How's the country?" Bruce attempted a southern drawl.

"It's quiet, well, mostly." Dev chuckled. "Did you get my email?"

"That's why I'm calling. I thought you wanted quiet, not a huge FBI investigation thrown in your lap."

Dev scoffed. "You mean you guys are looking into it?"

"Have been for a while, but there's not much there. About six or seven years ago, another person put in a call about a missing person and how the cases were piling up. Let me see ... A Laurel Ashburn?"

"She didn't tell me she called it in." Dev chuckled.

"So, she's the one who's got you looking, huh?"

"Not really. I mean, she did mention it after her attack two days ago."

"Wait, she was attacked?"

"Yeah, some guy tried to kidnap her, but he messed with the wrong woman. I rolled up on the situation and got her some help. She told me about the missing women in this area, including a friend of hers. I found it a little strange, so I looked into it last night."

"Well, we put in a call to a Sheriff Walter McGehee, just to get his thoughts. He said he was aware there seemed to be a series of disappearances from right when he took over being sheriff. But as far as he knew, there was no link anywhere in his town."

"Well, he would know. He's been around this town for a long time." Dev frowned. "So, you got anything you can tell me?"

Bruce let out a long breath. "Right now, we don't have anything concrete. There's a rumor of a human trafficking ring in the South. A small band that moves primarily through Oklahoma City. But with the interstate system, it can wrap through just about any other neighboring state."

"Makes sense. So, no players you can identify?"

"Not really. It's kinda need to know. But if something pops in your area, I'll give you a call."

"Thanks." Dev sighed. "I appreciate it."

———

ONCE AT THE OFFICE, Dev logged the cigarette butt and scanned in the plaster of the shoe print. He filled out the forms and sat back in his chair. This whole attack on Mrs. Beecham's rose bush seemed ... odd. Was it because he'd been snooping around? But wouldn't that come back on him and not her?

He exhaled and checked his email, finding one from the state crime lab with Laurel's case number on it.

A small piece of skin has been found lodged in the blade of the knife. It's being processed, and if any DNA matches from the system, you'll be notified.

About that other thing, well, it's just like you suspected. I'll let you know once we get a match on the knife.

Tray

Well, that was interesting. Tray was a good friend from years ago and had done him a favor with the black marker and getting prints. Laurel's prints, but Tray would keep it quiet. Now, they not only had a connection to her attacker, but proof someone was pushing awfully hard to set up Laurel Ashburn. But why?

"God, let there be an answer in that DNA," he mumbled.

With a grunt, he stood, stretched, and went outside to the corral. Laurel's car sat in the lot. Popping the trunk, he inspected the tire. It was just like she said, the head of screw stuck up between the tread. He went over the outside of the car, looking for any signs of blood, but the rain had washed everything away.

Frowning, he made his way inside and found Walter at his desk.

"You got a sec?"

Walter looked up and waved him in. "Yes, I wanted to ask what happened at Mrs. Beecham's?"

Dev stepped inside and shut the door, then sat down. "I need to ask a delicate question."

Walter frowned. "Yes, Mrs. Beecham and I have been seeing each other off and on. She's a remarkable woman and good friend."

"Okay, well, that's good to know. But that's not what I wanted to ask."

"Then what's your question?" Walter leaned back in the chair, clasping his hands over his chest.

"Did Laurel and Lester ever have a personal connection?"

Walter sighed. "Miles Lester is an ... interesting character.

He's had a lot of trauma in his past and matured into a dependable and reliable deputy."

"Trauma?"

"Sealed. But I can say that he's several years older than Laurel. As far as I know, they've never had any personal connection. He did have quite a few run-ins with her father when he was sheriff."

Dev frowned. "The claim that she attacked someone last night, did you see the footage from the diner?"

"I did. She wasn't there, there was nothing even showing an attack. I've started a trace on the call to see if we can verify the caller."

"So, there was a call?"

Walter shrugged. "All I can say is a call did come into the office around the time Lester mentioned. But I don't know where it came from. No caller ID, and so far the number hasn't been traceable."

"He really hates her." Glancing up, Dev noticed the stern frown across Walter's face. "I'm just trying to figure out why. He's already warned me to stay away, giving me some outlandish assertions about her character that I don't see."

Walter leaned into the desk. "Laurel is a remarkable person. Her father, Guy, was a good friend of mine. When he died, I promised myself to look after her. Her father dead, her mother disappeared, I needed to be sure she was cared for."

"Did he hurt her?"

"No." Walter narrowed his eyes. "He might've had a drink or two too many, but I never saw him hurt anyone." He stood and paced the room. "She was confused, hurt, and with all the rumors, I'm afraid it all went too far. I tried to protect her, sending her to Kendra Beecham's, but it didn't matter. The whole town heard what she said. It was in the paper."

Dev saw something more than worry cross Walter's face. "You really think she hurt her mother?"

Walter cut his eyes a second. "Not sure. Laurel had her

father's temperament, and no one to help her reign it in. Since Miles grew up here, he knew the rumors. He's very protective of the department and feels her presence complicates things. I know he would never do anything to compromise the integrity of this office."

Dev stood. "I can respect that. But the next time he comes after Laurel without any proof, I'm reporting it. That doesn't do any good for this office either." He turned to the door.

"You sure the office is all you're worried about?"

Pausing, he took hold of the knob. "Integrity is an important thing." He turned to Walter. "I've read about her time in the service and know at least a little of what she's had to deal with here. So far, I've seen more integrity in her than I have in Deputy Lester."

With that, he left the office and headed home.

———

AFTER FINALLY FINISHING HER CHORES, Laurel collapsed on the couch, exhausted. Lizzy picked up Johnny at 3:00, then Laurel passed out on her couch for an hour. Turning on the TV, she hoped the mind-numbing programs would distract her.

Every Wednesday after Lizzy picked up Johnny, she felt empty. Having that little boy to hold and cuddle, wanting her attention and smiling just for her, made her wish for things she knew were out of reach. Her heart would ache for an hour or so, then she'd sober up and get on with her life.

But tonight, loneliness overwhelmed her. Gripping the small cushion to her chest, she closed her eyes and leaned back. A vision of Dev Hollister came to mind, and she shook her head. He'd been so attentive and helpful and ... kind. The attraction between them would only get worse. It wasn't as if she hadn't noticed his handsome features.

Those green eyes that looked right through her, always concerned and worried. His stiff jaw, with a shadow of scruff that seemed to make his lips stand out that much more. Broad shoulders and a gentleness about him, she was surprised more women hadn't tried to lay claim. The things he said to her, the way he looked at her, his gaze landing too often on her lips, it was all burned into her brain.

"Good grief," she muttered. Shutting the TV off, she tossed the pillow aside and leaned on her knees.

Allowing herself to think he'd want something more seemed almost as ridiculous as her believing it could happen. It couldn't and she wasn't about to let that world of pain enter her life again.

Her phone chirped and she picked it up.

So, how do you feel? Better?

She sighed and shook her head. Why did Hollister keep trying?

I'm fine.

Just fine?

She groaned.

Look, I'm not interested in whatever you're trying here, Detective.

And what is it I'm trying?

That's enough, okay?

The phone rang and she sat back, staring at the screen for a moment. Sighing, she answered. "What do you want?"

"Why are you being like this? I'm just checking on you."

"Why?"

"To be kind. To be a friend. That's what friends do."

"Don't be condescending."

"Then stop acting as if I have ulterior motives." His deep sigh echoed. "Look, I really wanted to check up on you. You've had a ... busy day."

She leaned forward on her knees, unsure what she was supposed to say.

"So, how are you?" He punctuated the words.

"Tired."

"Did you eat yet?"

Her breath stalled in her throat a moment. "Um, yeah. Just finished."

"How about some ice cream? Ice cream makes everyone feel better."

She let out a chuckle before she could stop herself. "No, I—I was headed to bed."

"It's kinda early isn't it?"

The clock read a little after eight. It was pretty early. "I've had a busy day, and my body is worn out."

"Rain check then."

"No, no rain check." She sighed and stood, trudging to her bedroom. "I've tried to warn you, but you don't seem so interested in listening."

"You know, I can take care of myself."

She groaned. "It's not just that. You'll lose your job, no one will ... I mean, don't you see how they treat me? Just being seen with me will make it that much worse. So, I need you to stop."

Silence stretched for a moment.

"Laurel? I'm not pushing for anything here. I'm not trying to upset you or make you feel uncomfortable. I don't want to do that. But I do want to be your friend. You have friends here in town, why can't I be like them?"

She paused as her mouth opened. She really didn't have a response for that.

"Laurel?"

"I'm not interested in ruining anyone else's life, okay? Bye."

She hung up before he could say anything and fell back into the bed.

Wincing at the cuts, she reached over and turned out the light, rolling herself into a ball, taking the blankets with her. She needed sleep and some time alone, at least time away from Dev Hollister.

He burrowed into her head, making her think way too much about their "friendship." She couldn't do anything more than this. Besides, getting hurt by anyone, even someone as helpful as Dev Hollister, wouldn't happen. Not if she could help it.

16

A hand gripped her arm, hard. "You're not leaving."
The voice was familiar but ... Wrenching away, she tried to steady herself as her head throbbed and dizziness consumed her.

"Mom? Where are you?"

"Get her back! Now!"

Heart pounding, she raced from the house, blood trailing into her vision as pain pulsed through her body. She had to get away, had to get help.

Sitting straight up, Laurel looked around her room and groaned.

Another nightmare, another early morning. Falling on her side, she covered her face, drying the tears with the blanket. She missed her mother so much. It was a deep ache she couldn't fill. For some reason, each dream had another voice, another flash of memory. Maybe someday she would have an answer. Although she already knew her father had killed her mother that night. That wasn't anything surprising to her. Not that anyone would believe her...

Knowing she wouldn't be able to go back to sleep, she rolled out of bed, trudged to the bathroom, and splashed water on her face. The mirror provided proof of her tear-filled nightmares. Blotchy cheeks and puffy eyes stared back at her.

"You're a mess," she murmured as she got dressed.

Stretching out as much as she could, Laurel grimaced at the stitches across her back. Studying her arm in the bathroom mirror, she sighed. Those stitches were healing, slowly. Her back wasn't easy to see, but she could sure feel the pull.

By eight o'clock, she was ready to at least attempt a fast walk if her body couldn't handle a jog.

Turning left out of her driveway, Laurel walked to warm up. Memories flooded her mind again, only she pushed them away. With a sigh, she picked up the pace, and halfway down the dead-end road, she noticed tire tracks in the mud to her right, running into an old hay field. The gate had long rusted away, sitting in a heap to the side, and the tracks moved right though.

"That's where they went," she mumbled.

The field belonged to an elderly neighbor who no longer owned animals to graze the land. She knew his property eventually ran into another county road several miles away.

Shaking her head, she turned and headed back toward the house, passing it by as she picked up her pace.

Why would anyone try to run her off the road?

Considering it happened so soon after the attempted kidnapping, it'd crossed her mind that maybe the man wanted to finish the job. But why?

She'd already escaped his grip, injured him, and filed a police report. It would make more sense for him to give up and let her be.

Raindrops darkened the road, the smell of fresh rain filled her senses. Taking a deep breath, she rotated her head, popping her neck as she settled into a slow trot. She needed exercise. It lifted her mood, and with her body sore, it would relax her tense muscles.

The sound of gravel crunching shifted her focus to a truck barreling down the road toward her. Based on the shape and color, it was the same one that followed her the other night and tried to run her off the road.

Instinctively reaching behind her back, she groaned. Her weapon was still at the house. Pausing at a damaged hole in the fence, the truck pulled to a stop about twelve feet away. Rain pounded her head, trailing off the bill of her hat.

Suddenly, the door flew open, and a rifle barrel aimed her way. She darted into the field, hopping over the damaged fence.

"Hurry! Stop her! Shoot!"

The sound of rifle fire made her zig-zag, hoping to reach the trees before they closed in. Just as she reached the tree line, a bullet lodged in the trunk of a pine to her right. She flinched as the wood and bark sprayed her.

Weaving through the trees, Laurel splashed through the mud holes and found an old rusted-out tractor. Weeds covered the form, creating a small shelter. She knelt down, and the sound of rustling leaves echoed over the rain. The footsteps of whomever was chasing her sounded on the other side of the woods.

She pulled out her phone and texted Hollister.

He's back.

The MESSAGE NOT DELIVERED icon displayed, and she stifled a groan. No signal. So much for help.

Peering through an opening in the metal, Laurel saw no movement, so she started off again, stooped over, until she reached the tree cover. She needed to find shelter, somewhere to hide until they gave up and left.

Her back burned as exhaustion set in. Sprinting toward the fence line, eager to find a way to get to the road, she hoped for a signal away from the trees.

The sound of truck tires on gravel made her pause, then resume her trek toward the dense forest. Finding a fallen tree, she pushed herself underneath, letting the branches fall over and cover her. On her belly, she shoved her hat aside to lay flat on her stomach, rainwater and mud freezing her body as it pooled around her. Everything ached, and her back burned.

Crunching gravel to her right reverberated through the quiet of the forest.

"She has to be there." That strange, eerie voice from her attacker spoke, making her blow out a breath and close her eyes.

"No trace. I saw some blood back there, but then, it disappeared." The gravelly voice sounded almost familiar.

"She didn't come out here," her attacker's voice echoed with a loud sigh. "Just get back in before someone else comes driving down the road."

Slamming doors made her jump, her body stilled, and her breathing slowed as she closed her eyes. Knowing there might be someone left behind to wait her out, she decided to stay put.

"Just wait a little while longer," she whispered as she passed into unconsciousness.

17

"You realize if you don't get her out of here, we'll have another issue on our hands?"

"What issue?" Tobias's voice heated. "You're supposed to take care of things on your end, remember?'

He seethed at the incompetence. "I've run out of patience with you. It's not just the girl that's the issue. That new detective has taking a liking to her, been hanging around her. If she disappears, he'll open an investigation, and questions will be asked."

"You know I'm good. They can't rattle me."

"Oh yeah?" he spat the words. "What about that friend you've hired? You confident he can keep his mouth shut? If you've so much as breathed a word about me to him—"

"Relax. He wants money, and I've given it to him. He knows nothing about you anyway," Tobias mumbled.

"You have two days. Then I'm taking care of it. All of it."

He gritted his teeth at the silence. Surely Tobias knew that meant he would require a new distributor, and he never left loose ends. Never.

"Consider it done."

The call ended, and he sat the phone down.

Stroking his chin, he leaned on the edge of his desk. He'd also learned that he wasn't the only one gunning for Laurel. Seemed she'd made a few more enemies. That could work too ...

18

Laurel's eyes popped open at the sound of her phone vibrating.

"What—what's that?" she mumbled.

Pulling her phone from her pocket, she sighed. From underneath the tree, the phone now showed a full signal. Strange.

"Hello," she whispered, her head pounding.

"Laurel? Laurel where are you?"

"Hollister?" she muttered.

"Laurel what's wrong? Where are you? Mrs. Beecham called and said you've missed lunch and she can't reach you."

"What—what time is it?"

"A little after 1:00."

"Oh, I didn't ..." Her mind felt foggy.

"Laurel, where are you?"

She frowned at his pointed words. "I'm in the woods. There was the truck—"

"Wait, what woods?"

She heard the sound of the door slamming and the engine of his truck starting through the line.

"Down the road, about two or three miles from the house. The truck—"

"Can you see the road?"

"No, no, I can just hear the road."

"When you hear me, tell me."

She sighed. "Okay," she muttered and closed her eyes.

"Laurel? Laurel talk to me."

"I—I'm just tired. Wait, I hear the gravel." The sound of a honking horn made her flinch. "Yeah, must be you."

Rolling from her spot, she groaned loudly as she landed on her back. Pushing herself up on all fours, she took a few breaths.

"Laurel? Laurel, which side are you on?"

"Over here." She tried to call out, but her voice was almost gone.

"Laurel?"

Hands pulled at her shoulders as she tried to stand. "I—I'm tired," she whispered.

Feeling herself being lifted, she looked up to find Hollister cradling her, her head leaning against his chest as her mind once again faded.

STANDING NEXT to Laurel's bed, Dev gently held her fingers, waiting on her to wake up. According to Lizzy, Laurel's back was badly torn, the stitches barely hanging on.

Watching her rest, her hair hanging down over her shoulders, she looked peaceful, but he wondered what she'd seen in her lifetime. The things she experienced as a child and what she did in the Navy to earn those medals—it must've been bad.

Her jaw clenched as her breathing jumped and her body tightened.

"Laurel? You're okay. Laurel?" He leaned over, stroking her cheek and watched her body ease.

Bright red lips opened a moment, then pursed and her

eyelids fluttered. He felt his own breathing spike just watching her.

"Man, Laurel, you're beautiful," he muttered, brushing her hair back. Blowing out a quick breath, he pulled his hand back.

Her eyes popped open, and she sat up.

"Laurel? You're in the hospital."

Wincing, she pushed her hand to her back, and he helped her lie down, holding her hand tightly.

"I—what happened?"

"They found you, chased you into the woods. Remember?"

Closing her eyes, she gripped his hand, pulling it under her chin as she rolled to her uninjured side.

"I remember running. What are you doing here?" Her words slurred, the pain medicine apparently wreaking havoc on her brain.

"Laurel, what happened when you were in the Navy? Why did you leave?" He sat on the edge of the bed, holding her hands with both of his. The question rattled around in his brain and even though it might not be the best way to ask, he figured it might be the only way he could get her to open up.

"I didn't leave, they said I couldn't go back." She sighed heavily and faded back to sleep.

He frowned as her hands released his, and he stepped back. A quiet knock made him turn. Mrs. Beecham entered, frowning.

"How is she?" Pale and worried, Mrs. Beecham walked over to the bed. Dev moved aside to let her near Laurel.

"She's better, woke for just a second, but I think the medicine—"

"Regular pain medicine doesn't work for her. She'd need something strong, and she won't be happy about what they gave her when she wakes."

Laurel groaned and flinched.

"Don't get too close." Mrs. Beecham stepped back, holding her hands to him. "If you happen to accidently wake her when she's dreaming, it's not good," she whispered.

He nodded, waiting for Laurel to calm. "Do you know what happened? Why she left the Navy?"

"No." Mrs. Beecham sighed. "I asked once, but she ... she told me she wouldn't talk about it and not to ask again. So, I didn't."

"When she came back, did she have a lot of nightmares?"

Mrs. Beecham sighed, taking Laurel's hand gently. "She did, but I only saw it when she napped in the living room. She didn't want to be around me at night, so she moved to the guest house." Mrs. Beecham leaned against the bed.

"They called me after it all happened, told me she was injured and in the hospital. It would be a few months before she could return home. She called a few days later, letting me know everything was okay, not to worry, and not to come check on her. It was almost ten months before she came back."

"Ten months? Did she tell you why?"

Mrs. Beecham shook her head. "Just that she wanted to be completely healed before she came back." She sighed. "I wish she'd stayed elsewhere. Here, she's ... things aren't good for her here. I would miss her terribly, but she might find happiness somewhere else. It's only been four months since she got back, and nothing's changed. Everyone still—they all treat her like a confused child."

He swallowed at the comment.

Laurel moaned and rolled, her eyes opening as she strained to sit up with a groan.

"Laurel, easy." He moved closer, shoving his hands in his pockets to keep from reaching out.

"What—how did I get here?" She winced and leaned back with a groan.

"I called Detective Hollister when you didn't show for lunch. He found you."

"The woods ... yeah, I ..." Laurel looked up at Mrs. Beecham. "Can you go get the doctor? I need to get home."

"Laurel, no, you need to rest."

"Please, Mrs. Beecham?"

Mrs. Beecham sighed. "You either start calling me Kendra, or —" The older woman looked ready to cry.

"I'm sorry, Kendra." Laurel swallowed. "I just need to get ..." she winced and gripped her side.

"I'll get the doctor." Mrs. Beecham left, and Dev stepped toward the bed.

The door slammed and Laurel tried to sit up. "We need to get back to the woods."

"Why?"

"They were shooting. I know they hit a tree—"

"They were shooting? And you think you can find what tree they hit?"

"I know where. It was right before I went into the tree line." Blowing out a breath, she rolled her face into the pillow.

"Let me see if the stitches—" he reached for her side, but she gripped the hospital gown.

"No." She rolled and glared.

He nodded and moved his hand to hers, pulling it down and holding onto her fingers.

A quick rap, and Lizzy and Dr. Carrington walked in.

"You can't leave. Your stitches are barely attached to anything, you don't have enough healthy skin." The doctor glared, her gaze drifting to their hands.

"I need to leave. If you can just take out the IV—"

"No. I won't do that." Dr. Carrington crossed her arms.

Laurel's face went to stone, glaring at the doctor as she sat up. "You can't keep me here against my will. Either you take it out, or I will."

"Fine, but I'm not signing your release." Carrington took one more look at their hands, glared up at him, then left.

Lizzy sighed and walked around to Laurel's left side.

"Can you—" Laurel motioned toward the door, and he released her hand with a nod.

"I'll be outside."

Once in the hallway, Dev found Walter speaking with Mrs. Beecham.

"Hollister, you know what's going on here?"

He sighed as Walter gave Mrs. Beecham a hug. "I'm afraid I don't. Two attacks like this and then being run off the road—"

"Run off the road? She told me someone hit the back bumper."

Dev frowned as Mrs. Beecham wiped more tears from her cheeks. "Someone has it in for her. You know what we discussed last time?

"Now look, I realize Lester has been protective, but I don't think—"

"You think Miles has something to do with this?" Mrs. Beecham turned to Walter. "I know things were bad, but I had no idea he held such a grudge."

"What happened?"

"I doubt it's Miles, Kendra. He's a good man now, dedicated to his job."

"What happened?" Dev repeated as the two finally turned toward him. "Did something happen between them?"

Mrs. Beecham shook her head. "No, of course not. He was several years older, they never had any contact." She let out a long sigh. "Miles lived with me for a short time. He had ... issues with his father, and I was glad to take him in. He only had a few years left before he graduated, and we all thought a move would help him, get him away from bad influences."

"Kendra, this is all sealed and private information." Walter frowned. "Miles is a changed man."

"Of course, of course he is." She turned back to Dev. "He made several mistakes, and the judge asked if he wanted to go to prison or into the military. I helped convince him the military would be good. He needed structure I couldn't give. He came back a changed man."

"Then why does he hate her so much?"

Mrs. Beecham shrugged. "I—I'm not sure. I know he was

upset with me when he left. I told Laurel I was afraid he might hold a grudge against her simply because of me. Surely he doesn't believe all those rumors." She let out a sigh. "Laurel would defend herself or someone else in a heartbeat, but kill someone for no reason? She has a good head on her shoulders."

Dev narrowed his gaze at Walter. His jaw clenched, Walter's lips formed a thin line across his face. Walter didn't believe Guy had ever hurt Laurel or her mother. Although it was obvious Laurel had a lot of buried personal trauma, it was hard to believe she would hide it from Walter. They were close.

Maybe she had a reason to kill her father. Maybe she was defending herself or her mother. The thought made him sick. Her pain, the fact she could've been put in that position as a child—it was devastating.

He sighed. "I'm going to see if she's ready to go." Giving a quick rap before entering, he stepped through the door.

"Laurel ..." he paused.

Her bare lower back was exposed as she leaned against the bed, the skin scarred and stretched as Lizzy changed out the gauze pad.

"Go." Her haggard voice sounded, and he backed up, closing the door behind him.

Fire. She mentioned the smell of fire bringing back the memories. He sighed and leaned against the wall. Somehow, whatever got her discharged involved a fire, and she must have been stuck in the middle.

Lizzy came out and barely made eye contact before rushing away. Laurel appeared a few minutes later, her left arm holding her injured right one.

"I don't—don't ask," she whispered.

"Okay, I won't." He straightened, stepping to her side.

She shuffled her feet and approached Walter and Mrs. Beecham. They hushed their voices.

"Are you all right?" Walter took hold of her shoulder. "Do you know who chased you?"

She shook her head. "You didn't have to come check on me."

Walter shook his head. "Of course I did. We're both very worried, Laurel. I might have to take you into protective custody until this is all over."

Her cheeks reddened. "No, I—I'll be fine. Mrs. Beecham, she needs to find another place." Laurel cut her eyes up to his.

"Don't worry about Mrs. Beecham. She's in good hands." He gave a wink.

Although Walter didn't look convinced, Mrs. Beecham nodded. "Thank you."

"I need to get back to the office." Walter motioned him over.

"Excuse me." Dev gave Laurel's elbow a squeeze before he followed Walter to the door.

"Told you, stubborn." Walter pulled on his rain jacket. "I expect you'll take care of her? Not leave her alone?"

Dev shrugged. "I'll do what she'll allow me to do. I can't say that'll be much." He paused and ran his fingers through his hair. "You really don't think Guy hurt them? I mean, not that he deserved to die or anything, but do you really think she made it all up?"

Walter's jaw tensed. "Guy Ashburn had his faults. He drank too much on occasion and had a temper. But I never saw him hit anyone."

That really didn't answer his question.

"I'll ask around, see if anyone saw a truck heading down Laurel's road. Maybe we'll get a good description."

"Yeah, thanks," he muttered as Walter headed toward the exit.

Admitting that Laurel's father had abused his wife and child would be detrimental to Walter. It would mean he knew and didn't report it. But knowing Laurel, learning about her, there was no way she made it all up, even as a child.

"We need to get back." Laurel's hushed voice came from behind him.

He turned. Laurel's pale face stood there, still gripping her arm.

"Let's go."

Wrapping an arm around her waist, he waved Mrs. Beecham forward and kept a firm grip on Laurel. With a sigh, she leaned into him, and he couldn't help but smile.

19

Once in the truck, Dev glanced backward. "I know this has been a rough day, but you both need to leave the house for a while, go somewhere safe."

"I'll call Molly." Laurel said.

"Oh Laurel, I don't want to bother her."

"You'll be safe there, and you know it won't be a bother." Laurel reached to the front seat, and Mrs. Beecham gave her a cell phone.

As he pulled up to the house, he paused before getting out. "Don't get out of the truck until I clear the house, okay?"

Laurel nodded.

Stepping into the house, he was thankful the sun still shone in the sky. Without any backup, the last thing he needed was darkness hiding someone lying in wait. After checking each room, he cleared the house and motioned in the women. He watched as Laurel helped Mrs. Beecham pack, then they loaded back in the truck.

"What about you, dear?" Mrs. Beecham's concerned tone echoed.

"I've got some things to do before I can go. I'll figure it out later. We just need to get you somewhere to rest," Laurel mumbled.

He bit his tongue. Now was not the time. Laurel was too concerned with getting Mrs. Beecham to safety to worry about herself.

Molly Gresham was a close family friend, her house thirty minutes away past the county line, and by the time they returned, he decided he needed to call for back up. Walking in the woods with the sun ready to set within an hour, he didn't want to be on that road without cell service.

He pulled out his phone to make a call. "Hey, Morris."

"What's up, Hollister?

"I need some backup."

"Okay, where?"

"Laurel was attacked in the woods by her house. I need you set up on her road, making sure her attacker doesn't come back. We're going to see if we can find any evidence."

"Sure, sounds good."

"Once you get there, set the handheld to channel six. We won't have much cell service. You're looking for a large, dark truck—

"A dark blue GMC truck with a chrome bumper and damage on the passenger side," Laurel said.

Dev smiled and pressed the phone back to his ear. "You got that?"

"Yeah, I'll head that way."

He hung up and chuckled. "Guess you didn't need my help with the truck after all."

Glancing over, he noticed her taught shoulders as she gripped her hands together in her lap.

"I texted you," she murmured.

"You did? When?"

"I—I ran a bit, then found a place to stop and listen. I tried to get a text out to you."

His mouth dropped open. "I'm sorry it didn't go through."

He pulled over as she pointed to a break in the fence. "Laurel, I would've come and got you."

She only nodded and pushed open the door.

Taking a deep breath, he slid out, then took his bag from the back. They stepped over the broken fence, the wet grass still flattened from where she and her attacker had run through. As he followed her to the trees, the wind blew Laurel's hair around as the rain clouds moved in again.

"I went in around here." She motioned as they paused.

"You okay?" His hand went to her side, but she turned and pulled away.

"Fine." Her jaw clenched as she walked slowly past the tree-lined field.

He sighed and looked as well, studying each tree trunk. He finally found a mass of splinters. "Here."

She stepped in next to him, her breathing heavy.

"Take a seat, this might take a while," he mumbled.

After gathering the bullet, he wove between the trees, finding some tracks and blood drops on a few leaves and branches. She must've been bleeding a lot as she ran. He scrubbed his face with his hand, working to ease the irritation at her being injured and not being able to get a hold of him.

The thought struck him. She texted him, asking for help. Pausing, he turned to see Laurel sitting on a stump, her head in her hands, and her hair blowing in the breeze. He really thought once at home, she'd grab her hat and sink back into her usual demeanor.

But the revelation that she'd tried to call for help made him smile.

Was she changing? Was it him?

Focusing back on the ground, he snapped some pictures of the shotgun shells littering the leaves and grass. He then pulled out some evidence bags and stuffed them inside.

As the sun started to sink, he headed toward her.

"Let's get back to the truck before dark."

Escorting her into the truck, the radio clicked.

"You almost done?" Morris's static-filled voice sounded.

"Yeah, we got what we needed. But I want you to stay until we come through. Laurel needs to pack a bag and to find another place to stay for the night."

"Got it."

He could feel her eyes glaring as he put up the handheld radio, shifted the truck into drive, and moved out.

"I can stay at home. I'll be fine."

"They know where you live. Stop acting as if you can defend yourself like this. You're injured, and you need to realize these people mean business. You know how many shell casings I found?"

"Twelve, fifteen? I was the one being shot at, Hollister." Her voice dropped. "Look, thanks for helping me, but I need—" she paused.

"What, Laurel? What is it you need?"

She turned and glared at him as he pulled into her driveway and parked. He sat back, turned in his seat, and stared at her.

"What?" she glowered.

"Talk to me here. This is getting ... combative. Whoever it is in this truck has tried to run you off the road and now this?"

"It was him."

"What do you mean him?" He stared at her a moment. "The man who attacked you?"

She nodded, gripping her arms tightly.

"How do you know?"

"His voice, I heard his voice." She cleared her throat, looking away. "The other voice I didn't recognize, but his ... I think he was driving the truck."

"Okay, that information would've been useful earlier." He frowned as she turned and glared at him.

"Sorry. It's been a long day."

"I know, but if I hadn't made you sit here and talk to me, I still wouldn't know the connection." He reached out to her arm, but she yanked on the door handle and slid from the seat.

He jumped out and jogged to get ahead of her, stopping her at the door to the guesthouse. "Let me clear it."

"I can do it."

"You don't have a gun." He returned her stare, then headed into the small house.

Flipping on the lights, he went through the rooms and cleared them, seeing the neat and orderly military style he expected. She stopped in the hallway, pulling a small duffle bag out of the closet.

"Let me help."

She glared a moment. "Look, I can do this. I'm not an invalid."

"I can see you're able to take care of yourself. I just want to help."

Shouldering the bag, she pushed past him to her bedroom, setting the bag on the bed and grabbed clothes.

"Where are you staying?" He leaned up against the doorframe.

"I—I guess a hotel." Her body language was stiff and unwelcoming.

"No, that doesn't sound like a good idea."

"Well, I'm not risking anyone else, and you really don't have anything to say about it." With an echoing huff, she stepped into her bathroom. Doors and drawers slammed. She returned with a small bag and stuffed it into the duffle, then went to her closet.

Letting her have her silence, he slipped to the living room, trying to figure out a way to talk to her.

Lord, give me some opening, something. He sighed and sat on the couch, leaned on his knees, and wondering exactly what to say and how to say it.

She entered the living room, awkwardly carrying the duffle, then set it down by the coffee table. Moving to the small antique desk, she pulled out a gun, checked the chamber and clip, then stuffed it into the back of her pants.

"Why don't you come to the station?" He watched her mill around the room a minute. "You can stay in the back room while I work on this truck and see what I can figure out?"

"No, I can't."

"Can't?"

"You know Lester has it in for me. I have no desire to be around him," she murmured, heading into the bedroom.

He tried to wait her out, but there were too many questions pulsing through his mind. Stepping into her bedroom, he saw Laurel going through drawer after drawer.

"What do you need?"

"Just looking ..." She tossed a few things on her bed. A well-worn Bible fell open on the blanket.

Smiling, he picked it up. "Looks like you used this quite a bit."

Laurel paused for only a second. "No, that's Mrs ... Kendra's." She sighed.

"You don't have one?"

"Don't need one." She glared at him a moment before moving to her other dresser.

"Can I ask why not?" He leaned against the doorframe as she packed.

"Don't see any point in it."

"In the Bible or God?"

"Both." She must have found what she was looking for, since she sat down on the chair in the corner. Her hands held a black sheath, revealing a military style knife she inspected before standing and brushing past him.

"So, that's more effective, huh?"

She sighed and shoved it in her bag, then sank onto the couch. "Look, not interested in the God talk. Kendra has been at that all my life. She was my Sunday School teacher."

"So, you were raised in church?"

"No, holidays only. Guy wasn't the church-going type, just the keeping-up-of-appearances type." She frowned. "Let's go."

"We have time."

"I'm serious, God and I aren't familiar with each other, and I'm fine with that." She huffed and crossed her arms. "I have no problems with you believing, so why are you so determined to butt into my business since I don't believe?"

"Because I know you need him."

She rolled her eyes and winced as she picked up the duffle. He tried to take it and she turned.

"I can handle it."

"But you don't have to."

A grunt escaped her lips as he pulled the bag away.

"You keep saying that. Why?"

"Because you've done this life on your own for so long, you don't realize you don't have to anymore. You have people around you who care and want to help. You should let them."

She exhaled sharply.

"Laurel, the reason Mrs. Beecham has been talking to you about a relationship with God is because she understood something else was happening with your family. I'm certain she knew you were living in a bad home situation and wanted to give you some hope."

Her face went red as she stepped into his space, her arms crossed and looking as if she were about to deck him.

"You don't know what you're talking about, so maybe you should be quiet," she hissed.

"I don't." He dropped the bag on the floor, then shoved his hands in his pockets. "I have no idea what went on in your childhood. For the record, I'm really sorry no one was there for you. But God was waiting on you."

"Waiting?" Her jaw dropped. "He was *waiting?* If God was there, He could've fixed it, right? That's what He is, mighty and all powerful. So why didn't He? As soon as my dad started drinking, he started hitting, throwing, shoving. Why didn't God stop him?"

Dev swallowed. "I don't know."

"Then you don't have a right to talk about how much I need God. I did need Him, a long time ago when I couldn't defend myself, when I didn't have the ability to defend myself. I can now, and you think I still *need* Him?"

"Laurel, I don't know why you had to go through all that. I hate the fact that you did. But your dad made a choice, a bad choice, to drink and to hurt." Dev paused, fully expecting her to lash out.

But she just stood there, her breaths heavy as her jaw twitched.

"I can't give you those answers. But I do know that God can make something good come from all that."

"Good? You've got to be—" she turned and started pacing, pushing hair away from her face. "You have no idea what I went through, my mom ... my mom has been gone for almost fifteen years, and I have no idea what happened to her. I mean, I do, but I don't know where she is."

"What happened?" he whispered.

"He killed her and buried her somewhere."

Dev blanched. "What?"

"I know he did. My memory, it's not good. I got hit in the head so many times I don't remember that night. But I know he finally killed her, hid her somewhere, and then everyone blamed me." She fell to the couch with a huff.

Pushing past her knees, he sat down on the coffee table. "I'm so sorry Laurel. I can't—I don't even know what to say."

"You got your story. You done with *conversation* yet?" She took a few quick breaths.

Dev shook his head and leaned forward, trying to will her to face him.

"I really do believe we're given chances in life, Laurel. Many chances to find Him and see what He can do. He gives us reasons to be alive." Dev swallowed hard. "I was shot right before I came here."

Her narrowed gaze bounced to his.

He continued, "I was working a case where under-age kids were being targeted, used as drug mules. I—I struggled with my job. I hated to see the innocent caught up like that. Most of them didn't have a choice, it was a life-or-death decision." He ran his fingers through his hair. "I'd decided after that case, I would retire. It was too much, and I couldn't handle seeing the chaos anymore.

"After months of undercover operations, we found the man who ran the whole operation. SWAT and the DEA were on standby. A few of my guys went into the warehouse to scope it out, and said there were kids still inside, something we had hoped to avoid. I went in with my partner, and we were able to round them up, get them somewhere safe before SWAT came in and the shooting started."

He took a deep breath. "I made a move to go in a side door and ran into a teenaged kid. I pulled him behind some pallets and gave him my vest, told him to stay low and not to move." His jaw clenched as he focused on her swollen hand. "I advanced on the men and we rounded them all up before too many were injured. We were busy cuffing when a shot rang out, and I suddenly felt winded.

"The leader noticed I didn't have a vest on and shot me from the catwalk. The kid I saved, wearing my vest, ended up grabbing a gun we'd piled up away from the bad guys and shot the leader. The bullet—it missed my heart by centimeters, but I survived. That shot could've killed me instantly, but it didn't."

Dev rested his hand on her knee. Looking into her wide eyes, he sighed. "Laurel, none of that compares to what you've been through. I'm just trying to show you, God takes the bad and can use it for good. That kid I saved? He called me right before I took this job. Said he's going into the military. His life was basically over. He was eighteen and could've been charged as an adult for everything he'd been involved in.

"But because the lives of his mother and sister were threatened, he agreed to move drugs. And because he took out the shooter right after I got shot, he saved the lives of more officers, and the judge gave him a choice." Dev paused and watched her a moment. "And I'd like to think that me being shot came out as something good too."

"How can you being shot be good?" She frowned.

"Because I ended up here." Dev shrugged. "A good friend of mine heard about this job and encouraged me to apply. I didn't want to go back in, I was done. But God was prodding my heart and I applied, thinking I wouldn't get it. My injury is healed, but most people see a gunshot wound in the chest and back away. I got the job, and I'm here, willing to help you." He smiled, seeing her eyes intently searching his.

"I'm sorry you got shot. But I'm not sold on something good coming from what's happened to me."

"You were in the military."

"Don't … I said I don't talk about it," she whispered as a sheen formed over her blue eyes.

"You saved someone, maybe multiple people. That's why you earned the Bronze Star. You were there."

"Someone else would've done it," she muttered.

"Maybe." He nodded. "But *you* did. That won't make up for everything that happened to you, I'm not saying that. But to those people you saved, their families and kids or future kids, it means the world to them."

A few tears trailed down her cheeks before she stood and pushed past him to the door, grabbing her duffle. "I'm leaving and taking my truck."

He stood and followed her out, making sure her truck started before locking up her house. Getting into his truck, he followed her out the driveway. "Lord, please let her see You. Let my words sink in and help her find You."

20

Sleep wouldn't come. Laurel's mind raced from the adrenaline and pain medication that always backfired and wired her. Pacing the small room, she tried to ignore the heat creeping up her neck and face.

Hollister's story, it was a heartache. He could've died, and for some reason, that hit her hard. After saving a child's life, sounded like a lot of kids actually, he ended up getting shot. She shook her head. No, it wasn't anything like her past. Those kids he saved might have some idea of what living in fear felt like. But he didn't know. No one knew.

As a child, the school nurse checked her out a lot, because a cut would bleed or a bruise would hurt. As far as she knew, it was never reported. But then again, who would the nurse report possible abuse to? The sheriff was her father, and he controlled the deputies and had a lot of influence over the county officials.

Sighing, she sat down, willing the memories to fade and the hurt to go away. There was too much to deal with right now to sort through the pain and heartache of her past.

"God, you just … how can you just sit by and let all this happen? Those kids Hollister saved, they deserved to be happy, not be enslaved because of fear." She shook her head.

It was a concept that was beyond her. A loving, caring, all-powerful and mighty God who allowed evil to conquer and innocent lives to suffer. How could that happen?

Her phone chirped and she snatched it from the nightstand.

I'm praying for you Laurel. Tim told me you were attacked again and I wish I could stop it for you. But I can't. So I'm praying God will put a stop to it or at least have Dev put a stop to it for you! If you need anything, let me know.

She sat and stared at the words. Lizzy was a new convert. She recently started attending one of the churches in town, saying she needed some guidance with Johnny, and he could be around other kids. So, for Lizzy to say she'd pray for her, made her feel, happy. The fact she cared, that was nice.

Then, the comment about God using Dev Hollister to stop the men from hurting her ... she'd never thought of it that way. Is that how God worked?

Lying down, Laurel thought about her job in the Navy. Her unit was there because of the evil that lurked in the far corner of the world used fear and big weapons to take down the innocent.

They were there to protect and administer help, just like every other military faction from the US. But everything went wrong ... Her heart pounded.

She jumped as her phone rang. Calming her breathing, she picked up the phone.

"Hello?"

"Hey, just wanted to run something by you." Hollister's voice sounded in the air.

Blowing out a haggard breath, she closed her eyes and suddenly felt comforted. "Okay, what is it?"

"First off, are you okay?'

She smiled. "Yeah."

"That wasn't convincing."

"Just tired."

He sighed over the line. "Okay. Next, does the name Tobias Rutherford sound familiar?"

"No. Not at all. Who is he?"

"I think he's your attacker."

"What? Why do you think that?" She sat up and groaned with the sudden movement.

"What did you do?"

"I just sat up too fast. Now, why do you think it's him? Did you find out his license plate number?"

"I've been going through traffic cameras and found the truck. The damage, the chrome, I think it's a match. It took some guessing to the get the plate match, but I've got his license photo. Do you think you could pick him out?"

She sighed. "It was dark and with the shadows, but I can try."

"Okay, I'll send you a picture array and see if any look familiar. He doesn't have any priors, but there's a flag on his name. I'll look into that and see what's going on."

"Okay." She laid back down.

His deep sigh carried through the line. "You need some rest."

"I am resting."

"No, I mean, no working tomorrow."

"I'm not. I usually only work a few days a week unless Chuck is busy, which he isn't right now."

"Good, just give me a heads up if you plan a trip somewhere, okay?"

"I don't need a babysitter." She sighed.

"It's not like that. I just wanted to know in case you have trouble. Then, I'll have an idea of where you are. It's a precaution."

She frowned, but said, "Okay."

"You want to talk about anything?" His soft, calm voice carried through the line, and she smiled.

How did he do that? Bring peace to her turmoil with just his calming voice?

"I'm good. I think. I just need to go to sleep."

"Okay, talk to you later."

"Yeah, bye." She hung up and tried to get comfortable on the lumpy mattress. Her phone chirped again, and a series of faces lined up on the screen.

What do you think?

Studying each one, she kept going back to the second picture. It didn't look exactly like the man, but remarkably close.

Could be the second one. He had a weird smile and he's older than this picture. But I think it's him.

Yeah, it is. I'll see if I can get a different shot, that one is from several years ago. I should be getting a definite answer about the evidence on the knife too, so if you're not positive it's him, we might have a DNA confirmation to back it up.

Okay.

The silence carried a while in the room as she watched the bubbles pop up and back down on the screen. Seemed Hollister was struggling with what he wanted to say.

I wanted to ask, what's your friend's name who went missing?

She sighed.

I told you not to go into it. That's probably what started this whole mess.

It's not what started it, trust me.

She sat a moment.

Tara Ramsey.

Thanks, I'll look into it discreetly. I have a friend at the FBI who might be able to give me some info.

Hollister, don't get too caught up okay? I know you said you weren't chained to this job, but you'll be looking at getting fired if you're not careful.

She frowned at his need to push into a case that would end badly for him. Lester already had it out for her, and Walter trusted him implicitly. If Lester thought Hollister was helping her and influenced Walter against him ...

As much as I appreciate your concern, I can handle it. Call me later if you want to talk. I'll be up for a while.

Night, Hollister.

Night, Laurel.

21

Tara Ramsey was alive and well, living in an Illinois mental hospital.

Dev stared at the computer screen, comparing her high school graduation picture to the one on the screen labeled Missy Jane Doe.

Five years ago, she'd been found wondering the streets in Illinois, beaten, bruised, and confused. Without a missing person's report plus missing memory, the police found no evidence to determine her identity.

He'd have to ask Laurel why her parents didn't file a report, just in case. But then again, Tara was eighteen, and maybe they were talked out of it.

In an email to Bruce, he sent the info and the pictures, explaining his thoughts on who the missing person might be. As he typed, another email arrived from the state crime lab.

"That was quick," he muttered with a smile, saving the unfinished email and opening the other.

DNA from the knife will be run against Tobias Rutherford's DNA from warrant search on 10/14. Get you the results ASAP.

-Tray

Dev smiled and added the name Tobias Rutherford in the email to Bruce. His name was flagged by the FBI for a reason, and he wanted to know why. Finally, everything was coming together. It felt good to see a trail and possible end to all this.

As he drove home, his mind wandered to Laurel. She was just ... *man*. He didn't have the words. Beautiful, smart, and strong—so much more than what she appeared. If only she'd open up, allow herself to be more, be that woman he kept catching glimpses of.

After clearing his house, he showered and collapsed in bed. At almost midnight, he groaned at another late evening. But at least he felt accomplished.

"God, thanks for helping me through today and finding a possible connection. If this isn't the guy, please lead me to him. Let me find him and stop him. Please guide Laurel to You, and let her understand she's not in this all alone."

He sighed and felt the weight of her soul on his. She needed God much more than she needed him, and the thought made him a little sad. Especially since he was realizing just how much he was falling for her.

SITTING at the compound's gate, he frowned as it slowly opened.

"Come on," he mumbled under his breath.

Reaching the inside, he parked and climbed the porch steps. The door opened, and Tobias stood there, a frown on his face.

"Well?"

Tobias's shrug sent rage through his body. Gripping the man's shirt, he thew Tobias against the wall.

"Easy!"

"No! I warned you what would happen!"

"I've got eyes on her. My guy—he's keeping watch and is supposed to let me know where she is, and when we can get to her without that cop around."

"And you think that will come before that detective puts it all together? I'm sure by now your truck is known, and your name will be next if he hasn't already figured that out. If he ties you to me—"

"My arm," Tobias whined.

Releasing his grip, he stepped back. "I've built my life on this —it's my retirement plan. You screw it up, you'll have an enemy," he hissed. "Just remember, I can get to you when no one else can, Tobias. You've got until tomorrow to redeem yourself."

Tobias's face went crimson. "I don't need your threats. I've got it under control."

He huffed. "Not likely." Throwing open the door, he paused. "Tomorrow. Then *I'll* be the one taking care of everything— including you!"

22

Dev looked up at the sound of the door opening. Mrs. Beecham walked in, and he stood.

"Detective."

"Dev, please."

She grinned. "Dev. Is everything alright?"

"I was about to ask you the same thing."

"Oh, yes. Everything is fine. I spoke to Laurel this morning. She sounded as if she got some sleep."

"Good."

"Is Walter in?"

He shook his head. "No ma'am. But I'm sure he'll be back soon."

With a frown, she glanced over the room.

"Can I speak with you a moment?" He walked around the desk and offered her a chair.

"Thank you. You're such a gentleman." She sat, hands in her lap. "What you would like to discuss?" Her grin made him chuckle.

"Actually, I wanted to know about Guy Ashburn."

She looked up at him with a frown. "Why?"

"Just feel like I don't know the *real* man." Dev shrugged. "Only the one the town remembers."

"He was an evil man." Her shoulders slumped. "You could see it in his eyes. I never was fond of him, but his wife was a darling woman. Very caring, passionate, and concerned. I see a lot of April in Laurel."

Dev could see all those things and more.

"He was a good sheriff, did some good things, at least he did before he started drinking. I didn't meet him until after he changed. He tried to hide it, but this is a small town. Everyone basically knew what everyone else did. It wasn't as if anyone was surprised."

"So, everyone knew Laurel was right, but still treated her so badly?"

"No, not about that." She sighed. "When Laurel ran away and was found in the field, her comments about being attacked by her father went into the paper. It didn't help that he was no longer around to defend himself, plus, no one wanted to believe what she said was true." She swallowed hard before continuing. "There were always people who thought Laurel was lying, the ramblings of a child. Just because Guy drank didn't mean he did all those awful things."

Dev stood and walked to the other side of the desk, his fists clenched at his sides. "I can't believe this whole town went against her just because her father beat her, and she told the truth."

"You have to understand. Laurel was a troubled child. As I learned more and more about her past, it all made sense. Quiet, shy, yes, but she has a stubborn streak a mile wide. She'd had to defend herself all her life, but all most people saw was a disruptive child.

"We had always connected at church. So, I told her she could stay with me after everything happened. I knew there was something going on, but I, I never knew the extent." She sighed and dabbed her eyes.

"The case was never closed, her mother never found. Laurel went on with her schooling and joined the Navy after graduation."

"So, Walter never found her mother? Never determined what happened?"

She shook her head. "Walter believes there was an intruder, and that April tried to defend herself. Maybe Laurel stepped in and that's how she was injured. Guy appeared and was killed during the attack. April went missing. No one really knows what happened. Laurel was the only witness, and she doesn't remember."

He sat in the chair, his mind churning. "Walter believes Guy was a good man, a good sheriff. That he would never hurt anyone."

Mrs. Beecham sighed. "Walter wants to see the best in everyone. That's why he's been such a great role model for Laurel. He's supported her when so many are afraid or really think she's a danger. But to see Laurel's eyes when the subject comes up, her nightmares, her aversion to a simple hug." She shook her head. "I can't believe she would be scarred like that for any other reason than something violent."

He nodded along in complete agreement.

"Dev, I'm so happy you're working hard to help her. She needs someone who can prove to her how important she is."

His face heated at the comment.

Mrs. Beecham grinned. "You can't fool me, Detective. But just so you know, I see it both ways. I'm not sure I've ever seen Laurel talk to anyone like she does you. She has friends from when she was younger, but with you, there's something ... different."

"I'll, um ... keep working her case." He grinned.

"And I'll let you know if I find anything out." She stood and headed out of the office.

"Hey, Hollister?" Deputy Stack's voice echoed through the station.

"Yeah?" Dev stood with a huff and walked through the bullpen. "What's going on?"

"I've heard some things lately." Stacks eyed him with a smirk.

Great.

"And what have you heard?"

"Laurel's pretty, but trust me, big mistake."

"Laurel is pretty, beautiful actually. But what kind of mistake are you talking about?"

"Look." Stacks chuckled. "My brother has been after her for a while. They dated for a bit, then she broke it off with him for no reason. She's messed up in the head. Just being honest, man."

Working his jaw to keep from lashing out, Dev narrowed his eyes. "And who would your brother be?"

"Mitch Stacks."

Dev scoffed. "Mitch says they dated, and she's the one messed up in the head?"

Stacks shot to his feet, moving in fast and ready to strike. "What's that supposed to mean?"

Keeping his cool, Dev stood his ground, hoping this could end peaceably. Although, based on what he was about to say, that might not happen. "I saw him at her shop the day after she was attacked—came into the station for his car. He grabbed her arm so hard it made her injury bleed. She told him to back off, and that if he didn't, she'd file a report against him. Now I understand why she'd never done that. You wouldn't take it."

"He didn't do that. You're just in it with her, trying to mess with people." Stacks's finger pushed into his chest.

"Apparently, Chuck has a new video surveillance system. Wanna go down and check it out?" Dev glared at the deputy, once again frustrated at how badly the law enforcement in this town acted. "You don't have to take my word or Laurel's. Just go look at the video before you go around calling me, or her, a liar."

Stacks stared for a moment, then took off past him. Dev sighed. At least Laurel wouldn't be there today for Stacks to mess with.

"That was bold, man. He has a temper." Deputy Lester glared at him.

"Must run in the family. Mitch has one too. If he'd hung around, I would've arrested him right there for assault."

Lester glared a moment before returning to his desk.

Man, this was turning out to be a crazy day.

23

"Yeah, I can be there in ten," Laurel said.

"Are you sure?" Chuck asked. "I'm having a hard time getting everything done before the weekend, but I know you've been busy too."

"Don't worry about it. See you in a few."

Laurel rolled off the bed and closed her book, then pulled on her boots. Pushing her hair into a ponytail, she pulled on her hat, grabbed her keys and phone, and headed to the truck.

The fall breeze hit her face, the sun poked through the clouds. She wondered if she'd have to deal with Hollister for getting out. Smiling, she slid into the truck and headed for the shop.

She debated calling him but didn't want to. Well, she actually did want to call, to hear his voice. Unfortunately, he still had no idea just how deep all the hate in this town ran. It was a situation she didn't want him in the middle of, no matter how wonderful it felt to finally have someone on her side.

Pulling into the shop, her heart leapt at the sight of a police cruiser sitting in the parking lot. Rushing inside, she found Chuck behind the counter with Deputy Stacks.

"Chuck? You okay?"

"I think maybe I need to ask you the same thing." Chuck looked up with worry in his eyes.

"I'm fine. Why do you ask?"

"You didn't tell me you were having problems."

She shrugged. "Problems? With who?"

"My brother." Officer Stacks glared at her. His jaw tensed.

"Who said I was?" She pushed her hands on her hips and glared back at the officer.

"Hollister."

She frowned.

"How often?" Stacks moved from behind the counter and Chuck followed.

"How often what?" She crossed her arms and returned his glare. She'd been in the Navy. It would take a lot more than Deputy Stacks to intimidate her.

"Mitch. How often does he come in here and bother you? Did you ever go on a date?"

"No. He'd ask, I'd decline."

"He grabbed your arm."

She nodded.

"He won't bother you anymore." Stacks muttered as he headed out the door.

"You should've told me sooner, dear." Chuck's voice made her turn back. "I could've talked to him for you."

"It's fine. Besides, he's not a bad guy, I guess. Just doesn't know how to take 'no' for an answer."

"And a man who, apparently, spread rumors about you two dating."

"Oh?" She clenched her jaw a moment. "I didn't know that." Now she *did* want to punch the guy out.

Chuck only gave a quick laugh and patted her shoulder. "You sure you're feeling all right?"

"I'm fine. Just a little sore. I can sit here and help people just as easily as I can sit in my hotel room." She smiled.

"Okay, then, I'll be in the back finishing up on the car I'm working on. We have three coming in to pay, and four more are coming to pick up parts they ordered. It'll help me out a lot if I don't have to keep running up here to wait on them." Chuck winked and headed back to the bay to finish up.

She slid onto the bar stool, the video still on the screen. Pressing play, her eyes focused on Dev. He had taken a few steps before Mitch finally backed off.

Seemed he did want to take care of Mitch for her. A smile etched on her lips as she leaned her chin in her hand. Of all the people in this town, the ones who heard the rumors and stayed away, the ones who planted the rumors out of their hate for her, it took an outside man to step in to help.

Darrell was right. Maybe she should let him help.

"WHAT DO you mean you can't tell me?" Dev paced his living room.

"It's a need-to-know case," answered Bruce from the FBI, his voice filled with frustration.

"But he's a suspect in my attack and attempted kidnapping case. Why is he flagged?"

"Has she identified him?"

Dev blew out a breath. "It was dark, and she picked his picture from an array. She thinks it's him, but he's older now than that license picture. I'm waiting on DNA—"

"DNA? You have his DNA? From what?"

"The knife he attacked her with was left at the scene. The blood was hers, but there was a small piece of skin wedged at the base of the blade. I'm hoping it's our attacker's and not hers. There's a sample from a case back in 2014. He was ordered to give up his DNA in order to convict him of an assault. He ended up walking because of a technicality."

Something that wouldn't happen with his case.

"So, you're not sure yet?"

Dev winced and ran his hand through his hair. "No. Not until the DNA is finished."

"Call me when it's done. I've got some things to do on my end. If it's positive, don't go chasing after him without calling. I mean it."

"Yeah, I will. Then you'll let me know?"

"Then you'll be read in. I'll put in a word about that DNA, see if I can help it along."

"Thanks man." Dev huffed and tossed the phone on the table, rotating his neck, trying to release the tension in his shoulders.

He'd just grabbed a snack when his phone went off again. Laurel's name flashed across the screen.

"Hey, you, I was just about to call you and see if—"

"They're here."

"What? At the hotel?" He stood and grabbed his keys, taking off to his truck.

"No, I'm at the shop."

"You're out? What—" he muttered under his breath, trying to keep his tone civil. "It's going to take me about five minutes to get there. Are you inside?"

"No, as soon as I saw the truck, I locked the doors and headed out the back toward the feed store. Chuck just left, and I was cleaning up when I heard the truck pull up. It's the same one from the other day." Her heavy breaths echoed through the line.

A lump formed in his throat and his heart picked up its pace. "Look, just keep moving. I'll call Morris—"

"No, he's off today. Lizzy called this morning and said they were going on a date."

He groaned. Of course, now would be the time the one deputy he got along with would take his advice. "Just keep your phone on, I need to be able to talk to you when I get there."

She grunted, then moaned. Running was a bad idea, if she split her stitches this time, there might not be a way to fix them.

Speeding down the highway, he hung a right then crossed

traffic to turn onto Main Street. The feed store was a large area, on at least a few acres and held a silo and granary for the local farms. He passed the mechanic shop but didn't notice her or the attacker's truck anywhere.

"Where are you?"

"I'm in the back field between the feed store and the shop."

The crack of a rifle made him jump.

"Laurel?"

"I'm fine, they're trying to flush me out. You need to hang up and call for backup." She ended the call.

Putting a call in to the station, he jumped from the truck and headed inside the feed store.

"You need to get everyone out."

"We're working on it. Heard the rifle shot, what's goin on?" A man with the handlebar mustache motioned to the others as they headed for their trucks.

"Sheriff's office."

His attention turned back to the phone. "Lester?"

"Detective Hollister, what can I do for you?" The long-winded rambling tone just made Dev mad.

"Shots fired at the feed store. Seems Laurel's attackers have come back."

"What? What attackers? Look, I know you're new here—" Another shot rang out and Lester cursed.

"Get here now!" Dev hung up.

He rushed through the store to the back of the building. The bed of a dark blue truck barely stuck out from behind one of the outlying buildings. Drawing his weapon, he stepped outside and sidled along the wall, looking for the men and Laurel.

His phone buzzed and he pulled it from his belt without looking. "Hollister."

"You're out in the open, going to get yourself killed." Laurel's ragged voice breathed through the line. "Double back to the truck, I'll jump in."

"You need cover."

"No, I can make it. But if they see you, we're both in trouble."

"Fine." He sighed. "But one more gunshot, and I'm coming back."

"Make it two." She hung up.

Dev smirked at her ability to handle the situation with a little humor. Backing up, he slid through the door and rushed back to the front, got in his truck, and cranked the ignition. He pulled up to the edge of the building as another shot echoed. Laurel's hat came into view as she sprinted toward him. Reaching across the seat, he opened the passenger door.

"Let's go!"

She barely got the door shut when he took off, ducking as another rifle shot took out his rear windshield, littering the backseat with broken glass. The sound of sirens filled the air as he drove past Main Street and took the shortcut to the sheriff's office.

"Where're you going?" Laurel's breathless voice sounded above the truck's engine.

"The station. They won't attack us there, and maybe with the cameras around the building, we might get a picture of the men in the truck."

"Seriously? Is there even anyone there?"

He frowned and pulled out his phone. The station line rang and rang, proving she was right—the only two deputies on duty were probably headed to the feed store. He punched in Stacks's number, but it went straight to voicemail.

"Need you to be on the lookout for a blue GMC with a chrome bumper, they're the ones doing the shooting." He hung up and grunted. "I still think the station—"

Another round of shots cracked from behind them, and he swerved, turning onto the highway.

"Okay, no station. What do you suggest?" he yelled over the sounds of the air rushing through the truck.

"Just keep going until exit 115."

He sighed and nodded, weaving through the cars and trying to squelch his anger. As they took the exit, she directed him right, and he flew down the road and through the red light. Horns blared and cars swerved, slowing the truck chasing them.

"What are you doing out of your hotel room? I thought I asked you to keep me updated on where you were?" Slamming his horn, he tore through another light.

"Chuck called and needed a hand. I had to go help."

He groaned, trying his best to cover his irritation that she hadn't let him know. Taking a hard left, he flew down the old highway. Glancing in his mirror, the truck sat several cars back, caught in the rush-hour traffic.

"I'm just saying, that could've been bad if I wasn't so close."

"Would you just drop it and focus on the road?" She shouted, then pointed at a turn. "Right, up here."

Barreling down the county road, he followed her directions, making a right and then left off the rural road as they climbed a hill.

"Keep going till the fork, then go left."

They bounced and flew over the dirt road, hitting the potholes and the gravel that lined the drive. Pulling in behind an old barn, he cut the lights and turned off the truck. Laurel jumped out and he followed her inside.

24

The air thickened as droplets of rain pelted the ground. Following Laurel into the boarded-up barn, Dev hesitated. "I'm not sure this is the safest spot."

"We'll be fine," she mumbled.

Pushing through the space between the broken planks, they stepped inside. Dank air and the stench of rotting wood filled his senses. Laurel rushed over to a boarded-up window and peered through a slit.

He took the spot beside her and angled to see the road. But they were too low, the hill kept them from seeing beyond the field.

"There's a loft, I'll go look—"

"No, you stay here." He frowned.

She nodded and turned back to the window. The evening sun shone through the rainclouds, casting an orange glow through the barn. Missing timbers and slats allowed enough light to help him find the rickety ladder and make his way to the loft.

Through some gaps in the boards, he viewed the road. The flash of a chrome grill kicked up his heartbeat. The truck paused and the sounds of slamming doors echoed. Frowning, he waited.

More slamming doors and the truck soon rolled backward, then turned and headed down the other road.

Blowing out a breath, he climbed down and found Laurel still at the same spot, looking out.

"I saw them leave. They stopped then headed back the other direction." He pulled out his phone. "We don't have any cell service here. I need to get some backup headed this way before we leave, just in case they circle back. Who's property is this?"

"Darrell's."

He frowned at her deep breaths. Laurel leaned against the wall and grimaced. She probably hadn't slept in days, and after all the running, she had to be exhausted. What she needed was a distraction.

Grinning, he pushed at the bill of her hat until she looked up. "What're you doing?"

"You did need me."

She huffed and placed her hands on her hips. "Are you crazy? Just because I called—"

"Yes, you called me because you needed help. Everyone needs help, Laurel. Just making sure you realize that."

"Fine, *Dev*, I needed someone to distract the guys with guns."

His smile fell as he reigned in his surprise. She called him by his first name.

"What? What's wrong now?"

Before he could think, he stepped forward and pushed her hat back. Taking hold of her elbow, he kissed her hard and fast. His heart raced as he eased back just enough to see her blue eyes searching his.

Wide and surprised, she barely glanced at his lips before he leaned in again, holding the back of her head gently.

As he pulled her closer, her arms wrapped around his neck, bringing him down to her. Breathing her in, he reveled at her lips, her body pressed up against his as he tried to catch up to her eagerness.

Slowing, he continued, kiss after kiss, trying to make the moment last before she finally released his neck and lowered herself back to the ground.

"Laurel ..."

Breathless, her hands all at once fell off his chest, and she backed away.

"No. Hang on." He caught her elbows.

But her hands raised in front of her as if to ward him off.

Releasing her arms, he took a firm grip of her belt loops. "Laurel, look at me." He worked to ease his breathing and slow his racing mind. "Just ... wait."

Feeling led to let go, he groaned and stepped back, releasing her and shoving his hands in his pockets. "Talk to me."

She crumpled to the floor, then ripped the hat off her head, pulling her ponytail halfway down with it. Putting her knees to her chest with a moan, she rested her head on them. He sat down opposite her, stretching out his legs as he leaned against the wall. Waiting for her to speak felt like an eternity. His heart pounded.

"Look, that was not—you can't just do that, Dev," she muttered.

As much as he tried, he couldn't help but smile that she used his first name. Again.

"Do what? It seemed an awful lot like you were involved too." He grinned again as she shook her head.

"That's not it," she whispered.

"Then, explain it to me."

"I can't. You just, you wouldn't understand."

"I don't know. I'm a pretty smart city guy, remember?'

She looked up for just a second, her blue eyes catching his. A glimmer of a smirk flitted across her lips, and his heart eased. The lump in his throat lessened as he stood. Stepping across the room, he sat next to her. She pulled her legs underneath and sat on her feet.

"This is just like with Mitch—"

"You think I'm like Mitch?" He frowned as she made eye contact, a red flush noticeable even in the dim light of the barn.

"No. That's not it."

"Okay ..." he waited again as she pulled tendrils of hair from her face.

"This is just an attraction. That's all."

"That's what it was for you? Because it didn't feel like that to me."

"Look, I've been trying to warn you, but you won't listen." She sighed. "You think Deputy Lester is the only one who will treat you differently? Everyone in town will dispise you, just because of me. You need to stop this."

"Laurel, I'm not stopping anything. I don't kiss a lot of people. I'm a gentleman that way." He winked.

But she shook her head, wiping her face and refusing to make eye contact.

"And those I have kissed, have never kissed me back like that. This is more than attraction, although, I am very attracted to you. You're beautiful."

She shook her head again and stood with a grunt, making him stand as well.

"You need to back off. I won't—I won't ruin anyone else's life."

"Laurel, I need a different reason." He stepped in front of her. "You looking out for my well-being is one thing. But I'm not giving you up without a better reason. I told you the other day, God put me here for some purpose, and it's become more and more clear that it's because of you."

The corners of her mouth titled down. She stared up at him, tears forming in her eyes. He saw her change in an instant—that strong-willed fighter transformed into a woman who was alone, with her body bearing the brunt of being alone for too long. Her shoulders shook as she held her face, and he slowly stepped in.

Pulling her close, she rested her forehead on his chest, and he wrapped his arms around her.

"What is it that upset you so badly?" He swallowed hard, his mind rushing to find the words God would want him to say. "The fact someone cares deeply about you, or the fact God would care enough to send me?"

Her hands gripped the front of his shirt, her body weakening as she leaned heavily into him. Leaning down, he kissed her cheek, breathing her in, and sensing so much more than attraction moving between them.

"I really do care about you, very much. And as attractive as I find you, as any man would find you, that's not the only thing I see. You're an amazing woman, giving up so much of yourself for everyone else. You have an astounding character, and I know there's another side to you. I've seen only a little, but I'm very eager to see the rest of who you are. If you'll just let me."

She shook her head, and he frowned.

"Do you trust me?" He swept her hair away from her face, tucking it behind her ear and rubbing the back of her neck gently.

"I trust you, but this is different. I'm just—I can't ..."

"Okay," he sighed, the lump in his throat welling up again. "That's fine. But I'm not going anywhere, and I'll prove none of that matters. I do care about you, and that's not going to change." He felt her stiffen and squeezed her gently. "Now, let's go see if we can get a cell signal and get out of here."

Taking her hand, he led her through the barn door and up the ridge to the tree line.

The mist falling around them cooled his body from their earlier interaction. Attraction, yeah, there was a lot of attraction. But her character still amazed him, moved him. God had placed him here for this purpose. He was certain.

Laurel Ashburn. He was meant to find her and help her. And just maybe, God willing, there could be something more between them.

25

U sing his phone's light, Dev hiked until he got a signal.
"Sheriff's office."

"Hey, Stacks.."

"What is it, Detective?"

He frowned at the tone. "Is there a problem at the office?"

"No."

"Then I need some backup."

"Backup for what? We just got back from the feed store. There were a lot of worried people to calm down. Who was shooting and why? What is she into?"

Heat hit his face as Laurel pulled from his grip. He turned and pulled her back in, wrapping his arm around her.

"Look, a little professional courtesy would be great here. Besides, she's not getting into anything—the men trying to kill her and then us would be trouble-makers."

"You know, Lester said—"

"Lester has a vendetta against her and won't listen to truth," Dev snapped as Laurel pulled away again. "Now, I need you on County Line Road 119, and I need you there now. You're on the lookout for a dark blue GMC truck with a chrome grill and a scratch down the passenger's side.

"We're trying to get out of hiding. You either be there and offer some support, or you can take Lester's point of view to the county reprimand board." His heart pounded as he finished. Anger and irritation clung to him.

"Fine."

The call ended, and he pocketed the cell phone, noticing Laurel was gripping her hands at her chest level, watching him intently.

"I told you, it's not just Lester," she murmured.

"And I told you, none of that bothers me." He grinned and reached for her hand, but she just frowned. "Look, I'm not pushing here. I'm not trying for anything. But that doesn't mean I'm not going to take care of you when I can. I rather like that part." He smiled and led her back to the vehicle, wrapping his arm gently around her side.

Piling into the truck, he slowly backed out and waited at the edge of the barn. Several minutes later, headlights lit the darkening sky and paused. He pulled out from the safety of the barn and passed Stacks at the end of the road. Dev called him again.

"I need any footage from the feed store, anything that can give us a picture of the truck or the shooter. Check the cameras at the stop lights around town too."

"I'll take care of it," Stacks muttered.

"Keep me updated, and I'll be back at the station as soon as I can."

After arguing about where she would stay, Dev agreed to take Laurel back to her hotel and gather her belongings, but left her truck at the shop.

"I do need a vehicle," she huffed.

"I realize that. But right now, I'm much more concerned about you being somewhere safe."

"I'll be safe at Molly's. But I don't like not having a vehicle, just in case."

"Have you called Mrs. Beecham?"

Laurel shook her head and pulled out her phone. Watching her place the call, he smiled. She'd been working to shrug off everything that happened between them, but he wasn't blowing it off. It didn't matter how much she pushed. He wasn't going anywhere.

Pulling up to the station, Laurel groaned.

"It's just for a second. I need to see if we've got any footage of the truck."

She nodded and slid from the seat.

As he opened the door for her, she stepped inside and found Mrs. Beecham, waiting.

"Laurel? Are you okay?" Mrs. Beecham's face paled.

"Yes ma'am. I told you that on the phone."

"Hollister?"

He closed the door and faced Walter. "We've got to cinch this up. Those guys are pushing too hard, and I don't like it."

Walter pulled Laurel in for a quick hug. "Kendra, the two of you go in my office."

Kendra took Laurel's hand and walked off, as Walter steeled Dev with a glare.

"This is cutting too close. I want to know everything you have and where it's going."

Dev grabbed the original file from his desk and handed it over. "The truck we're chasing, as well as the identity of the man who attacked Laurel."

Walter stared at the file. "Tobias Rutherford?" He shrugged. "Doesn't ring a bell."

"His name is flagged by the FBI. I've got a buddy looking into it for me."

Walter's mouth dropped to a frown. "Why's the FBI involved?"

Dev shrugged. "No idea. He says it's need-to-know, and so far, I don't. We do have some DNA—"

"DNA? From what?"

"The first attack. Rutherford left the knife at the scene, and

I retrieved it. It had a piece of skin wedged in the blade. My buddy is going to help push it through if he can."

"Good. I want this guy off the street and Laurel out of danger." Walter took off the with file. He turned back to face Dev. "And Hollister—"

"Yes?"

"Keep me in the loop."

Dev nodded as Laurel stepped out of the office to grab a water bottle from the cabinet.

His heart pounded in his ears.

God, why did she have to go through so much?

Storm after storm, and she weathered each one as if it were nothing. The fact that someone kept coming after her, her injuries, she took everything in stride. Each storm seemed to steel her more, make her stronger. And more withdrawn.

Would she ever let him in? After all this was done, the case solved, her safety ensured, would she allow him to get close? Because now, that was all he could think of.

God, give her some peace, lead and guide her. And lead me too. Help me to protect her.

His phone rang, and his jaw jerked.

God, please.

Her gaze jumped to his for a second, a red flush falling on her cheeks as she hurried back into Walter's office.

"Hollister."

"You got a sec?" Bruce asked.

"Yeah." He wandered over to the wall to lean against it with a sigh. "What's up?"

"It's Tara."

"What? The Jane Doe?" His breath hitched in his throat as Bruce's chuckle echoed. "You better not be playing around here."

Bruce huffed. "It's her. Her parents just made the ID. They want to keep it quiet in case whoever took her wants to make sure she can't talk."

"She remembers who took her?"

"Not sure about that. I didn't get a chance to speak to the parents or to her doctor to see if she remembers. But I guess anything's possible. How's your case going?"

"It's ... complex. I'm hoping to get that DNA and get this thing cinched."

"Like I said, I've put in a word. Don't go around telling anyone, especially the friend, about Tara."

"I wouldn't do that, Bruce ."

"Good. Let me know if you need some intervention down there."

"I might just take you up on that." He sighed. "Good people are hard to come by around here."

"Good luck, man."

"Thanks."

26

"Laurel, are you sure you're okay?" Kendra watched her intently.

Laurel offered a nod. "Just tired. Other than that—"

"Kendra, you know she's stronger than everyone thinks." Walter gave her a wink before he sat behind his desk.

"I know that, Walter. But it's always nice when someone asks." Kendra shot him a glare before turning back to Laurel. "Can you identify who's chasing you? I would think by now you've gotten a good look at something."

Laurel shook her head. "Not really. I recognize the man's voice, the one who tried to take me. He chased me through the field. Other than that, I never see a face. Just the truck.

"Excuse me a moment." Walter snatched up his jacket and headed out the door.

Following Walter's exit, Laurel watched Dev pacing the lobby.

"How are things with you and Detective Hollister?"

Laurel's face heated "We're fine. He's ... helping. I didn't think anyone would. I mean—"

"Laurel, he's a good man. I can see how much he cares for you."

"He doesn't really. It's just an attraction." She huffed. "I do think he's a good man and that's why he's helping. That's all."

Mrs. Beecham frowned. "You can't keep hiding who you are, and you sure can't keep pushing a man like that away. He's an eligible bachelor who could have his pick of any free woman in this town, and he chose you."

"He can't. You understand. You talk to him. He won't listen to me." She sat up with a groan. "He'll get fired, or run out, or—"

"Laurel, he's made his choice. It's a good choice, and I won't convince him of anything else. I'm actually hoping he'll take you away from here."

"What?" She stared at Kendra's smile.

"You need to find a nice place where you can be happy, and this town isn't it. I'll be fine here. I have my quilting club and the church. I have friends here to help me out. You needn't feel responsible for me."

"I'm not going anywhere." She clenched her jaw, her back burning as she looked up to see Dev heading toward them.

Why'd he have to be so good-looking? And that smile ...

"Are you ready to go?"

"Yeah, take Kendra, I'm going to the hospital to see if Lizzy—"

"I thought you said she was out."

She sighed, rubbing her forehead. That she had forgotten about. "Never mind."

"If you need someone to look at your back, let another nurse do it."

Shaking her head, she stood. "It's fine."

Before she could move, Dev stepped into her space, and she flinched.

"Laurel, you need to take care of yourself. I don't want to risk you being so injured if someone got to you ...." he whispered, his voice trailing off.

Looking up into those green eyes, she felt a pull she didn't think she'd ever have. His hands on her hips, that worried and concerned look on his face ... her heart pounded in her chest as she forced her eyes from falling to his lips.

"I—I'm fine," she stammered.

"You're not. But if you won't get it checked out, I guess I'll have to stick closer." He narrowed his eyes with a smirk.

Laurel frowned when he finally released her and turned, letting her go in front of him. His hand went to her side, and she tried to keep from tensing up, but it seemed even he couldn't break down all her walls.

As they walked to the parking lot, she did her best to keep from letting her mind go, allowing herself to fall into his arms. After all, it was being here with him that would make things worse, for him and for her.

"Where are you staying, dear?" Mrs. Beecham asked.

"I haven't decided." Laurel shrugged.

"I have an extra bedroom at my place." He neared his truck. "I think until this guy is stopped, you need protection."

She paused at the comment. Her eyes wide as Mrs. Beecham just stood there, grinning.

"No, I can't. That's not a good idea."

Dev huffed. "Laurel, I want you safe."

"I understand that, but I ... that just doesn't seem like a good idea."

"Why not?" Dev crossed his arms.

Trying to understand why he would offer to personally protect her, she opened her mouth to protest. By morning, they'd be the talk of the town, and his career would effectively be over.

"Then that's settled. Come on." Dev opened the door for her as Mrs. Beecham chuckled and slid into her car.

Laurel stood and stared a moment as he prodded her to get inside. Turning, she gripped the door handle and his arm.

"Dev, you can't. You'll lose your job. You just don't understand."

"I do understand. If that's not comfortable for you, then the sheriff's office it is. There's a bedroom in the back, and—"

"No." She felt nauseated just thinking about staying the night there. "I—I can't stay there." Her body trembled, and she held her head a moment, closing her eyes and taking a deep breath.

Dev wrapped his arms around her. She fell against him, relaxing and enjoying the rest as her fears disappeared.

"We'll find a different option then, one where I can stay with you. I'm not risking you being out of my sight. These guys must be getting desperate," he whispered in her ear, causing chill bumps to cascade down her body. "Cold?"

She smirked at the humor in his voice. Looking up, she swallowed at her mistake. His green eyes focused first on hers then dropped to her lips. Her hands gripped his shirt, and she could feel his heart pounding beneath her palms.

Finding some strength, she made herself push him away.

"Let's—we need to go," she muttered.

"Yeah." His lips curled into a smile.

She slid onto the seat and sat back. He shut the door for her, and she sighed.

Being in close quarters would effectively eliminate her chances of keeping distance, letting the attraction ease up. Even if he didn't realize it, she wasn't the kind of woman he needed. Her reputation and past had already ruined her life—letting it ruin his as well wasn't an option.

They followed Mrs. Beecham to Aunt Molly's, then headed to Dev's for some of his things.

She stood just inside the door, uncomfortable and out of place in his home.

"You can sit down, you know." He stood at the kitchen island watching as she shoved her hands in her pockets.

"I'm fine," she muttered.

Hearing his sigh, she looked up as he strode down the hallway and out of sight. The smell of paint still hung in the air, and she remembered the night he called asking about an alibi.

Someone trashed his house and wrote something on the wall. He must've painted over it already. She scanned the walls, trying to find the marked spot.

A family picture caught her eye. She moved in closer to see a younger version of Dev, a huge smile on his face and a couple who must be his parents next to him. Several others surrounded him, and he held a certificate of some kind.

"That was when I became a detective."

She spun around, surprised at his close stance. "Oh."

Stepping closer, he pointed around her. "That's my brother Harry, my sister Pam, and her husband Luke."

"It must be nice to have such a big family."

"It has its drawbacks. But it's nice to know I always have backup, someone on my side no matter what."

She nodded. That intense loneliness hit her again. Besides Mrs. Beecham, she'd never experienced that closeness. Her mother was always kind and loving, but she was so caught up in her own lies with Guy that she was too busy to really be there for Laurel.

Lizzy and Tara, well, they'd been there for her at one time. But there was little they could really do to help with Laurel's family situation. Although she stayed with Tara as often as her parents allowed. Her memory hung on Tara's face and laughter. She missed her.

"Laurel, you have that too."

She shook her head and tried to walk away but he stepped in front of her.

"You have more than just Mrs. Beecham," his whispered voice made her want to fall into his arms once again.

Why was he suddenly so irresistible?

"If you're going into the God lecture again, I'm not ... just don't." She sighed and took a step back, crossing her arms and hoping he got the message.

"It's not just God who's there for you. I am too." He propped his hands on his hips, tilting his head as he watched her. "Do you even want someone on your side?"

Laurel felt her eyes widened. "Why would you ask that?"

He shrugged. "You seem so adamant against me helping and I—I wonder if you just don't want help."

"It's not that, but, I mean, usually, help comes with a price."

"Such as?"

"Silence." She clenched her jaw. "Or the fact that Lester has tried so many times to get me locked up that it seems no matter what I do or say, it gets twisted and used against me somehow."

"Come here." He gently clasped her elbow, guiding her to the couch.

She sat on the cushions with a wince. He pulled up the large ottoman in front of her.

"What kind of silence?"

Like she really wanted to get into this. She blew out a haggard breath. "Look, I don't want to talk about the past. It's not pleasant, and I've worked to just forget."

"I can see how hard you've worked to forget. But the problem is, you've also worked hard to push everyone aside when it comes to anything personal. Or maybe it's just me." He leaned forward on his knees.

"It's not just you, I—I'm just careful." She groaned. "I've been through too much to just let anyone around, okay? Anyone who might hurt me in any way. If I can stop it, I just don't let it get to me."

"It makes sense, I get it." He sighed and took her hands in his. "But the thing is, I don't want you to stop me." His green eyes looked up into hers. "You said you trust me."

"I do, but there's a difference in trust and what you're— what's going on here." She swallowed hard, hating to see the look of disappointment on his face. "Dev, I just want you to know, I do appreciate everything you've done for me, but I—I'm not going to be worth it."

He chuckled. "I think it's interesting you believe you know what's good for me."

"I do know. You're a great detective and a good cop. You don't need a distraction or someone who will ruin your reputation. That's what this is." She pointed between them and scooted to the front of the couch to stand.

Standing with her, he pulled her in. She sighed and let him, wrapping her arms around his middle and enjoying the comfort.

"Laurel, when I said I didn't need this job, it's because God gave me this job. I wasn't looking for it, and I didn't even think I'd get it. So, when they called and gave it to me, I was more than a little surprised. If this job doesn't work, if I get fired because I want to be with you, I have faith God will give me something else.

Dev backed up and pulled her chin up. "You have me to depend on. I'll always come looking for you, I'll always find you, and you can always lean on me for anything."

"Why?" She furrowed her brow.

He chuckled and tucked away some hair behind her ear. Her skin heated as he ran his fingers across her cheek.

"Because I see a side to you I don't think a lot of people see. You're an amazing woman, inside and out. And I know God wants me here to help you."

Uncomfortable with him always saying that, always calling her amazing and referring to God's plan for her, she pulled back. None of it made sense.

"Come on." He sighed. "We need to get out of here and find a place to stay."

27

After a few phone calls, they made plans to stay at Darrell's. He'd built a one-bedroom guest house behind his home for his aging mother, who hadn't moved in yet.

They stopped at the diner and picked up a to-go order, then headed out to Darrell's.

When they arrived, their host ushered them inside.

"Are you sure, Darrell?" Laurel frowned, worried he was once again being dragged down because of her.

"Stay as long as you want. You know you're always welcome here or at my barn anytime." Darrell winked and she stifled her grin as Dev chuckled from behind her. But then Darrell turned serious. "Laurel, I want you safe."

"And I don't want to drag you into another—"

"Don't." Darrell shook his head, crossing his beefy arms over his chest. "I'm not willing to let anything happen to you either."

She simply nodded and smiled. "Thanks."

"Come on, I'll show you around." Darrell motioned and they followed him to the side door and out to the yard.

Several yards behind Darrell's home sat a quaint cottage. Laurel followed Darrell inside, smiling at the immaculate woodwork and new furnishings.

177

"Did you do all this yourself?"

Darrell beamed.

"I can't believe it." Dev let out a whistle. "This is amazing. You could do contract work all over the state."

"It's just a hobby, no need in making it work." Darrell shrugged.

Dev chuckled and held out his hand. Darrell shook it with a nod.

"Like I said, stay as long as you like." Darrell looked at her for a moment, then back to Dev before he left.

"I guess you're one of the lucky few." She tossed her bag on the floor.

"Why's that?" Dev turned with his hands in his pockets, that amazing smile of his shining.

"Darrell's not usually so friendly. He doesn't talk much because he sometimes stutters, and he doesn't like outsiders."

"Well, we've talked a few times. The stuttering thing, I've not heard that."

She sat down on the sofa with a grimace, working to ignore the searing pain across her back.

"Let me take a look. I'll get the first aid kit from the truck."

She glared up at him for a minute. Trust with anyone besides Lizzy or her Navy team members wasn't something she did. She didn't feel comfortable with anyone seeing her back. But since he'd already seen it once ...

"Fine."

As he left, she lay on her stomach, burying her face in the pillow and trying to relax. Her body hurt, her heart ached, and now, she was in this ... whatever this was with Dev.

What was she going to do? And being under the same roof? That just seemed like an even worse idea.

"Yeah, well, I'll take sick days then. I have two weeks, start taking it out," Dev said.

She rolled over, her hand holding her head as Dev walked in on his phone with his med kit, his face red.

"Do what you think you have to Lester, but I'm telling you, this is bigger than you know. If someone from the crime lab calls, you better send them to my phone, or I'll have your badge." He hung up and tossed the phone on the table.

"What was that about?"

"Just a difference of opinion. Lester's decided since the incident at the feed store that something else is going on, and I'm involved somehow. He thinks I need admin leave."

"What did Walter say?"

He shrugged. "Didn't ask. I don't have time to deal with Lester's grievances. He can take them up with Walter, and then, hopefully, Walter can straighten him out." He pulled out the gauze and tape before he knelt next to the couch. "You ready?"

She studied those amazing eyes of his for a moment. "Just remember, I don't talk about it."

He nodded and she lay back down, lifting up the back of her shirt slightly to reveal the stitches.

"You have one busted, must be from running this evening."

Despite the cold sting of the alcohol, she let her body relax into the cushions. Closing her eyes, she focused on Dev being there and being comforted by the fact he was helping, but her mind slowly moved toward the past.

"You're done." He finished up and pulled her shirt down. "That should hold, but we need to take you to get them fixed up tomorrow sometime."

She sat up, her body trembling.

"Let's eat."

While Dev busied himself with the food, she held her head and tried her best to hold back the wave rolling over her shoulders. Her mind disengaged, heat burned at her skin, yells and screams echoed in her mind.

A hand gripped her shoulder and she jumped up, seizing the fingers and spinning around before making eye contact with Dev.

"Sorry," she said breathlessly and released his hand.

"Talk to me." He helped her back to the couch, then sat down next to her, pulling her in.

She closed her eyes and took a few deep breaths, covering her face. Her body trembled. He lifted her to his lap and held her tight. Pushing her face into his neck, she held on and took some deep breaths. The nausea eased, and her muscles relaxed.

"What triggered it?"

"I'm not sure." She swallowed hard to keep from crying. "Just ... being on my stomach, someone messing with my back ... it all just ... I'm so tired," she muttered, and her tears let loose.

He held her as she cried. For the first time in forever, she felt safe and comforted. Her eyes closed, and her mind drifted.

AFTER CARRYING Laurel to the bed, Dev hated to let her go, but knew she'd sleep better if she wasn't curled up in his lap.

Covering her with the blankets, he pushed the hair away from her face, enjoying the view of her without the hat. He was impressed with how she dealt with everything hitting her at once.

How could she think she wasn't worth it?

He closed the door and scrubbed his hands over his face and through his hair. She needed help, much more than a doctor to stitch up her back. The mental dump she carried was too much, between her abused childhood and whatever happened overseas.

Sinking to the couch, Dev let out a breath, emotionally and physically spent.

"God, You've got to get through to her. You've got to show her there's a way out of all of this if she'd turn to You. She's hanging on to way too much."

Leaning back on the couch, he closed his eyes, exhausted from the day's events. As appealing as the food smelled from the kitchen, he was too tired to eat. He put the boxes back into the fridge, then lay on the couch and tried to relax enough to sleep.

Between mentally sparring with his feelings for Laurel and the physical toll of escaping men determined to kill her, he needed to be rested for the next day's events.

The problem was, until the DNA on the knife came back, they were in limbo. He couldn't arrest men they couldn't catch, something that would have to change tomorrow.

There were several chances to catch the man with the truck and even with the BOLO, he'd struck out. How could that happen in such a small area? Between the other officers and himself, they should've seen the truck again by now.

His eyes popped open. Unless Lester hadn't followed through with the BOLO. He groaned and sat up. Worry for Laurel had superseded everything else, and he'd left the BOLO and video up to Lester.

He pulled out his phone and stepped outside. If this went the way he assumed it would, he'd get loud enough to wake Laurel.

"What is it Hollister?"

"Lester, we need to talk."

28

Laurel's eyes popped open at the smell of something amazing in the air. Pushing herself up with a groan, the bedroom walls and pictures lined her vision.

How did she get in the bed?

The memory of crying against Dev, his arms wrapped around her and holding her tight surfaced, and she lay back down with a huff. She was pitiful. Between her flashbacks and her exhausted sobbing, he must think her a huge mess.

She rolled off the bed, found her duffle bag on the chair by the door, and sifted through it for clean clothes. Quietly opening the door, she slipped through the hallway and into the bathroom.

Making sure the door latched, she undressed and stepped into the shower. The warm water eased the ache in her neck as she sighed. This had to end soon. Her body, her mind couldn't take much more.

And then there was Dev. She closed her eyes and tried to figure out why he was so adamant about being there for her.

Was it the God thing? Was he just pushing his religion on her? Was there something else he wanted?

She groaned and fisted her hands to keep from hitting the

tile. Dev Hollister was a good man. There was nothing backhanded or tricky about how he'd helped her through all this. But for some reason, her mind couldn't grasp that idea.

Was it so different from when she dated Mason?

Dev had been there for her just like Mason, treated her with respect and kindness, put up with her attitude and anger. Trusting him was easy. But setting her mind free, convincing herself he was worth it—it just wasn't working.

After dressing, she checked her stitches. Her arm was sore, but looked better than her back. With a sigh and the help of the mirror, she managed to tape a clean gauze pad over the stitches.

Digging through her bag, she found the brush and headed back to the bathroom. As she pulled the brush through her hair, her thoughts went back to Dev. It was the town. Nothing good could come from this town, at least, nothing good for her. Dev was here, defending and protecting the people, just like Guy had.

Closing her eyes, she took an even breath, then perched on the edge of the tub. Dev wasn't her father. He wasn't even the sheriff, but for some reason, even knowing how good a man Dev was, her mind couldn't separate the two.

"Laurel?" Dev's voice through the door.

"Give me a sec." She gathered her clothes, opened the door, and hustled into the bedroom. After packing everything back into the bag, she pulled out the hair dryer.

"Darrell brought us some food." Dev leaned in the doorway. "I had no idea he was married."

She nodded, working to keep her eyes from his. She plugged in the hair dryer, sat in the chair, and turned it on, letting the hot air and the sound drown out everything but her thoughts.

How? How was she going to fix this? She wanted his attention, wanted to have him come in and rescue her, save her from herself. That was a new idea and something she'd never thought about since leaving her childhood home.

The dryer shut off, and she looked up. Dev held the plug.

"You okay?"

She nodded, fluffing out her hair and pushing off the chair. He took her elbow and she paused.

"What's going on? You've got something on your mind."

His green eyes mesmerized her, and she smiled as she leaned into him. His arms wrapped around her waist as he chuckled.

"Okay, want to share?"

She shook her head, tentatively wrapping an arm around him. Breathing in, she felt a sense of peace washing over her. His fingers moved through her hair, and for the first time since Mason, she felt herself giving in.

"You hungry?"

"Yeah." She stepped away, biting her lip, and tucking her hair dryer back in her bag.

Dev perched on the edge of the bed in front of her and tugged on her elbow. "Hey, talk to me."

She blew out a long breath. "Not in a talking mood," she whispered. There was too much going on in her mind right now, too much she needed to sort through.

"Okay, just let me know when you're ready."

"Why do you do that?" She smirked and shook her head.

"Do what?"

That warm smile on his face, his hair a mess and a prickly shadow on his chin. He looked so good.

"You don't need to always be there. You've got a job, and this is not—"

"This is not what?" His brow furrowed.

With a sigh, she paused, and he stood in front of her, his hands firmly gripping her waist, his eyes searching hers.

"You have to understand, I can't, I don't even know how—" she sighed. "If you're wanting a relationship from me, I'm not that person. I don't even know how—"

He moved his thumb across her lips, silencing her as a shudder tingled on her skin. "Right now, I'm your friend. Right now, I want to go on a date with you, enjoy your company in a more relaxed situation than this." He licked his lips. "Laurel, I care about you too much to walk away. I told you the other day, all that other stuff, it's in your hands now.

"I know you have a bad past, but I want to help you. Not for me, but for you. I can't stand to hear you think you're not good enough or needed when you already mean so much to me and several others in this town. It's not all bad you know," he whispered as tears ran down her cheeks.

He pulled her in, holding her as she cried, her emotions so raw from years of keeping them hidden away. Now, he seemed to just pluck them out, and here she was, crying and struggling to find her footing.

"I'll be here. Whether you ever want more or not."

Shaking her head, she pushed away, wiped her face. "See? This is the problem. I can't handle you being here like this. You keep saying I deserve all these things, but what about you? You deserve all those things too. Things I'm not sure I can give you." She rushed out of the room.

In the kitchen, she grabbed a can of soda from the fridge, poured it over ice, and sat at the table, her head in her hands.

"You know—" Dev sat down next to her, pushing into her shoulder. He pried a hand loose and held it with both of his "—just the fact you're thinking about it makes me pretty happy."

She let out a deep breath and sat back.

"Laurel, really, let's table as much as we can until after we clear everything else up. I've already got a lead, and hopefully, we can get an end to all this soon. Then, maybe we can talk about other things."

She glanced over, that great smile of his lighting his face. "You need to shave."

His smile fell, and she smirked.

"You don't like the rough look, huh?"

"Let's just say, I was in the Navy. Clean cut, clean shaven."

"I'll remember that." He laughed and leaned in, planting a kiss on her head as he stood.

He took off down the hallway. She heard a slam of the door

and then the shower start. Sipping her drink, she propped up her legs on the opposite chair and sighed.

Munching on the bacon and biscuits, she stared out the window. Once this ended, could she really allow herself to let him in like that? To try at a relationship when she had no idea what one even looked like?

A knock sounded and she jumped. Frantically searching the room, she finally found a letter opener on the coffee table. Armed and ready, she eased to the door and looked out the window to see Darrell on the porch.

Blowing out a deep breath, she undid the latch and opened the door. "Hey, come on in."

"You sleep good?" Darrell smiled and stepped inside.

She set down the letter opener. "Yeah. Thanks again. And thank Mary for us. The breakfast is great."

"So." He followed her into the kitchen, took a seat across from her. "What's going on with you and the detective?"

"Look, right now, nothing." She rolled her eyes. "He's ... pushing."

"Do I need to stop him?"

She chuckled. "No. it's fine. I'm just, with everything going on, I'm having a hard time dealing." She pushed her glass back and forth on the table. "Dev's a good man. No one besides the few of you have ever tried to believe me, to help me. He's actually looking into Tara's disappearance."

"Wow. That's impressive." A grin lit Darrell's face.

"What's that for?"

Darrell shrugged. "Finding someone to believe in you, someone who you can trust."

"Well, it's not been easy." She sighed and leaned back in the chair. "I know Dev's not ... I know he's different. He's not Guy. But still, he's in the office, and I just can't ..." she trailed off.

"He reminds you of Guy."

She nodded with a frown. "My brain seems to engage that image, and I can't break away. That's crazy but—"

"Laur, you've been through too much. Your past, dealing with Guy, you need help. I told you Mary knows a really good therapist. You need help to get your head on straight."

"Yeah, I know." She licked her lips. "Not that I have time for anything like that at the moment." She almost laughed. "The thing is, I feel this need to push him away. But I—I don't want to. He deserves someone who can give him much more than I can."

"Good." Darrell leaned over and slid his hand over hers with a pat. "I'd hate for you to miss the fact that he's head over heels for you. And he is a good man. Don't push him away."

She smiled and squeezed his hand. "Thanks for everything."

"Anything for you." He grinned with a wink and stood. "You staying another night?"

"No idea."

"As long as you need, you stay here, okay? No hotels or nothing, just here, where it's safe."

"Thanks."

Darrell stood and stepped out the door, closing it behind him. She grabbed another biscuit, her hunger breaking through again.

Leaning back, she tried to wrap her mind around relationships. So far, Darrell and Mary were the only couple she knew who had made a marriage work.

With Mrs. Beecham losing her husbands, Lizzy and her ex, Tonya and her on-and-off boyfriend, and then, of course, her parents, it's not like she knew what it even looked like to be in a real relationship.

Love. Such a strange concept. She'd always thought she was in love with Mason. But the more she considered it, it was an enduring trust with a close friend. She trusted him indefinitely, a new concept for her at the time.

Now, here she was with Dev, and she not only trusted him but wanted much more contact than she'd ever had with anyone, including Mason. With Mason, just a quick hug, a rare kiss when they were alone—physical displays of affection were few and far between.

With Dev, they were in constant contact, and she shivered at the thought. His kiss, the hugs and closeness he gave so freely— none of it hurt, none of it scared her, and she found herself craving it.

It would all eventually end, that was certain. So, could she accept that hurt when it did?

29

L eaning against the wall of the bathroom, Dev smiled and bowed his head.

"Lord, please guide her, lead her to some help. Give her peace around me. Let her see me for who I am, and help her understand I'm here for her," he whispered.

Eavesdropping wasn't something he normally did, but it was more a mistake than anything. After heading down the hallway, he'd heard Darrell and Laurel talking, and his name coming up in the conversation.

Hearing her compare him to Guy hurt, a lot. But he understood. After her enduring many years of abuse and distrust from a police officer, he understood her point of view. The fact she didn't want to push him away—that made his heart ache.

He'd already promised moving forward was all on her now, and he couldn't take it back. Even though not kissing her when he walked back into that room would be difficult.

Heart pounding from overhearing her comments to Darrell, Dev did a quick shave. If she didn't want to push him away, maybe when this was over, she'd be willing to move on to something more. He dressed, then packed everything back into his bag and headed down the hallway. Laurel was humming.

Peering around the corner, he leaned against the wall and watched her wash dishes. Her hair was pulled up, and he smiled to see her so relaxed. Her voice carried smoothly in the air and he dropped his duffle bag.

Her singing stopped, and she froze for a moment. Turning to look over her shoulder, she sighed. "You know I don't like to be spied on, Dev."

There it was again, something about her saying his name, finally. He grinned. "Just enjoying the sight and sound. You have an amazing voice. I think you should sing more."

Red stained the back of her neck, and he chuckled and stepped into the kitchen, grabbing a towel, and drying the washed and stacked dishes.

In silence, they finished cleaning up the dishes. After putting everything away, he found her sitting on the couch, glass in her hand, and her legs nervously bouncing up and down.

"Now what? Don't you have police work to do or something?"

He chuckled and sat next to her, placing his hand on her knee. She stopped bouncing.

"Laurel, why are you still nervous? I just told you, all the other stuff can wait. I'm just here as a friend, someone to protect you and keep you safe."

Though her eyes wouldn't meet his, she nodded. Frowning, he took the glass from her hands and set it down on the coffee table.

"What—what're you doing?"

He took her hand in his, stood, and led her out the back door.

"Darrell wakes up really early, did you know that?"

She chuckled as he pulled her down the steps of the back deck.

"Anyway, when he woke me up, I couldn't go back to sleep, so I walked around for a bit."

Her fingers threaded between his and he smiled. Weaving through the trees, they reached a cliff.

"I found this. Thought it was, remarkable." He turned and saw her smiling.

"I—I haven't been here in forever." She sat on a nearby boulder, and he settled next to her.

Holding her hand in both of his, he grinned and leaned forward on his knees. He rubbed his fingers over her left hand, noticing the scars and feeling the bumps and probable previous breaks under the skin.

"You shaved."

He chuckled, her smile warmed his heart.

Man. How was he supposed to step back and let it all go? Standing, he released her hand.

"What's wrong now?"

"You know, I brought you out here because I thought it might distract you enough to make you more comfortable around me. It seems when you're confined, either in the car or the house, you get anxious. But out here, I hoped it would help."

She nodded, furrowing her brow. "It did," she spoke softly, making his heartrate jump up again.

Giving her space, he hiked down the edge of the bluff, convincing himself to not push for something more. He turned and jumped, and she stepped close behind him.

"You know what? You're a little too stealthy."

"Come on." She gave a smirk and tugged his hand. They headed down the path leading off the side of the cliff.

"Um, where are we going?"

"Don't you trust me, Hollister?"

He grunted and pulled her back to him, wrapping an arm around her. "Not if you go back to Hollister instead of my first name."

What started out as irritation, moved quickly toward tension as she stared up into his eyes. Those bright blue eyes of hers ...

Without the hat, he could see flecks of gray as the sun hit the side of her face.

"Sorry." Her gaze dropped, and he muffled a groan.

"You know, I've been trying hard to keep my word. But right now, you're making me regret some things," he mumbled.

She looked at his lips, her body so close. "Dev, what if—"

"No, no what ifs here. You know how I feel about you, at least, by now I hope you do. I'm here, I'm not going anywhere. But if you, if you don't—" He couldn't even finish the sentence.

"Dev." Her gaze narrowed as she met his, her arms pushing around his neck, making his pulse kick up. "How can you ... I mean, you know I'm messed up."

"You're not messed up. You've hung on to everything and finally reached your limit. There's no more room for you to keep it all inside. You'll have to find some help, someone to talk to, someone you trust. That's not messed up—that's a woman struggling to survive."

A sheen covered her eyes, and he pulled her into a hug, gripping her tight and breathing out.

"I want more for you. I don't just want you to survive, I want you live." He clamped his mouth shut, trying to hold back all the other things that moved through his brain he knew she wasn't ready for.

A soft kiss landed on his cheek, and he stilled.

"Thanks."

"For what?" he mumbled.

"Just being you. I don't trust too many people. I still don't understand why you ..." She trailed off.

Until she understood love, that wouldn't happen. He loved her, it was there, he was there, and she didn't understand.

"I'm kinda hoping I can explain it to you."

She nodded, her hands slipping from his neck and resting on his chest. He didn't want to let go. He wanted to stay here, explain everything, show her just how much he loved her. Her gaze never left his chest as her fingers moved around his collarbone and down his sides.

"Laurel? You have no idea, do you?" He clenched his jaw.

"About what?" her muffled voice came from being pressed into his chest, her arms wrapping around his waist.

Avoiding her injury, he rubbed her back, kissed her head. Something more seemed to kick into gear, something he felt moving in his heart. Admitting to himself he loved Laurel allowed him to see something different in her. *Touch*.

She'd probably had few instances of touch that didn't hurt in her lifetime. Her holding him, allowing him to hold her back, it probably meant something different to her. As he rubbed her back gently, she leaned in, and he smiled.

The attraction was still heavy, and it took a lot to keep himself from pushing for more, but understanding this one thing, it brought him an insight from God. She needed to be able to trust him in other ways before they could move on to any other form of relationship.

"We need to get back," he whispered, his fingers sifting the ends of her hair and threading through the strands.

"I know," she whispered back, and he closed his eyes.

"Lord, watch over us, keep us safe and guide our footsteps. Show Laurel how much she means to You. Amen."

She stiffened as he finished, and he simply gave her a squeeze before he released her. Stepping back, she looked up at him with furrowed brows.

"Why ... what was that for?"

"The prayer?"

She nodded.

"Protection, guidance." He shrugged. "A way for you to see Him."

"So, we don't get that if we don't pray?"

"Asking for things that are in God's will is allowed." He frowned and pulled her hands up to chest level. "I want you to understand that. I'm here to help, but what you need, who you need is God. As much as I want to be it." He sighed. "He's the one you need."

"So far, all I see is you, Dev." She raised up and kissed his cheek again.

Pulling her in, he lowered and kissed her lips softly, waiting for her to take over. Her hand on his neck, her blue eyes focused on him, she pushed up and kissed him firm on the lips. Breathing her in, he let her pull back first.

Resting his forehead against hers, he kept his eyes closed, trying to find a way out of this. He'd messed up, let his body take over and now ...

"What's wrong?" she whispered.

"I'm sorry, Laurel." He opened his eyes. "I shouldn't ... I can keep my promise okay?"

"I'm not mad." She gave him a smile.

His arms pulled her tighter to him. "I just, do you know? I mean—"

"I'm not blind. Between this and the barn, it's not like I've never been attracted to someone before. Even if none of this makes sense. I just hope after all this—"

"Nothing's changing my mind. I want you to trust me, okay?"

"Okay," she whispered, her face red as he ducked his head, stealing another quick kiss.

"Now, we really need to go," he muttered.

Her smile made his heart pound.

"I need you to know, this isn't just attraction. But I don't think I've ever been this 'attracted' to anyone."

She started to pull back, and he held her tight.

"It's a compliment, one that I intend on repeating over and over again until you believe it. You're beautiful, strong, and smart. You have the sexiest smile and blue eyes ..."

Her face went crimson, and he chuckled.

"I want you to know you're an extremely attractive woman. But I see the woman inside too. You've got a great big heart, and that's drawing me in. You care for everyone around you, take care of them, do your best for them, endure for them."

"Dev—"

"I wasn't done."

Her jaw went solid, and he sighed.

"I hope one day you see how amazing you are. I hate to think that this town and your past have made you think you're worthless, when I see you as so much more."

As she avoided his gaze and nervously shifted, he could tell she was done with his compliments. He took her hand and started back up the bluff. She didn't hold on, but he gripped her fingers, making sure they stayed connected. The sooner she realized he could be trusted even if she was upset, the better. Because now, he wasn't going anywhere.

God, I need your guidance here, show me where to go and what to say and do. Because I'm all in.

30

"We need to get to the station."

Laurel narrowed her gaze as Dev came inside, his jaw clenched and face red.

After their amazing hike, they watched a few shows on TV, and the tension between them finally eased. Things were great, until Dev returned from outside and a heated phone conversation.

"What happened? What's wrong?"

"Morris said I needed to get to the station. There was something going on with Lester, and it has to do with your case. He's messed something up."

She sighed and jerked on her jacket and followed him out the door. He held open the truck door, then slammed it hard as he moved around and slid in behind the wheel.

"I'm sorry," she mumbled, holding her hands tightly in her lap.

"What? Why are you apologizing?"

"You realize what this is, right?" She faced him. "Retaliation. No one at that office likes me or thinks highly of me. This is all messed up because of me."

"No."

She stilled at the anger in his voice. His hands gripped the steering wheel, his knuckles white.

"You're not to blame. When are you going to realize that? These people are making their own bad choices. You're not to apologize for their mistakes."

Her breathing hitched as she turned away.

The truck pulled to the side of the road, he hit the brakes abruptly. Laurel pulled at the seatbelt as it tightened on her.

"Laurel, I'm sorry."

She turned and found Dev's hand over the console, reaching for her.

"I'm upset because we found a lead, and I just knew we were going to cinch all this up. I don't need Lester stepping in and messing it all up." He sighed. "I didn't mean to lose it with you."

"That was losing it?" She frowned.

"Yeah, it was." He took her hand in his. "But I'm upset that you still think you need to apologize. Honey, this is about them, not you. They've chosen to believe a lie, followed it down so far they can't give it up now. I don't want you to apologize for them anymore."

He leaned closer. "You okay?"

Unable to form words, she nodded. If he thought that was losing his temper, he had no idea what anger really was.

Pulling her hand up, he kissed her knuckles and grinned. "Let's get this thing wrapped up. My friend from the FBI is very interested in what we've found out." He winked and faced the front again, pulling back onto the highway and heading into town.

As THEY PULLED up to the front of the office, Dev jumped out and grabbed Laurel's hand. They climbed the steps to the station and opened the door revealing a standoff.

"You can't explain this away, man."

Morris stood in front of Lester, a piece of paper in his hand. Stepping toward the men, Laurel's hand fell from Dev's.

"What's going on, Morris?" Dev asked.

"We got the DNA back on the cigarette butt from the rose bush. It's Lester's."

His jaw dropped. "What?"

"You can't prove nothing! Besides, my DNA isn't even accessible, so you can't match it," Lester spat the words.

"That's why I lifted a butt from outside in that empty plant pot you use as an ashtray. I noticed yesterday. You smoke the same brand of cigarettes that we found outside Mrs. Beecham's house."

Lester's face went crimson as he glared at Morris. But Morris wasn't done.

"The lab also confirmed diesel on the ground, probably what caused it to burn for so long. Did that come from your daddy's gas station?"

Looking down, Dev frowned at the cowboy boots. "What size boot you wear, Lester? 'Cause that looks an awful lot like the cast we made at the crime scene."

"Humph. There is no crime scene."

Stepping into his space, Dev barely managed to keep his hands down and stop himself from decking the guy. "Why? Did you trash my house too?"

Lester just smirked.

Shaking his head, he glanced at Morris. "We have enough to hold him. Get a warrant for his shoes, the judge will be in by now."

Morris nodded and headed to his desk. Stacks came up behind Lester, taking the gun from his holster.

"You either cooperate here or I'll call state and you can spend your time up there until you see a judge." Dev mumbled.

Morris put the handcuffs on Lester. "Let's go."

"You don't deserve her!" Lester squirmed from under the

cuffs, a glare on Laurel. "She's a good woman, and you've ruined her reputation!"

"What?" Laurel's face paled. "What does that mean?"

Lester huffed. "You know you killed your own parents—just admit it."

"I—I didn't," Laurel stammered.

Dev stepped between them. "What's going on? Why do you hate her so much?"

"Mrs. Beecham took me in, took care of me, then shipped me off. It was the best thing for me. Then you came along and ruined everything! You were supposed to stay away!"

"Why did Laurel coming back ruin everything?" He pressed closer, trying to calm Lester down.

"She's *my* family, *my* mother. Not hers. I couldn't prove that you killed them, but we all know you did it. You just don't remember. I can't let you near her and risk her life either!" Lester lunged toward Laurel, but Dev grabbed his shoulders and wrangled him to the ground.

"Get him to the cell!" Dev shouted as Stacks and Morris wrestled the large deputy into the back.

"I—I need some air."

He turned. "Laurel, stay inside. You can't go outside without me."

His desk phone rang, and he rushed to pick it up. "Hollister."

LAUREL TRIED to steady her breath, but Lester's hate, his complete disbelief in her crushed her spirt. She wasn't a killer. She could never kill her mother or father, no matter what her father did to her. And to think she'd hurt Mrs. Beecham?

Gripping the doorknob, she rushed into the open air, breathing in deeply and pacing outside. It was early enough the roads were clear, and no one was there to see her fall apart.

"Why is this happening?" she murmured.

Leaning against the brick, she closed her eyes. Even after having at least one good night's sleep, her body was exhausted. Dev's comments about needing God came to mind.

What possible good could God do at this point?

So many people were scared of her, believed the same as Miles Lester. She was ruined, scarred, hated. The time to help her was forever ago, when her father was so evil and mean ...

The fear overwhelmed her again, crushing her chest and taking her breath. She held her head and tried to forget, ignore the sensation of being thrown around.

A hand gripped her shoulder and she grabbed it hard, looking up.

"Uncle Walter," she murmured.

"You look tired. Are you okay?" His gray eyes narrowed.

A sharp pain hit her neck. Fighting the urge to pass out, she leaned into his arms. "Everything—everything is so confusing ..."

Her mind drifted as darkness took over.

31

"Hey, man." Dev muttered into the phone.

"We might have a connection on this end. The DNA isn't in yet, I just checked. But that BOLO you gave me describes one of the trucks we've tracked. The license plate matches. I think we have enough for a warrant."

Dev blew out a breath at Bruce's decision. "That's great, I—"

The sound of the door took his attention as he turned to realize Laurel was gone.

"I'm headed your way. I've got a lot to catch you up on. This Rutherford guy is bad news, and I'm surprised you haven't been informed."

As much as Dev wanted to check on Laurel, he figured she probably needed some air. He turned his focus back to the phone. "What does that mean?"

"Tobias Rutherford has a long rap sheet, a lot of complaints from the neighboring counties. Did your search not bring him up?"

"No. I didn't find anything in our system about him." Dev gritted his teeth at the new information. Could Lester have gone so far as to hire Tobias Rutherford to kidnap Laurel? And even remove Rutherford's records from their database? His attention swung back to the door. "Hey, let me call you back." He slammed the phone down and rushed outside.

The street was clear. He frantically ran to the edge of the building, thinking she might have needed a walk. Snatching his phone, he called hers, but it rolled straight to voicemail.

"Laurel, call me, now." His heart dropped as he ran back inside to Morris's desk. "Pull up the video of the street view, now!"

Morris clicked through the computer, and Dev stepped in behind him, dread weighing on his shoulders. He already knew, he just knew. Tobias had taken her.

"Here."

The video played as Morris fast-forwarded to a few minutes prior to him rushing outside. Laurel appeared in the screen, pacing back and forth for a moment before. Then, she froze, backed up to the wall, leaned her body in, and held her head in her hands.

A man appeared.

"Who—who is that?" he murmured.

The man took Laurel by the elbow, then she leaned into his chest. With the man's head down, Dev couldn't see his face. The man picked Laurel up, and as he turned, Dev's heart dropped.

"That's Walter."

NAUSEA WORKED its way through his body. Dev paced the room, swallowing the bile burning his throat.

"I should've seen it before now. All the interference with the BOLO, the case—"

"I thought Lester suspended the BOLO?"

He glared at Morris. "Yeah, well, it doesn't mean they aren't in it together." He grabbed Morris's arm. "Let's go. Stacks, when the FBI shows up, tell them to give me a call."

The door opened, and Bruce walked in. "Where are you going?"

"Laurel's been taken—by Walter McGehee."

"Laurel Ashburn? The sheriff? What're you talking about?"

"I'm going after her." He pushed past him, through the door. Bruce grabbed his arm.

Dev shrugged from Bruce's grasp. "Let go, man! I have to find her."

"Let me call this in. We'll get a team ready—"

"We don't have time for a team." Dev spoke through gritted teeth.

"Let's do this right." Bruce stood his ground. "We know where Tobias's compound is, and with the sheriff involved, we need to have a solid case. "

"Compound?"

Bruce guided him back inside. "Let me make a call."

Pacing the office, Dev waited while Bruce spoke on the phone. As much as he trusted Bruce's experience, his patience was running out.

"Got it." Bruce hung up. "We've got the warrant. The DNA from the knife came back, it was Rutherford."

"Then what? What is Walter doing in the middle of it?" Dev followed Bruce to the waiting SUV and slid into the back seat. As the driver pulled away, he leaned back and prayed.

God, please protect her until I can get there, please.

"Dev?"

He sat up and nodded, steeling himself for whatever Bruce was about to reveal.

"This is our guy."

He snatched the file from Bruce's hands.

"All those girls that were reported missing were not just while McGehee was sheriff. There's several the years prior to that happening. I'm not saying he's responsible for all of it—"

"I am. Laurel trusted him completely. Walter defended Guy

this whole time, saying he would never hurt anyone ..." Dev trailed off. "She trusted him. How could he do this?"

"We need answers, Dev. If Walter really is involved, this case just got a lot bigger and heavier. A sheriff helping to kidnap girls?" Bruce shook his head. "Back to Tobias Rutherford. He's been in and out of the state, picked up on harassment and then there's the assault charge he slipped away from. But here's what we do know.

"We've been tracking the network for the past year, trying to get a lock on how he moves and where he goes. About a month ago, we got a description of the truck, but only a partial license plate. After running through the system, we've been narrowing down the list of who it could belong to.

"Last week, the same truck was noticed in this area with expired tags. The guy driving said it belonged to a friend. On a hunch, we followed it, and ended up at Rutherford's compound."

Dev glanced up. "Yeah, the compound. You mentioned that. The address I was looking at is barely an hour up the road on a farm."

"That's his home address." Bruce huffed. "He owns a large camping compound. High tech fence surrounds about an acre and a half, a large two-story building sits there, in the middle."

Dev flipped through the file, and his heart leapt to his throat. The pictures showed the enormity of the compound and the large fence that surrounded it.

"This isn't the first time we've looked at Rutherford for kidnapping. Several years ago, we had a hunch he was involved in a string of disappearances, and we staked out his place a few times. But he either got wind of it or was conveniently gone at the time. If the sheriff is involved, I guess we know why we always missed Rutherford. We have little info to go on when we do manage to rescue the girls."

"Girls?" Dev stared up at Bruce's frown.

"Yeah, young girls. We do what we can to track them down. But his network is growing. From here, he can jump on the interstate and be gone before we even know where he hit. The few men we've caught are just the lower-level street walkers. They look for targets. But we want the whole network."

As the information built up in his brain, the only thing Dev could think of was Laurel.

"The compound sits a couple of hours away, so you'll have to find a way to be patient."

Dev ignored Bruce's glare.

"Just get me there," he mumbled.

God, please, I need You to save her. I'm not sure how much more she can take.

His heart ached as his legs bounced up and down. The car wasn't moving fast enough, and all he could do was sit there.

Pray, he could pray. Closing his eyes and lowering his head, he blew out a ragged breath and began an in-depth conversation with his Creator.

32

H er mind swam.
    Groggy and disoriented, Laurel's head ached as she let
out a groan. She flexed her fingers and realized her hands weren't
bound, neither were her legs. Working herself to a sitting
position, she blinked away the dizziness and nausea.

She sat in a cell, bars all around her, and a plywood floor
beneath her. A rancid smell permeated the air—body odor and
human waste combined, with some kind of cedar air freshener.
The cell was tall. The bars reached high, but she noticed they
weren't attached to the ceiling. It was basically a box—the walls
holding together without a top.

After trying a few times, she finally stood, gripped the bars,
and forced her body to move. A large chair sat in the middle of
the room, raised with armrests and a footrest.

Muffled sobs echoed, sounding as if they came from above.
Dim lights drifted back and forth as wind whistled through the
drafty room, pushing at the bare bulbs hanging off wires from
the ceiling.

A chill swallowed her.

"God, You can't do this. If you really wanted me to believe in

You, You can't do this," she muttered as she worked her way around the cell.

It made no sense. She was too old for trafficking, right? Women her age weren't targeted and used like this. But yet they had kept trying to catch her so many times ... Why?

The sound of metal scraping metal made her pause. She peered through the shadows. Footfalls echoed, and she tried her best to contain her fear, hoping the adrenaline pulsing through her body would shake off the effects of being drugged.

Two large men appeared at the cell door. Backing away, she hid behind the large chair, gripping the edge as she worked to ease her heartbeat.

"You're awake. No one has woke up that quick before." A man with a long beard and long dark hair smiled.

As he opened the cell, another man appeared from behind, carrying what looked like a cattle prod.

"Why am I here?" She stiffened her voice, deciding which one to attack first.

"You're here because *he* wanted you here. You're too much hassle, but he was adamant."

The man with the cattle prod headed to her left, a stern expression on his face.

She couldn't wait any longer. Acting as if she'd throw a punch, the man reacted, shoving the prod toward her. She caught it with the crook of her elbow and spun, hitting him in the back of the head with her other elbow. He hit the floor and she pried the cattle prod away from him and spun it around to his chest.

As the other man approached, she hit him with the prod to no effect. He slammed her into the bars, knocking the breath from her. She groaned, dropping the prod. He picked her up and shoved her into the chair.

After he restrained her left arm, she yelled, "God, you can't do this to me!"

"It's not God honey, just us," the bearded man smirked as he moved to restrain her right arm.

Kicking out, she nailed him in the groin, then stood and pivoted in the chair, kicking him as hard as she could in the chest. As he slammed into the bars, she unbuckled her left wrist and picked up the prod, shocking the bearded man until he went unconscious.

Searching both, she found a handgun and set of keys. Her heart pounding, she stood on shaky legs and rushed from the cell, pulling the door shut behind her. Aiming the gun down the corridor, she eased quietly along the dark hallway.

Whispers and shuffling echoed, but she couldn't tell if they were real or side effects from the drugs. Turning a corner, the darkness revealed nothing. She held the keys at her side and worked to contain the tremor in her hands.

As she paused, someone tugged on her hand.

Snapping a look down, the gun followed. A small hand stuck through the busted-up board, pulling at her fingers, searching. She released the keys, and the hand guided them through the wooden slats. Laurel returned her focus to the hallway and took a steadying breath. Going back to help would be her priority after she took out her attackers.

Corridors of locked doors appeared before her, a maze that left her disoriented and frustrated. With all the turns, she could end up face to face with someone aiming a gun at her, or they could come from behind ...

"God if you're there, please help me," she whispered.

Taking a few deep breaths, her nerves eased, and she continued her search. The main corridor ended, and a door stood between her and the unknown. Swallowing her fear, she opened it.

Tobias Rutherford stood ten feet away, a smirk on his face, his arm in a sling.

Her anger surged.

"You've caused a lot of trouble, girl," he growled.

"THIS IS IT?" Dev's voice faltered as he stared at the large building. The pictures in the file didn't do it justice.

Bruce turned. "I've got SWAT on standby, and my guys are on their way. We've got to find a way in, something that will take them by surprise. If they've got more than just your friend in there, they'll use them as hostages."

Swallowing the constant lump in his throat, Dev nodded.

"Sir? There's a lot of movement going on." The driver of the SUV held out the binoculars and motioned toward the compound.

Dev snatched the binoculars before Bruce could grab them and peered through the lenses.

Windows were opened on the top floor, and a few small figures moved out on the ledge.

"Those girls will kill themselves if we don't get in there. Now." Dev handed off the binoculars and slid from the car.

"You can't get in. That gate is motorized and—" Bruce was interrupted as several SUV's arrived, men and women filing out. "Here's our backup."

Bruce gathered his people together and went over the situation. Dev stood at the gate, praying they weren't too late. The figures on the rooftop took his breath as one slid from the roof to a ledge.

"Hey." Dev turned to the driver of the SUV. "Flash your lights, let those girls see us. They'll jump and kill themselves just to get away."

The agent reached back in and flashed the lights several times until the girls finally noticed. Several waved their arms, hugging each other as they nestled together.

Pacing the gate, Dev wondered why now? What had changed to make them go out the windows? They looked disheveled, as if they'd been there for a long time ...

"Laurel," he mumbled. A slow smile formed on his lips.

Someone to his left whispered, and he walked the fence until movement within a large bush made him pause. Gripping his gun handle, he knelt down.

"My name is Detective Hollister. My friends from the FBI are here. We want to help."

A small face appeared, a girl no older than ten. She offered a faint smile.

He smiled back. "Where did you come from?"

The girl looked over her shoulder at the compound.

Burning bile filled his throat, and he swallowed hard. "How did you get out?"

She bit her lip and reached behind her. Another girl appeared, older, with a fat lip and bruised face. His heart clenched.

"One of the girls got some keys," she whispered. "Someone— someone escaped, with keys."

"I'll get some help to cut the fence and get you out. Stay here."

The girl nodded and he rushed back to the FBI crowd.

"Bruce." He motioned him over and lowered his voice. "A few girls are hiding the bushes. Get some of the women and get them out of there."

Bruce's face went red. "Jeffries, Austin, over here."

Two women hustled over to them.

"There's a few girls in the bushes." Dev pointed. "They need help."

"Let's go." The agent motioned.

Dev led them back down the fence row to the bushes. "Hello? My friends would like to help."

The older girl appeared again, tears streaking down her face.

"Hi. I'm Geena." One of the agents knelt down. "We're going to get you out of here, okay?"

"I—I need some other clothes," the girl's haggard voice barely whispered.

"We've got it. No worries." The agent gave the girl a reassuring smile.

More agents flooded the area, cutting the fence so the female agents could get through. They handed out blankets and jackets.

Dev headed back to Bruce. "I need to get in there. Now."

"Yeah, and I've got to get some medical personnel in here to help those girls." Bruce's jaw clenched as he turned to the other agents. "Hannon? Call in the medics. The rest of you, we're spreading out and heading in. There are innocents in there too, so watch yourselves."

With his heart in his throat, Dev followed the FBI team through the cut fence and approached the outskirts of the compound.

God, don't let me be too late.

33

L aurel glared at Rutherford, his crooked smile, the evil in his eyes.

Rushing down the narrow corridor, she got within a few yards when a gun pushed into her back. The sound of the hammer being cocked back echoed in the quiet room. Rutherford grinned.

"Put it down or you'll die," the voice murmured from much too close behind her.

"Then so will he, because I'm not releasing the gun." She kept her aim at center mass, using both hands to hold the gun steady. "You shoot, I automatically pull the trigger, and he dies too. Even if I fall or my arm waivers, he'll still be mortally injured. I don't have anything left here on earth. I've got nothing to lose."

Stepping away, she paced down the aisle, the gun relenting from her back. Rutherford narrowed his eyes as she approached. The sound of her cell phone ring tone made her pause. Her phone lit up, sitting on a paper laden desk.

"They're on their way. He already knows who you are." She smirked up at him, suddenly realizing she didn't want to die.

Dev was on his way here, to rescue her. He made her

happy, and she wanted happy. In her entire life, there were only a handful of times she could actually say she was happy. Even with all the chaos, she was happy with him by her side.

Standing between Rutherford and his accomplice, it would be too risky for the man to shoot. Rutherford would be in the way of any bullet aimed at her.

In one swift move, she slammed into Rutherford's injured arm, turned, and shot the man behind her. He fell as Rutherford cursed and grabbed at her with his good arm. She turned the gun on him.

"Move, and I'll kill you right now." It was all she could do to keep her finger from pulling the trigger.

He slunk to the ground. She found a pair of handcuffs on the desk. Strapping his injured wrist to the metal shelving unit, she turned at the sound of someone approaching from behind.

"Laurel." Walter stood a few yards away, arms up and a frown on his face.

She lowered the gun. "What—what are you doing here?"

"I'm here to get you out."

"Get me out of these cuffs!" Rutherford moaned from the floor.

Laurel's eyes cut from Rutherford back to Walter. "Wait. You —you were there, outside the police station."

Walter's face reddened.

"I was upset, and you were there ..."

"You don't remember. I'm here to help."

"Walter—"

"Shut up, Tobias!" Walter's voice dropped as he glared. His gray eyes cut to hers. "You've made a mess of everything! Why couldn't you just stay away?"

Her breath hitched as she backed up to the wall. "Uncle Walter?" she whispered.

"You really do have no one in this life, girl." Rutherford's chuckle echoed.

Leaning against the wall, she shook her head, not able to understand Walter's hatred of her.

"Why? What have I ever done? You said you didn't believe I killed them. You— you were one of the few who believed me, protected me," she whispered, barely containing the pain of betrayal surging through her body.

"She showed up." Walter struck out and knocked the gun from her hands, pinning her to the wall. "You weren't supposed to be there. You weren't supposed to see."

"See?" she stuttered. "See what?"

His gray eyes turned dark as they stared. "Your father. It was all his fault. Trying to stop me, trying to step in and do the right thing—after all those years of screwing up his own life, he picked then to become a do-gooder."

Laurel shoved her arm up, severing Walter's grip. Stumbling from the wall, she backed away from the two men now staring her down.

"What was he trying to stop?" She stared at the men, her mind trying to piece together that night.

Walter straightened with a grimace. "He was a drunk and a monster, and he told me what I was doing was wrong? That he planned to stop me? Hah!" Walter snatched some rope from the desk. "April was there. Somehow, she knew. I guess Guy just had to tell her."

"This—this is all you?" Laurel backed away as Walter started toward her. "It was you? You killed them?" she whispered. She felt a tear trickle down her cheek.

Walter lunged, and she spun away from him, taking out his knee. Laurel slammed the back of his head with her elbow, and then kicked him to the ground.

"Why? Why did you have to kill her? She did nothing wrong!" Her heart pounded in her head—she did her best to keep from keeling over.

"She knew ... too much," he groaned from the floor.

"But why? Why are you doing this now?"

"You saw." Walter peered up at her from the floor. "You saw what happened that night. The blood, Guy on the floor, your mother ..." He narrowed his eyes. "You'll remember. And I can't let that happen. You should have stayed away, Laurel. But now—"

"Sheriff McGehee!"

The sound of a blowhorn shattered her thoughts. She turned toward the door, but a force from behind threw her to the ground.

"Now you'll be my way out of this too," he gritted into her ear as she struggled to breathe.

Laurel screamed as he hiked her arm behind her. She did her best to release his grip, but to no avail.

"Walter, get me out of here!" Tobias rattled the handcuffs against the metal shelves.

Walter's grip increased, Laurel's body falling forward from the pressure.

"You put yourself there. I told you, I warned you, and you didn't take me seriously!" Walter shoved her forward. "Move. You don't, I'll start taking you apart little by little."

His breath on her neck sent tremors through her body.

"You said, 'get her,'" she muttered as Walter pulled at the locks on the doors.

"I knew you remembered."

"No, just pieces, parts of dreams. I—I can't remember wh- what happened," she stammered.

He opened the door. Dozens of officers took cover, all wearing FBI vests.

"Laurel!" Dev's muffled voice echoed.

"Shut up, Hollister!"

Searching past the uniforms, she finally found Dev's face peeking out from an old truck, his weapon aimed.

"You've got no out, Sheriff McGehee!"

Walter's arm tightened around her neck. "Don't try and

negotiate. I know the book, I know how you guys work. Get me a chopper and a clear path or she dies right now!"

"No!"

Walter's right hand pinned her arm behind her back, and his left arm wrapped around her throat holding a gun. If she could just break his grip ...

"Walter! Don't do this! Think of Kendra."

"Hah!" Walter backed up against the wall of the building. "You think I care anything about her? A means to an end, Hollister. You should've seen all this sooner!"

"Laurel!"

Clearing her vision, she looked up to Dev. Walter was yelling something, her mind struggled to keep up as exhaustion and pain overwhelmed her. Walter pulled her arm, her body, toward the back of the building, and she forced her legs to keep up.

God, what do I do now?

34

There was no way he'd go down without a fight.

Walter drug Laurel to the back of the compound, hoping for less guns aimed at his head.

"Why—why, Walter?"

He tightened his grip around Laurel's throat, and she strained for breath.

"Because—I fill a need, and the profits provide for me. This little circle has proved most useful for getting what I need, what I want. Then your father had to butt in," he muttered as he picked up his speed.

If he could reach the back where the SUV sat, he would have a way out. Bullet proof windows, tires, everything. An urban tank, just for him.

"Walter."

He froze. Hollister's voice rang out from behind him.

"Stop, or I'll shoot."

His voice sounded much too close.

Fight it was.

Releasing Laurel's neck, Walter swung the gun around. A burning sensation filled his senses. Pain flashed through his stomach, and he fell to the wooden floor. Legs and feet filled his vision as intense pressure stole his breath.

Staring at the large SUV, he tried to inch closer, until his vision left.

"LAUREL!"

Falling into Dev's arms, Laurel hugged his neck, holding him close.

"Laurel, we need to get you out of here, get you checked out."

"Just hold me for another second," she whispered as she pushed her face into his neck, enjoying the way he smelled and felt, his arms keeping her safe.

"I'll hold you as long as you want, but let's do it elsewhere," he whispered.

"Okay, yeah." Her energy bottomed out, her body giving in to the adrenaline crash. "I think ... I think I'm tired," she mumbled as she felt herself being lifted. "Dev?"

"Easy, your back is bleeding again. You need to be checked out."

She opened her eyes as he sat her down, the smell of the ambulance making her frown.

"I'm right here." He grabbed up her hand, capturing her attention for a moment.

"Hey, Laurel?"

A figure stood outside the ambulance. She focused and realized it was Detective Morris.

"Thanks for getting this guy. You did really great."

Her mouth dropped open as Morris walked away. Dev's chuckle made her turn.

"Not everyone thinks badly of you, Laurel." He smiled and reached over to close her mouth.

The doors of the ambulance slammed shut. She winced at the sound.

"Head hurts?"

She nodded at Dev. "Yeah, the drugs I guess."

"We'll get a full tox screen as soon as we get to the hospital, okay?" The medic said.

The door to the front closed and Dev grinned, leaning down for a quick kiss. "You ... you had me a little worried. I thought I lost you." His green eyes searched hers, and a smile formed on her face. "What're you thinking, Laurel?"

"I ... I made a choice earlier." Her exhaustion took over, but she needed to tell him. "I could either give up the gun or die. I told them I wasn't giving up the gun. I had nothing to lose by dying." She swallowed, seeing his green eyes tear up. "But after that, I heard my cell phone go off, and I realized, you were coming to find me." She smiled. "I may have nothing to lose here on this earth, but I think I have a lot to gain."

"Laurel, don't ever do that again." He wiped his face and leaned close, pushing his forehead to hers. "I never want you to think you don't have anything to lose. I need you here, with me," he whispered.

She gripped his hand, her eyelids heavy.

"Go to sleep, I'll be here when you wake."

"You ... you will?" She forced her eyes open to see his.

"I love you, Laurel." He leaned down, giving her a gentle kiss. Her eyes went wide.

"Don't look at me like that." He chuckled. "I've done good to keep it in this long. I can't wait any longer. I love you. Don't ever doubt it." He gave her another kiss.

She smiled, her mind washing away again as her eyes closed.

35

I t had been almost three full days since Laurel had been
rescued from the compound. Dev waited with her as much
as he could, seeing her open her eyes briefly and offer a nod or a
hand squeeze before falling back asleep.

She'd been going non-stop for almost a week, evading
capture, being injured and attacked. Without sleep and her
world crashing, her body was begging for rest.

It was Tuesday afternoon. Dev had been in briefings and
meetings since they found the cache and details of the whole
operation. The FBI dismantled the human trafficking ring with
the information gathered at Rutherford's ranch. They ended up
saving eight girls at his compound and another 119 at a drop-off
in Oklahoma City.

The newspapers credited Laurel with uncovering the
smuggling ring and assisting in the capture of the men involved.
Although there were still a few nay-sayers left in town, it seemed
the report turned most people's head about who Laurel Ashburn
really was and the kind of character she possessed.

He'd just finished up another debriefing when Mrs. Beecham
called his cell.

"Hello?"

"She's awake, and she's asking for you."

His heart dropped. "I'll be there as soon as I can. Um, make sure she knows I'm on my way."

"I'll let her know."

With a groan, he grabbed his keys from the desk, rushed to his truck. Although he was there the few times she woke, he knew she wouldn't remember. In that ambulance, he'd promised he'd be there.

Stopping at the florist, he picked up a bouquet and headed to the hospital.

He rushed up the stairs to her floor. At his soft knock, Mrs. Beecham opened the door with a smile.

"Come on in, I was just leaving," she whispered, with a wink as he stepped through the door.

"Thanks." He looked past Mrs. Beecham to see Laurel sitting up in bed, a smile on her face.

Dressed in sweats and her hair piled on top of her head, she looked amazing.

Setting the flowers next to her bed, he smiled at her wide eyes. "Hey, you feeling okay?"

She nodded as her eyes teared over, her hand covering her mouth.

"I'm sorry I wasn't here when you woke up, I promised and—"

"No, I'm not mad Dev," she whispered and reached up for him.

"Laurel?" He sat down and pulled her in, confused at her reaction. "What's wrong?"

"Nothing I ..." She sat back with a grin, wiping her eyes. "Thanks, for the flowers."

He squeezed her fingers.

"No one has ever brought me flowers," she muttered, turning her focus to the glass vase filled with roses.

Leaning down, he kissed her forehead and wiped her cheek. He took a breath, realizing just how much she'd been denied all her life. "You deserve much more than a vase of flowers."

She shook her head, with a sigh and looked up at him. "I'm having a hard time with all this," she whispered.

Pulling her in, he shifted in the bed and gently pulled her onto his lap. She pushed her face into his neck and wrapped her arms around him. He smiled at her willingness to let him hold her after everything that happened. She didn't cry, but he could feel her shaking beneath the blanket.

"Talk to me. What do you want to talk about?"

"You talk." She sighed heavily, dropping her left arm to rest against his chest.

"Well, because of you, we were able to free eight girls in the compound you escaped from."

"Eight?" She sat back.

"There were five more upstairs who got out and made it to the fence. All younger than 18, all set to be sold."

She pushed back into him. He sighed, closing his eyes and remembering the fear that overwhelmed him when he realized just how close she came to the same fate.

"With all the evidence we found, the FBI were able to take out a large human trafficking organization. They stopped over a hundred girls from being sold. You made that happen."

Her arm tightened around his neck as she started to cry. Rubbing her back, he did his best to soothe her, waiting for her to calm. A lot was left untold from that compound, including the dead man and the two unconscious men found in a back cell that held a chair with restraints. Not to mention Walter McGehee's role in everything. Although with the money in his account and the vast paper trail, Dev could only speculate Walter's guilt. His heart pounded at the thought, not sure he could handle her story once she was ready to tell it.

"Who needs to know what happened?" she whispered, sniffing and taking steady breaths.

"Special Agent Bruce Curtis with the FBI. He's a friend of

mine. He's been waiting to get your statement. I'll call him. You just tell me when."

She nodded and sat back, her blue eyes looking into his. Dev swallowed at the red puffiness of her face, hating she was dealing with so much more than anyone should.

"Are you ... I mean, will you be here?"

"If you want me to stay when you talk to him, I will."

"I can't keep telling it, I ... if this goes to trial and I have to retell it ..." she sighed. "I just can't keep going over it. As soon as I tell it, I'll want to be done with it."

"Okay. I'll give him a call. You need anything?"

She shook her head and leaned back into him, making him smile as he wrapped her up.

Lord, please give me a chance to talk to her about You again. I don't think she'll ever be free of all of the bad memories in her life until she accepts You, understands just how much You can help her. Just give me an opening, Lord.

He sighed, rubbing her upper back.

"I do have some good news."

Her glassy eyes looked up to him.

"The FBI found Tara."

"What?" her mouth dropped open. "She's alive?"

He nodded. "Her parents are with her, and she'll be coming home with them soon enough. Physically, she's fine. But mentally she's struggling and hasn't remembered everything that happened."

"You think she'll remember?"

"I don't know." He shrugged.

Her gaze dropped, staring down at his chest. "I ... I want to see her."

"I'll see what I can do."

WHAT THOSE MEN did to Laurel and what she went through was awful. Dev barely made it through the conversation. If she hadn't stayed so calm, he would've lost it.

Bruce stopped the recording and filled out a few forms, then allowed her to sign. "I really appreciate what you were able to tell me. The details will help."

"Yeah, I just ... I want those guys in jail." She handed the forms back.

"There are a lot of reporters wanting an interview—"

"No, no press conference, no reporters, and no interviews. I don't want to talk about it, and I sure don't want to be on TV because of it." Her tone was solid, and Bruce looked up to Dev.

All Dev could do was smile.

"Okay. Well, I guess this is all for now. If I need anything else, I'll let you know." Bruce stood and motioned to the door. "Dev, a word?"

"Give me a sec." He chuckled as Bruce left.

"Something funny?"

Dev sat on the bed. "What you did, what you helped to accomplish, it's a big deal, and people want to congratulate you for it."

"I don't want to be congratulated. Surely you won't try and talk me into it."

"Laurel, I would never try to convince you to do something you don't want to do." He grabbed up her fingers. "I know you much better than that." He kissed her hand. "Now, I've got to go tell Bruce it's not happening and convince the news crews to head home. Will you be okay for a bit?"

She nodded, squeezing his hand. "Yeah. I think I need some down time."

"Get some rest. There's still an officer outside your room to keep the reporters and unwelcome guests out. Just Mrs. Beecham and I are on the list, besides the nurses and doctor. So don't worry about anyone coming in, okay?" He looked her over, worried about leaving her alone after reliving such a harrowing tale. "Maybe I'll stay until you fall asleep."

"Just go. I'll be fine." She forced a smile, but he frowned.

"You do remember I'm a big city detective, right?"

She huffed.

"I can see through all that. I'll stay."

"Just ... just go. I do need a little time, and knowing an officer is there, that helps. Just don't be gone too long, okay?"

He ached seeing the worry on her face. Nodding, he leaned forward and kissed her forehead gently. The need to stay hit him hard. "I—"

"Dev, you should go," she whispered, her fingers moving down his cheek and across his jaw.

"You make it awfully hard to leave," he muttered.

She was holding back so much. Her gaze focused on his lips a moment, her fingers rested on his chin. Not really sure what to expect after her reliving such a traumatic experience, he leaned forward tentatively. Her finger found his bottom lip, slowly running across it and making his pulse pound. Ever so briefly, her gaze shifted to his before she gave him a quick kiss.

"Go. I'll be fine," she whispered, her hands dropped to her lap.

"Laurel ... this ...." He swallowed, his body wanting much more, and his brain trying to come up with the right words.

"Just go. Please," she whispered.

"I'll be back in a minute. Okay? Call me if you need me." He forced himself to stand, then handed her the cell phone from the table.

Forcing his body to move, Dev clamped his jaw shut and entered the hallway to see Bruce watching him with a grin.

"So, that's interesting."

Dev blew out a deep breath and leaned against the wall. "What's interesting?"

"You and Miss Ashburn. After the way you acted when she

disappeared, I had an idea. But I wasn't expecting you to be a couple."

"We're not a couple." Dev clenched his jaw and crossed his arms over his chest.

"Not a couple?" Bruce chuckled. "Then why are you so red and look like you need to go run a couple of miles or take a cold shower?"

He glared. "Look, I won't be able to talk her into anything. No awards or interviews or anything."

"I know."

"Then why are you out here waiting on me?"

Bruce laughed out loud. "You've been a man holed up for years living the single life. You've broken hearts, you've dated and moved on, and now, you're obviously hung up on this woman. You don't think I want to know what's going on?"

"For the record." Dev smirked before he could stop himself. "I did not break hearts."

"Misty Coster, Carrie Thomas ...."

"Okay, okay. But I didn't break their hearts. They wanted a quick engagement and a wedding. After I figured it out a few months in, I walked away. They knew I wasn't ready for that kind of relationship."

Bruce shook his head. "Yeah, just them." He scoffed. "So, are you with her?"

"It's complicated. She's complicated." He grinned. "I mean, I'm ready when she is, but I have a feeling it might be a while."

"She's pretty amazing. Let me know how things go." Bruce winked and headed down the hallway.

"Amazing, beautiful, strong ..." Dev muttered under his breath as he shoved his fingers through his hair.

Man, he needed to get back in there. Although, what if she wasn't ready for anything more? He groaned and headed down the hallway, hoping to convince the reporters and news crews to back down.

36

Sitting in the silence, Laurel grunted as she pushed the blankets off her legs, then stood for a moment to get her balance.

Hobbling to the window in her sweats and socks, she looked out with a frown.

Walter's role in everything took away part of her heart. In the most devastating moments of her life, losing her mother, her father being killed, and everyone in town saying she'd killed them both, Walter had defended her.

He had made sure she could live with Mrs. Beecham. Of course, that was only so he could keep an eye on her, make sure she never remembered what happened. But at the time, he was a friend, a trusted friend.

Her heart ached. How could she move forward? How could she ever trust again?

Dev's words, although wonderful, unnerved her. She could never give him a real relationship, be that kind of committed to him. Marriage was a fantasy that couldn't last. After letting him in, letting him think he wanted to be with her, she wouldn't only hurt herself, but him too.

"You just have to mess everything up." She pressed her forehead to the glass.

All she could think of right now was leaving, leave behind the rumors, Walter and that compound that would forever haunt her. There was nothing here for her. Dev's face came to mind, and she hurt.

The door opened and Dev's image reflected in the darkened glass.

"Hey? You okay?"

"Not really," she murmured.

As he came up behind her, she tensed. Without a word, he leaned a shoulder to the wall, not even attempting to reach out.

"Talk to me."

She needed to tell him now. No sense in dragging it out, making things worse. "I think ... I think I need to leave."

"The doctor said you could go as soon as you were ready."

"No. I mean, I need to leave." She shook her head, wiping her face as the tears took over. "I don't think I can stay here anymore."

Refusing to look up at him, she turned and grabbed her duffle bag, setting it on the bed as she went to gather her things. She hit the button by the bed.

"May I help you?"

"I need to be discharged please."

"I'll send them in."

"I didn't mean to mess this all up, Dev." She didn't look up as she worked to hold back her tears. "I'm so sorry. I just ... I can't. I don't know what made me think I could be normal, and we could be normal, but I just don't think I can." She rushed to the bathroom to gather her things, shoving everything into a bag.

Her sudden vulnerability ate at her, and she started digging for her hat. She needed that hat.

"What are you looking for?" Dev quietly asked.

She looked up to see him still standing at the wall, his arms crossed and jaw set.

"My—my hat, I need it." Laurel dug through the bag, coming up empty. She groaned.

The door opened, and the nurse came in with an aide and a wheelchair. Laurel signed the slip and zipped up her bag.

"I don't need the chair," she muttered.

"It's hospital policy."

She glared at the aide. "I'm not using it."

Easing down into a chair, she shoved her shoes on and pulled the bag awkwardly to her right shoulder. Ignoring the aide, she pushed past Dev and got on an elevator going down.

As she stepped off, she noticed the vans and reporters camped just outside the doors, and her breath hitched in her throat.

A hand took the duffle and clasped her elbow.

"Come on, I'll take you out the back." Dev's clenched jaw stood out as he clasped her elbow.

As much as she wanted to protest, she didn't want to be with anyone else and allowed him to lead her through the doors to his truck.

The silence lingered in the vehicle, and all she could think of was her wanting him and him telling her he loved her. It had to be a dream, because right now, this felt like a nightmare.

He barely got the truck stopped before she jumped out, heaving the bag, and trying to climb the steps to get away from him. She held on tight as he came beside her and tried to pull the bag away. With a heavy sigh, he gave up and unlocked the door.

Rushing past, she dropped the bag in the floor and ran to her bedroom. She dug through her things, then went into her bathroom and found the hat she so desperately needed. Putting her hair in a ponytail, she then slipped it through the back and shoved the brim lower on her head.

Laurel sighed and leaned on the sink. She tried her best to work her breathing, ease the pounding in her chest.

"It's all over, just breathe," she muttered to herself as she made her way to the bedroom. Blowing out a deep breath, she looked down and saw Dev's sweatshirt on her bed, right where she'd left it. She perched on the edge of the bed, pulled the sweatshirt into her lap, and her emotions took over.

A gentle knock made her shake her head.

"Can you go, please?" she whispered through sobs.

The bed sank in as Dev sat next to her. "Normally, I would do what you asked. But not like this."

Pulling the hat down as far as she could, she nodded. His hand gently rubbed her back as he kept his distance, obviously worried he was the problem.

"You know it's not you, right?" she muttered.

"I was hoping not." He cleared his throat. "Just talk to me."

"I don't know what to say." She stood, needing to move as her brain worked around the words rolling through it. "Where to start."

His jaw tensed.

"I didn't mean to mess this all up, but being here ... I can't breathe. With all the rumors, Lester and all his hate, and there are others ... Then, Walter ... I have no peace here.."

"But you came back." He said gently.

She sighed and sank into the chair in the corner. "I was reeling, the—" she swallowed. "My injuries were finally healing, but the Navy said I couldn't rejoin, couldn't find another job with my unit. I was too overwhelmed to really notice everyone, I guess. I mean, it's not like it was any different from when I left. But knowing how much Walter hates me, Lester hates me ... I don't know how to process that."

"You just woke up, things are chaotic right now." He leaned on his knees. "Can I ask you to do something for me?"

She bit her lip with a nod.

Those sorrowful green eyes appeared, the worry and hurt just like the first day they met. "Don't make any decisions right now. Give it a couple of days. I promise, I won't ..." he sighed. "I won't try and convince you to stay. But you need some time to deal."

He looked so sad and hurt. It was all her fault.

"I'll wait," she whispered.

Blowing out a breath, he ducked his head to rub his neck. As he looked up, he focused on her, his gaze drifting to her hands. Looking down, she flushed at his sweatshirt wrapped around her fingers.

"Oh, I keep forgetting to give this back." She stood and handed it to him.

Standing, he placed her hands around the shirt. "You keep it."

She looked up and a smile formed on his lips. With a nod, she focused on the shirt and took a few steps forward, leaning into him. He grabbed her up, wrapping his strong arms around her, and she smiled.

"You're not mad at me?"

"No, Laurel." He chuckled. "You've been through a lot, and there's no way I can be mad at you for struggling." Lifting her chin, he gave her a smile. "Just talk to me, okay? I won't even talk back if you don't want me to answer, but please, talk to me."

She nodded, and her eyes focused on his lips for a moment before fixing on his chest. Holding her close for a while, he rubbed her back and let her just be there with him. He gave her a kiss on the head and stepped back, holding her arms.

"Are you hungry? We can go to the diner."

"Oh, I'm not ... I don't think..."

"Look, I'm not going to push, but I am going to be around. You're not getting rid of me as long as you're here."

Nodding, she wiped her face. "Okay."

"Do you want to go out? I can bring some food here."

She looked around her bedroom and felt contained, claustrophobic once again. "I need to get out."

"Okay, I'll be in the living room whenever you're ready." He gave her arms a light squeeze then left the room, pulling the door shut behind him.

37

Flopping on the couch, Dev did his best to breathe and keep calm. God's intervention was the only reason he'd been able to get through her need to leave. His pounding heart and fisted hands ached. Her leaving had never entered his mind.

"God, you've got to help me here. I thought this is what You wanted for me, for us. So, what now?" He leaned on his knees, holding his head with his hands.

She was obviously struggling. But he really thought once the shock wore off, she could get some help and begin to heal. He hadn't assumed for a second she'd just jump on board to dating. But this ... he wasn't prepared for this.

Peace, she mentioned needing peace. She needed God, the peace and love God could give her to escape all the madness of her life. But after talking to her, she still seemed separated from the subject.

He stood as her door opened, and he clenched his jaw shut. In her snug jeans and a red V-neck shirt, she looked amazing, even if he could barely see her eyes from under the hat.

"The hat stays, huh?" He chuckled as she crossed her arms.

"Why do you always comment on my hat?"

"Because—" he took a few steps in front of her, lifting the brim slightly. "I like to see your eyes. You have amazing eyes."

Her jaw dropped for a moment as she batted away his hand and pulled the hat back in place. Her mouth opened, then she turned silently, a red hue working its way up her neck and cheeks.

Grabbing a long cardigan, she pulled it on, and he held the door open for her. Once in the truck, he worked to ease his own emotions as he tried to end the silence separating them.

"So, how did you end up at the mechanic shop?"

"Chuck is my mom's cousin. He's always been kind, moved here with his wife a few years after I left. She died right after I came back." She cleared her throat. "I owe him a lot."

"What else do you like to do?" He felt her watching and smiled.

"What's that grin for?"

"I'm just making conversation, no need to be defensive." He winked and turned back to the road.

"I don't do much else. I take care of Johnny once or twice a week, when Lizzy needs me to, and I take care of Kendra' house —all the yard work and repairs. It's an old house." She sighed.

"What about the guest house?"

"What about it?"

"It's pretty outdated. I'm just surprised you haven't done more to fix it up."

"Well, it's Kendra's property. I don't, I mean, I don't feel like it's mine to fix up."

He chuckled.

"What now?"

"Nothing, just trying to see things from your perspective, Laurel."

AFTER BEING at the diner for thirty minutes, Laurel scarfed down the food, and Dev left part of his burger as she pulled him away.

Since the second they arrived in the parking lot, she'd been hounded by everyone. Some wanted information on what happened, others just wanted to shake her hand and tell her she did a good job. It seemed all the attention got the better of her.

Dev started up the truck. "Where to?"

"Just—just drive." She blew out a breath and rubbed her palms together between her knees.

He took off down the road toward Darrell's property. The bumpy road gave way to the Y, and he smiled as he took the road to the barn.

"What ... why did you come here?" She looked over, her breathing still heavy as sweat beaded her upper lip.

"I just wanted you to have some quiet, some peace." He frowned. "You okay?"

She shook her head and jumped from the truck, stopping short of the barn. Crossing her arms, she rubbed them, and he worried with the temp dropping she might get cold.

"Come on, I'll take you home."

"No. I don't want to go home." She shook her head, pacing back and forth.

Pulling out a blanket and an extra coat from the back seat of the truck, he set the coat on her shoulders and caught her elbow. "Come on."

"Where?"

"Trust me." He led her around the side of the barn, where the wind was blocked, and the moon shone high in the sky.

Laying out the blanket, he led her to sit. She leaned against the barn.

"Better?"

She looked over with a sigh and gave him a small grin. He forced a smile, working to keep his hands to himself. It wasn't often she smiled and even less often it was directed at him.

Settling beside her, he looked up at the cloudless night sky. The moon lit everything around them, and he closed his eyes a moment.

"He said something," she muttered.

"Who did?"

She pulled her knees to her chest and her arms wrapped around them, closing herself off completely. A shiver moved through her and he scooted closer, gently wrapping an arm around her waist.

"One of the men, with the long beard." She cleared her throat and he frowned.

Dev remembered each man's face from that compound, even the dead man's face. The guy with the beard was big and definitely an intimidator.

"What did he say?"

"I was ... crying, upset. After getting the one guy down, I couldn't believe I was getting strapped into ..." she paused, and Dev pulled her close. "He put my arm in the restraint, and I said, God, why are you doing this to me?"

His heart jumped, bile burning the back of his throat.

"He said it wasn't God, just them." She leaned back against the barn.

God, give me the words.

"I'm sorry. I hate you went through all that." He rubbed his eyes. "But, he ... what he said ... do you think God was the one who did all those things to you?"

"Kendra always said God was in control of everything." She shrugged. "He was more powerful than the strongest person—" She cleared her throat. "The strongest person we knew," she whispered.

"But he didn't save you from your dad."

She nodded. A few tears dripped from her cheeks. Dev lifted the hat off her head and pulled her in, letting her cry a bit before he finally figured out what to say.

"Look, I don't know why. I don't have an answer for that,

Laurel. I wish I did. But I can at least guess as to why you were in the compound."

"You think I *had* to be there?" She straightened and pushed him off, obviously upset and hurt at the comment.

"No, that's not it. Just listen, please." He faced her, cradling her hands in his. "God is stronger than any man. He created everything. If He can create everything, including us, He has more power than we'll ever understand. As far as your past, I can't ... I can't give you answers.

"And as far as what happened, I can't claim to know why God allowed that to happen. But I can tell you this. Because you were there, because of the abilities God gave you, your training, you saved eight girls. Then over a hundred more once we arrived, and the FBI got the information from the house.

"It might not be enough, and God knows I gave him an earful when I found out you were gone. I was terrified." Dev breathed through the wave of sickness just thinking about it. "But not only did you survive, you saved others. So, as far as I know, that's why you were there in that building, right then."

He let her have time, leaning up against the barn beside her. Her fingers threaded between his and squeezed.

"I'm having a hard time dealing with all this," she shuddered, and he looked up to see her staring at the sky.

Gazing at her profile against the night sky, he couldn't help the pounding of his heart. He'd never felt this way about anyone nor had this intense attraction before. As she closed her crystal blue eyes and sighed, her red lips looked much too inviting.

"Laurel, I meant everything I said in the ambulance. I haven't brought it up, but I ... I want you to know."

Her eyes popped open.

"I love you. I do need you in my life. Even if you leave town, I can't promise I won't follow you." He forced a smile as her eyes widened. "I know I said I wouldn't push you to stay, and I'm not. But I would consider following you."

She straightened. "You can't ... I mean, how can you know all that?"

"That I love you?" Dev smiled, his heart echoing in his ears. "I don't know how to explain it. I just feel like God led me here. He led me here for a reason, and since the moment I met you, I felt drawn to you. I've been a police officer for years, but I've never felt as protective of anyone as I do you."

Dev brushed the tendrils of hair that fell from her ponytail around her face. "I've already told you how attracted I am to you. But you're an amazing woman inside too. God made you special, even if you don't quite believe in Him yet. He doesn't need you to believe to make you special."

"I'm not special," she whispered as she shook her head, tears falling again.

He wiped them away. "You are," he whispered back, holding her cheek gently.

"You don't know me as well as you think." She forced a smile, one he desperately wanted to see as real.

"I don't need to know everything about you to love you. I know your character, your heart. That's more important than knowing about every single thing in your life."

"What about you?"

He smiled, pulling her hands up to his lips and kissing each one. "What about me?"

"I don't know anything about you. I think you've done enough searching on me and my past."

"What do you want to know?"

"I don't know." She shrugged. "Where did you grow up?"

"Chicago. I lived there with my parents for a while, then we moved to the South. Tennessee was the first place we lived where I started to enjoy being outside. I grew up hiking and canoeing."

"Why did you become an officer?"

"It was a plan God had laid out." He narrowed his eyes. "I was in college, getting my associates degree as a petroleum tech when I was told there was a surge in the program. I finished, but there were no jobs available. A buddy convinced me to go to the police academy and work until I could find another job." He shrugged. "It seemed like a good idea at the time. But once I was on the street, I loved it and couldn't quit."

Her eyes shone in the moonlight.

"Now, tell me about your time away from home."

"Not much to tell." She frowned.

"I don't believe that for a second."

Her gaze dropped to their hands.

"Did you enjoy the Navy?"

"Yeah, it felt like home. More so than being here." She glanced up, a wistful smile on her face. "I had some good friends, really good friends."

"Do you still talk with them?"

She shook her head. "When they told me I couldn't go back in, I didn't handle it well. I didn't handle being in the hospital well, in the rehab unit, or anything well, actually. I think I messed up a lot of those friendships." Her fingers moved over his, tracing the outline of his knuckles.

"You should try and find your friends. I'm fairly certain they understood your situation enough to know how frustrated you were with being there. I don't think it's as bad as you assume it is."

"I get an email every so often." She shrugged. "But I ... I always just delete it."

"Let me know when the next email comes." He sighed. "I'll be there with you when you read it."

She let out a haggard chuckle. "What makes you think I'll want to read it?"

He pulled a hand away and lifted her chin to see her eyes. "I think it would be a great place to start."

38

Laurel mentioned being tired, so Dev loaded her and the blanket up and headed back to her house. The ride home was quiet. As he pulled in, he put the truck in park and noticed instead of jumping out and bolting to the door, she simply sat.

He turned off the engine and waited, the lights clicking off and the sounds of the night surrounding them.

"It was a fire."

He shifted in the seat as she stared out the window.

"I was a gunner and usually had a great view as we moved through the country. We were escorting some members to a local village, a good neighbor type thing. I was in the lead Humvee. The attack sent us flying, I somehow ended up outside, and one of my guys was pulling me away from the fire." She cleared her throat.

"We made it to a nearby shelter, licking our wounds and calling in backup. Mine was the only one hit, and the guys took out all the insurgents around us. I really thought we were good."

He started to move closer, but she held up her hand, barely glancing at him before turning back to the window. She sighed heavily.

"We were headed to the air transport when we got hit again. The shelter exploded and threw me clear. I got up and saw the guys from the copter trying to keep the insurgents back, but no one was helping my guys." Her voice dropped.

"I made a hole and got inside, pulled a couple of them free. Backup showed and took care of the enemy while the first air transport helped me get them loaded. I went back when I realized we were missing three more, but right when I went in, another explosion hit and trapped me.

"My guys came in, and I told them to leave. I was stuck. A beam fell over my back. I just ... I couldn't move and then everything caught fire." She wiped the tears running down her face. "I managed to get out, but there was so much damage to my ... my skin."

He closed his mouth, making himself take a deep breath before he spoke. "How did you get out?"

"When I squeezed out, it took most of the ... skin, I managed to crawl through a hole, and one of my guys noticed me." She shoved open the door and slid to the ground.

The things she'd survived in her life ...

He followed her to the porch where she sat in the dark on the swing. He patted her leg, and she moved over so he could join her. Wrapping an arm around her, he sent the swing in motion as she curled her body next to his.

Holding her there on the swing, he closed his eyes and prayed.

Lord, please, please open her heart to You. She needs you so much. She's seen and experienced more pain than anyone should in this life. Please help her.

"You need some rest." Dev sighed and kissed her head, felt her nod against his chest, and he squeezed her shoulders. "Thanks for talking to me," he whispered.

Her face pressed close to his, making him still. Running her fingers over his jaw, she gently kissed his lips.

"Laurel, I—

She shook her head as her arms came around his neck. Pulling him in, she kissed him again, this time much deeper and more passionately. His body ached when she slowly pulled away, her blue eyes searching his as he struggled to control his breathing.

"Laurel, you can't do that and tell me you're leaving." He held her waist, trying to keep her close.

"I don't ..." She bit her bottom lip. "Want to leave." Her eyes found his.

"Then don't." He clenched his jaw a moment, watching her eyes search his face. "That's not a goodbye kiss, right?"

In silence, she watched him.

"Promise me you won't leave. If I come here to find you, I won't be able to handle it if you've left me alone without telling me goodbye."

She nodded, shifting in the seat. He pulled her in again, kissing her, and wishing she'd promise to stay.

"I should go inside," she whispered.

Tears trailed down her cheeks, and he wiped them away. He kissed her one last time, then helped her stand, and with his arm around her waist, led her inside. Holding onto the door, he held her close with one arm.

She wrapped him up, making him let go of the door. Kissing her cheek, he breathed her in and sighed.

"I need to go. Right ... now, okay?"

She looked up at him, and he couldn't turn away. He kissed her again, she pulled him in and once again, deepened their kiss. He groaned and forced himself to step back.

"Do you know what ... what you're doing?" he breathed out, forcing his fingers into her belt loops.

She only shook her head and slowly slid her hands down his chest to each side of his waist.

"I'm going, okay? Just call me if you need anything, anything at all. Lock up." He took a look at her blue eyes, seeing something there he didn't understand.

Taking her hand, he kissed it and turned to leave, run actually, down the steps and into his truck.

39

L aurel finished with her bag and let out a breath.

The sun was barely up, but she was ready to go. Staying here, being around every terrible memory and hateful person in her life ...

"I've got to get out of here," she mumbled.

Awkwardly carrying the bag to the living room, she sat it on the floor, when a knock on the door made her jump.

Swallowing an overwhelming fear, she pulled aside the curtain and gasped. She yanked the door open.

Tara stood on her porch, her dark hair cut short, and her hands gripping her shoulder bag.

"Tara?"

"Dad drove me. I ... I wanted to see you." Tears streamed down her face.

She gripped Tara's shoulders and hugged, holding on tight as her own tears let loose. "I thought I'd lost you."

"Me, too," Tara whispered.

After a moment, she straightened and wiped her face. "Come in, can you come inside?"

Tara nodded and stepped into the room. "I can't believe this is yours."

"Well, it's Kendra's. Not mine." She locked the door and sat down on the couch next to Tara. "How did you ... I mean, when did you get back?"

"A few days ago." Tara wiped her cheeks dry with her shirt sleeve. "Mom and Dad have kept it quiet. They don't want me having visitors yet. Memories are coming back slowly. A lot is in pictures, just moving frames in my mind." Her hands gripped the bag on her lap. "My therapist wants me to draw everything, get it all out."

"Lucky you. I get to talk about everything, over and over," she muttered as she pulled at her hoodie. "I'm so sorry, Tara," she whispered.

"What? Why are you sorry?"

"I should've come for you." Laurel shifted in the couch to face her friend. "When I finally came home and found out you were missing, I dug into everything, and then I had to report for the next duty. Each time I was able to come here for leave, I searched. But I couldn't find anything. No one was looking, and I—"

"Laurel."

She bit the inside of her cheek as she looked Tara in the eye.

"I never expected you to come get me. Everything that happened, it's still blurry. I don't remember who or what or even where. It starts to come into my mind, but I can't grip it long enough to remember." Tara sat down her bag and pulled out a spiral bound book.

"I remember the hospital. I woke up and they said I was safe. I couldn't remember my name or anything. They gave me some paper and pencil and I just started drawing." She opened the book and handed her a stack of pages.

The sketches took her breath away. Scenes from the diner in town, sketches of her and Lizzy, even Tara's childhood home.

"They tried to match them to something, but I wasn't reported missing."

"Why did they do that?" Laurel sighed, shaking her head. "Not file a report?"

"My dad, he tried a few times." Tara shrugged. "But Sheriff McGehee said I was too old to file a missing person's report. That it would just get drowned out by the missing children reports. It's something he's regretted a long time," she whispered.

Taking her friend's hand, Laurel squeezed. "I can't believe they found you."

"They didn't—you did." Tara's glazed eyes found hers. "You kept looking and told your friend. He found me. I was ... I remember being scared, a lot. They still don't know where I actually came from or the people who took me."

Tara cleared her throat. "But I just remember thinking, Laurel would be brave. She wouldn't make anything easy. She'd stand up against them. Sometimes I remember a face ..." Tara trailed off and took some deep breaths. "I was so scared, and I just couldn't see how you always stood up to your dad," she whispered.

A lump formed in Laurel's throat.

"I just wanted to be brave." Tara's tear-filled eyes looked up at her. "God's grace got me through—Him and you." Tara pulled a page from her notebook and handed it to her.

Laurel's hand trembled as she took the page, completely blown away by the sketch. It was almost identical to the one she'd carried around for years.

"I'm really sorry you went through all of this, Laurel."

"What?" Laurel's mouth dropped open. "You were missing, and—"

"No, I'm not just talking about the other day. This life, what you've dealt with. I'm so sorry you went through everything. I know I was young, but I should've done more, tried harder."

Laurel's eyes went wide as she tried to calm her breathing. How could Tara think her life was anything compared to being kidnapped and taken for a decade?

CINDY BONDS

"I do know one thing, I'm not going to live in fear. I won't run away, be scared to be on my own. Well, eventually." Tara chuckled as she wiped her face. "My mom and dad have been a bit overprotective since I got back. But, eventually, I'm going to move out and get my own place and ..." Tara trailed off and gave a smile.

Laurel grinned back.

"And I want you to take me to meet your detective friend. I can't wait to meet him. I owe him a lot."

"So do I," Laurel mumbled. Gripping the picture in her hand, she couldn't believe Tara thought her so brave.

"Are you leaving?"

Her attention went back to Tara who was staring at the large duffle bag.

"I just, I feel like I need to get away for a while. Everything is too much right now. The town and everyone ..."

"Dad told me what happened. You saved all those girls and stopped those men. You should be proud of what you've done. Not ready to run away."

Gritting her teeth, Laurel took a deep breath as she stood. "I'm not running away, I just, I ... I remember," she whispered. "I can't close my eyes without it hitting, and I'm alone and..." She paced, needing to move as the memories pushed into her chest. Spinning to Tara, her face heated. "I'm so sorry. What you've already dealt with and I'm here complaining."

Tara tilted her head with a frown. "I get it, it's fine. But you're not alone. We're all here for you. But I guess that's not what you want."

"What? What do you mean not what I want?"

"This is the same thing as after what happened that awful night." Tara pushed the book from her lap and stood. "We were at the hospital, and my parents said you could live with us.. But you said no. Lizzy even said she talked about you staying with Tonya, but you refused. Why didn't you want our help?"

"I didn't want you to deal with the fallout." Swallowing the lump in her throat, she took Tara's hand. "Look, everyone hated me. The doctor, the nurses, they all tried to convince me that what I saw wasn't what really happened. That I must've done something terrible that night to mom and Guy. Even then, people were trying to destroy my credibility."

"We're not kids anymore, Laurel." Tara gripped her hand. "And for the first time in forever, this town appreciates you, is accepting you. If you don't accept our help now, then it's because you're just too stubborn."

Laurel's jaw clenched.

"This is so familiar." Tara shook her head, letting out a chuckle. "All the times I tried to help, and you wouldn't let me. I remember you getting in a fight with Lizzy because she wanted to help buy you a bus ticket out of here. But you wanted to do it all yourself, alone."

"I ..." she trailed off, having no idea how to answer.

"Laurel. I don't know if you've changed in other ways, but I need to tell you something. The only reason I'm alive is because I felt as if someone was watching over me, protecting me, guiding me. God had a hand in all this. He led me out of wherever I was being held, and I walked away because He guided my steps.

"You escaped that place too. I read about it in the paper, Lizzy gave me the unedited version from her officer boyfriend. The only way you escaped is because someone guided you through all that, protected you."

She swallowed hard. "None of that changes the fact that I'm not better," she whispered.

"It's just been a few days! You won't get better in a few days. What you've dealt with—" Tara blew out a breath and dropped Laurel's hand, pushing both of hers onto her hips. "If I'd been in my right mind and not so scared of you getting mad, I would've marched into that police station and reported Guy Ashburn the second we became friends.

"All those years of abuse isn't going to just disappear, and neither will all this. Give it time. Let us help you. You've shouldered it all for everyone else for so long. Let us help you this time."

"I ... I don't know how." Her fingers twisted in front of her waist.

Tara chuckled and pulled her into a hug. "All you have to do is talk to your friends, and let us help you through all the memories."

"Yeah." She huffed. "Talking isn't my strong suit."

"You know, there is something different about you." Tara stepped back.

"Trust me." She sighed. "I think I'm just as stubborn as I was back then."

"If you decide to walk away from a man like Detective Hollister, you definitely are. I saw a picture online. He's hot."

She smiled and shook her head, pulling the hat down and hoping she wasn't as red as she felt.

"Laurel, trust us. Give us a chance to show you what it means to let others help."

As she chewed on the inside of her cheek, her friend's comments were interesting. Tara grew up going to church, but had never discussed God stuff with her.

"Are you ... do you feel peace?"

"What do you mean?" Tara tilted her head.

"With everything that happened to you. The fact your God let it happen. Do you feel peace?"

Tara sighed. "I'm getting there. I lost a lot, everything actually. And even though it was awful, I've had a few years to deal with it, to accept it. God didn't put me there, Laurel. Those men, it was their choice to do something evil. But God did get me out. I do have peace about that."

That was even more confusing.

"Just ask yourself what you want in life. So far, you've spent your entire life running away. You ran from Guy, from everyone in this town, and left after graduation without even a word. But now, we're all here for you. So, what is it you want?"

She blinked. Her mouth opened, but nothing came out.

"We want you to be happy here." Tara smiled. "Let us help you with that."

"Yeah, okay," she mumbled.

"I'm going to head out. Dad gets nervous when I'm out of sight for too long. I figure it's going to be a while before things go back to normal. But then again, I'm good with being home."

"I'm so glad you're safe." She smiled and a wave of emotions hit her as Tara gave her a hug.

"Same here."

After Tara left, Laurel collapsed on the couch, gripping her phone and wrestling with her decision. Running away, was that her answer to everything?

The phone vibrated and Dev's name flashed across the screen. She'd avoided his call first thing this morning, not wanting to tell him she was leaving.

"Hello?"

"Hey, I missed you this morning. How are you?"

"I'm better actually." She smiled, a warmth spreading through her heart.

"Oh?"

"Tara came by."

"Really? I didn't think her parents were good with letting her out and about."

She sighed. "Her dad drove her here. She said she wanted to see me."

"Sounds like you had a good visit."

"Yeah, just ... there were some things she mentioned. Apparently, I haven't changed much."

He chuckled, and the sound made her miss him even more.

"I called because I needed to talk to you about something. Mind if I come over?"

"Is this bad news?" She chewed on her lip.

"Well, I'm hoping you'll see it as some answers, something good. I'll be there in ten."

"Okay," she whispered.

"Laurel?"

"Yeah?"

"I love you."

The fear shattered long enough for her to enjoy the sentiment.

"See you in a bit."

"Yeah, bye," she whispered.

Even if she left right now, she would probably pass him on the road. She sat on her couch and studied the bag on the floor. Groaning, she leaned her head back and closed her eyes.

Running away again. First after graduation and now this. Since when did running away become who she was?

She got up and made some coffee, then leaned against the counter, looking out the back window.

Would this life be it from now on? This overwhelming fear and need to run? She couldn't be with Dev and offer nothing more than a shattered woman. He deserved so much more.

Once again, it seemed a foreseeable future with this amazing man wouldn't be possible. She did care about him, far too much to allow him to waste his time and life on her. But leaving him behind, she didn't want to do that either.

"God, what is the answer?" she muttered.

40

Dev took a deep breath and knocked on Laurel's door.

After kissing her last night, he was hoping the next time they met, it would be even better. But with the information he was about to drop on her, he knew that wasn't happening today.

"Hey." Her red-rimmed eyes met his.

"I thought you said you were better?"

She shrugged and stepped aside.

With a frown, he took her hand as she shut the door behind him. "Laurel?"

"I just ... you needed to tell me something?" She pulled away. Crossing her arms, she stared up at him.

He noticed the duffle bag on the floor. "You planning on leaving?"

"I don't know," she whispered.

Ignoring her stiffness, he pulled her in for a hug, closing his eyes.

God, please, please let her stay.

"I do need to tell you something, but I want you to talk first."

She shook her head, leaning her body into his, her arms finally wrapping around him.

"Okay. Since I know you like being direct, I need to tell you that a few days ago, I put in a request for a cadaver dog to search your family's property."

"Why?" Her head went up and her body pushed from his.

"Let's sit." He led her to the couch and urged her to sit down. "After discovering Walter's involvement in what happened to your mother and to Guy, we've discovered a few things. Tobias Rutherford is telling us pretty much everything we want to know.

"Walter had been running this ring for a while, long before he became sheriff. According to Rutherford, Guy found out and wanted to turn him in. Guy confronted Walter, basically gave him a head start to get out of the state, the country. Walter didn't like that idea, so he went to your house that night, to see if he could convince Guy otherwise."

Her face paled as she covered her mouth.

"Your mom was there, but Guy wasn't home yet. It didn't take long for Walter to realize your mom knew what was going on, and Walter ... well, Rutherford said he doesn't really know exactly what happened. Only that Walter doesn't leave loose ends. Ever."

Laurel jumped up. Dev followed as she paced.

"According to Rutherford, you were there that night."

"That's what Walter kept saying, but I ... I don't remember him being there!" she exclaimed through tears.

He stepped in front and took hold of her elbows. "Tell me what you do remember."

She wiped her face dry. "I ... there was yelling. I remember running and someone yelled, 'Go get her.' But I always thought, I thought it was Guy." Her red-rimmed eyes looked up at him. "Guy was trying to do the right thing?"

"That's what Rutherford said. It lines up with what you told us Walter had said." He rubbed her arms. "After you ran away, there was a fight, and one of them pulled a weapon. Rutherford swears he doesn't know if Walter was intentional or not when Guy was shot."

He took a deep breath. "Honey, since that moment, Walter's been terrified you'd remember what happened. That you'd remember, and then he'd be in trouble. That's why he tried to get you out of here.

"After everything we discovered, I called in the dog handler, because Walter didn't search the property. I got a call this morning. They found remains."

"Mom," she murmured.

Tears filled her eyes, and he drew her in, holding her close.

"I'm so sorry. You don't deserve to go through this again."

"How ... when will you know?" she muttered between sobs.

"It'll take a few weeks." He glanced at the bag again, a weight pushing on his chest. "I just want you to know, I'm here. We're all here to help you through this."

Just don't leave.

It echoed in his mind, and he pushed away the thought.

God, give her a way to handle this, to deal with all of this. Help her see You.

THE REMAINS WERE IDENTIFIED as April Ashburn.

It took almost three weeks for the ID and the cause of death to be confirmed. After examination, the ME declared blunt force trauma as cause of death.

Laurel had teetered between relief and anger, not able to find words to express herself. Keeping it all inside increased her nightmares as well as her flashbacks. She called almost every night for weeks, and Dev would go sit with her, soothe her until she was calm.

It was either waking up in a cell from her abduction or the heat of the fire searing into her body that took her sleep away.

Darrell convinced her to see a therapist, and the week her mother was finally laid to rest, she'd gone to her first session.

Laurel and Tara spent more time together, creating an even stronger bond. Dev could always tell when Tara had made a visit. Laurel would be happier, friendlier, and more talkative when he came by. Between therapy and friends, she was healing.

Dev's phone rang and he unearthed it from the mountain of paperwork on his desk.

"Hollister."

"Hey, man. Wanted to check in." Bruce's southern drawl worked its way through the line.

"Well, I've been a little bit busy."

"I heard about that. Something about human remains being found?"

Dev sighed. "Yeah. April Ashburn, Laurel's mother was identified two months ago."

"First the kidnapping and then this?"

"It's been a rough couple of months." Dev's jaw worked back and forth. "Thanks for handling all the case stuff so far. She's doing better, but I'd hate for her to have a set back by having to go through it all again."

"No promises, but so far, none of those guys have a leg to stand on. Laurel's not the only one who can identify them."

"Surely that's not the only reason you're calling."

Bruce chuckled. "I did want to see how your *friendship* is working out. Just wanted to know if you've got any news."

"We're dating, thanks for asking." Dev's smile grew as he leaned back in his chair.

"I knew it!" Bruce laughed out loud. "You know, with the open sheriff's position there ..."

Dev huffed. "Nah, not interested. I'm where I want to be."

"You sure about that?"

"Positive."

"Hey, I've got to go."

"Yeah, talk to you later." Dev hung up and tossed the phone on the desk.

He and Laurel were dating, a concept that made his heart swell. And Laurel, well Laurel had started to bloom. As her sleep caught up and her body healed, she laughed and smiled more. She'd become a different person, a new woman, and he loved her even more. They were looking at a wonderfully slow relationship, and he wouldn't have it any other way.

With a grin, he grabbed up his phone and found her number.

"Yeah?"

"Hey, beautiful."

Her annoyed huff came through the line, and he chuckled. "Want to meet for lunch?"

"Look, the shop is really busy. I'll meet you at the house tonight, okay?"

"Promise?"

"I've got to go." She groaned. "Yes, I promise I'll meet you tonight at the house."

"I love you. See you later."

"Bye," she murmured as the call ended.

He sighed. After three months from when he first met her, the roller coaster life of Laurel Ashburn was finally starting to slow, coming to a long straight stretch. Her mother found and buried, her injuries healed, and her town finally accepting her.

Now if she would just trust him as completely as he trusted her. With her past and her never ending distrust of the police and men in general, a wall was still there, marking her boundaries.

In the back of his mind, he kept seeing that duffle bag on the floor, ready and waiting for her to take off, to leave him behind and break his heart.

"God, I need some help here," he mumbled as he leaned his head in his hands.

41

"Um, thanks."

Laurel nodded as the last customer finally left the shop. Blowing out a deep breath, she sat back in the stool and swiveled around at Chuck's laughter.

"It's been like this for weeks. Is this a busy time of the year for you?"

"Nope." He shook his head and laughed. "But you're a bit of a celebrity."

She sighed as he walked past, her gaze centering on the pictures on the wall. The largest picture was of Chuck and his late wife, Toni. They looked so happy together. Her eyes moved across the other pictures as she stood, finding a wedding picture of the two of them.

"That was a long time ago."

"How long were you married?"

"Forty-two years."

"What?" Her mouth dropped open. "I didn't know people were married that long."

"She was a wonderful person."

"Are you mad because God took her away?" She bit her lip as Chuck frowned.

"God doesn't take people away. Everyone has a time to be born, a time to die. It's not God that takes us away, it's just part of life."

"But she ... the cancer."

Chuck blew out a breath.. "Cancer is hard. It's a terrible disease. But He didn't give it to her. This life ... When someone says that's life, it means bad things happen. Sometimes it's because we've done something wrong, and we suffer the consequences. Sometimes, bad things happen although we've done nothing wrong, and there's nothing we can do about it."

She frowned. That made no sense.

"Sit down, Laurel." Chuck led her to the stool, and she sat. "God isn't out to get us, He created us. This world is full of evil and sin. That's why there's disease and anger and hurt. But God doesn't put it on us. I mean, yes, it hurts that she's gone, and my selfish heart wants her here with me.

"But in heaven, she's cured. Her back doesn't hurt anymore, her hands are healed. Her arthritis was so bad, she couldn't play the piano anymore. But with God in perfection, she's playing her piano and singing. I'll see her again. It'll just take me some time to get there."

She sighed. "Does everyone go to heaven?"

"Those who don't believe, they don't go. Salvation means to be saved by Jesus, to accept Him as your Savior, to believe in Him, to believe He's with you. You know, your mom was a Christian."

"I don't remember that," she mumbled.

"When she and Guy met, he was a good man. I know you don't remember that about him, but he was good when they first married. It wasn't until he started drinking that things went badly. The devil got a hold of him."

"Humph." She slid down from the stool. "It's easy to blame the devil when he isn't here, Chuck."

Chuck let out a snicker. "I think you have a better grasp on the situation than you think. Guy let the bad get to him.

Sacrificed his family, his soul for what was in that bottle." He looked her over in concern. "You really don't remember your mom taking you to church?"

"High holidays only," she mumbled.

"She was an amazing singer, just like you."

"What?" Her face heated at the comment.

"I watch the security tapes from time to time. If I turn them up, I can hear the echo in the garage when you're working. You sound just like her."

Her jaw clenched.

"Laurel, this life isn't easy." Chuck's gray eyes studied her a moment. "You've been through much more than any one person should. But that doesn't mean God hasn't been there, trying to help you see Him. How many times should you have been badly hurt, or even dead, but then you weren't? Or you should've been there when something bad happened but you weren't?"

Chuck took hold of her arms. "If God weren't watching over you, I know you wouldn't be standing here right now. You would've been right there with your mom at the hands of your father's sin. It wasn't your time because God had other plans for you. Bigger, better plans."

Feeling the tears trailing down her cheeks, she couldn't breathe. The fire. She was thrown twice, cleared as the fire pulled at everyone else. She lost more than a few friends that day, but she got out with just the burns on her lower back.

"Laurel?"

"Yeah." Her gaze met Chuck's. "I ... I think I'm going home."

"Get some rest. I know this has been a hard time for you, hun. But things will get better."

She nodded as she strode to the truck, her mind spinning.

Had God really been there? As often as she was pushed into walls, her arms gripped and pulled, she'd never broken any bones. Just bruises and maybe a few cracks, nothing that ever needed a doctor.

While she drove, her mind rushed through the events of her

life, the terrible and sad, the times she tried so hard to forget. Her abduction and escape. A shudder zipped through her body.

"If You *were* there, why didn't I see You?" she mumbled.

42

"Hey, you." Dev smiled big as Laurel opened the door, her hair down and in a T-shirt and jeans.

She looked amazing.

"Hey." She grinned and pulled him inside, giving him a gentle kiss.

Before she could get away, he caught her up again, taking his time and enjoying the feel of her lips pressed against his.

"Hey." She repeated as she took a breath and looked up into his eyes.

"How are you today?" He smiled again, pushing the hair from her cheek, and tucking it behind her ear.

"I'm good. Kendra made dinner, you want to— ?"

"No." He chuckled as she crossed her arms, trying to appear upset with him.

"I told her we would come eat."

He sighed. Holding her upper arms, he squeezed them tight for a moment then let go. "Okay, lead the way."

Shoving his hands in his pockets, he worked to keep himself from grabbing her up. She'd been through so much, he wanted her to feel comfortable coming to him. As much as he needed that connection, it was something she needed to feel too, and he wasn't entirely certain she did.

With her auburn hair floating around her shoulders, blonde highlights shining in the sun, she looked good. Then again, she always looked good. But the past several days, the hat was gone. No longer blocking her out from everyone and from him, it was an amazing step she had taken for herself.

Jumping ahead of her, he opened the door, smiling at the smirk on her face.

"I'm so glad you came by." Kendra took his hand as soon as they entered the kitchen.

"You don't have to cook, Mrs. Beecham. Although, you know how much I enjoy it." He smiled as she slapped at his arm.

"Sit down and eat. Have you been busy today?" She pushed him back and got the plates from the cabinet herself.

"Not too bad." He grinned as he pulled out Laurel's chair, then brushed his hand along the back of her neck as he moved past. "Just glad to be off work."

"Good. I'm glad you're done, I have plans for tonight and wanted to make sure someone would be here for Laurel."

"Kendra, please stop treating me like a child." Laurel tried to ease her tone, but it was low and irritated.

"I have plans too," Dev said. "Actually, we both do."

Laurel and Mrs. Beecham both snapped to face him.

"What do you have planned?" Laurel asked.

He shrugged, gently nudging her foot with his under the table.

"Well good. And I'm allowed to worry Laurel, don't you forget it." Mrs. Beecham patted Laurel's shoulder as she sat down.

Mrs. Beecham entertained them as they ate, telling them all about the news she heard at her quilting meeting earlier that day. Dev chuckled and smiled as he glanced at Laurel. Pushing the food around her plate, she chewed on the inside of her cheek.

"Laurel?"

She glanced up at Mrs. Beecham and straightened. "Um, sorry, I wasn't listening."

"Dear, you need to eat."

"I know," she muttered.

"Well, I'm off. Clean up if you don't mind." Mrs. Beecham looked to him and he frowned.

"Yes ma'am." He nodded and sat down his fork as Mrs. Beecham hurried through the living room and up the stairs.

Standing, he slid the chair next to her. "Hey, talk to me."

"I'm not hungry." She sat down her fork with a huff. "Not much to tell." She leaned over to him with a grin, and he clenched his jaw. "What now?" That fire sparked in her eyes.

"As much as I want a kiss from you, I know you too well."

She huffed and stood, leaving out the back door. He chased her down.

"Laurel don't get mad. I just want you to talk."

"I talk all the time!" She groaned and faced him. "I talk to Kendra, I talk to the therapist, I talk to Chuck when I go to work, then I have to talk to you. It's been ... it's been two solid months of talking, and I need to just ... I need this to stop. Everyone is crowding around me, asking me to talk all the time, and I don't want to. You realize that before all this, I rarely had a conversation at all during the day?"

His face heated at the comment. It was hard to remember just how excluded she made herself before everything happened.

"Okay. Let's go." He grabbed her hand and pulled her to his truck.

"What? Dev, we didn't do the dishes, and I've got chores to do—"

"No talking." He paused, giving her a wink before opening her door.

"Dev—"

"Laurel, no talking. I'm trying here."

"But I have things to do."

With a chuckle at her irritation, he slammed the door.

Sliding behind the wheel, he started the truck, backed up and headed down the road.

"Now, I had this planned, but if you're too irritated ..."

"Does it have to do with talking?"

He grinned at her with a raised eyebrow, and she sighed.

Taking her hand, he held it between them as they drove in silence. He pulled into the back of Darrell's property, and opened her truck door.

43

The sunset was burning in the sky, and Dev grinned as Laurel let out a sigh. Without a word, he grabbed her hand, guiding her up the incline.

Ending at the top of the bluff, he led her in front of him, wrapping her up in his arms as they watched the sun setting in the sky.

"I love you, Laurel," he whispered in her ear.

Holding his arms, he felt her squeeze.

"You know, I've been considering a vacation to visit my family. But only if you come too."

She stiffened.

"Don't worry, they don't know anything about your past. All they know is we're dating, and I want you to meet them."

"Dev, I'm not ..." She looked more than a little concerned, her face shining in the dipping sun.

"Ready?"

She bit her lip and nodded.

"Then we'll wait."

"If you want to go, go." She frowned. "I don't need a babysitter."

"I'm not babysitting you." He groaned. "You know I hate

that. I love you, and I want to be here for you. Are you still not willing to accept that? That I *want* to be here?"

She pushed away. He let her have her space as he added wood to the fire pit. Starting the fire, he fed it until it glowed, crackled, and lit the area.

Upset with himself for getting so irritated, he settled on the blanket, and leaned back against an old stump. Laurel had been trying to find her footing, and his patience was admittedly spent. He felt so selfish for wanting more time with her, more everything. But after tonight, it was just another reminder that after almost three months, she was still out of her element.

Talking about anything was a struggle. Now she was talking twice a week with a therapist and apparently having some discussions with her uncle Chuck and Kendra. But the reminder tonight left him defeated. She still pushed at him, pushed just when he wanted to help.

She returned and sat next to him, wrapping her arms around her knees. He pulled her to him, draping an arm over her shoulders.

"I'm sorry, Dev. I do trust you."

"Look," he sighed and turned her to face him. "I'm the one lacking patience here. I don't want to push you, okay? I know I need to back off sometimes and I seem to—"

"Dev."

He looked up and frowned.

"Stop making excuses for me, okay?"

"It's not an excuse." He took her hand in his.

"It is. You do it all the time." She chuckled, surprising him. "I see it in your eyes even when you don't say anything. You want more, and you want me to stop pushing back. But it's just, it's a knee-jerk reaction, and I've been trying, really."

He nodded. "I know that."

"Okay, so, why the excuses? I don't blame you. I don't know how you don't get mad more often."

"I'm not wired that way. I don't get mad that easily." He

grinned. "Look, I get it. I ..." He nervously rubbed the back of his neck. "I heard your talk with Darrell when we were staying there."

"What?" Her eyes went wide.

"I was coming down the hall and heard my name. I just stopped. I wish you would've told me, but I do get it."

"I didn't want you to hear that." She bit her lip, ducking her head as she sighed. "That's the last thing. Dev, I don't see you like Walter and Guy, really."

"I understand. It's not me, it's the town, it's the department, it's the way I'm in charge. I guess that knowledge has been pushing me to make sure you see the difference too."

"This is really nice." She met his gaze. "The sunset, the fire, and everything."

"I was worried about the smell being too much."

She shook her head. "Other things seem to drown that out lately." She smirked and turned back to the fire.

Sighing, he pulled her back against his chest, leaned back, letting her rest against him as he wrapped his arms around her. Closing his eyes, he prayed that God would give him some clue, some path to take with her.

"Dev, how do you know what love is?"

His eyes popped open. Talk about an opening.

Sitting up, he leaned his head next to hers as he worked the words in his mind.

"Chuck said my mom loved Guy. He was good at one time," she whispered.

"I've heard that from several people." His jaw clenched.

"Then, if he loved my mom, why did he let everything happen?"

"I can't answer that." He sighed. "There are things in this life that pull at us, pull us away from God. Alcohol, drugs, other things can take our focus off Him. Guy got caught up in that."

"But what good is love if it can't stop that from happening?"

His heart dropped. "That won't happen with us."

"But what if it does?" She sighed and turned sideways to face him, gripping his knees. "My mom didn't know it would happen. How can I know? I don't even trust God yet, and Chuck said my mom was a Christian. So how can you say that?"

"Laurel, I can't guarantee nothing bad will happen, I can't." He pulled her hands up to his chest as he scooted closer. "All I can say is that I know in my heart, it won't happen like that to us."

She bit the inside of her cheek as her eyes searched his.

"It's not just love that makes this work. It's God. God is love. He created us out of love, He wants to be part of our lives because He loves us. He gave up His own son for us."

"I remember that ... John 3:16," she murmured.

"Mrs. Beecham did a good job."

"Dev, I do love you." She sighed. "It's as much as I can understand but I ... I'm not sure I know how to be together with someone, in any kind of romantic way."

"What does that mean?" Dev frowned.

She rolled her eyes.

"I'm trying to date you here. To have a future someday," he sighed and squeezed her hands.

"After everything." She studied him a moment in the shadow of the fire. "How can you even consider a future with me?"

His heart ached. She still had no idea.

"Because, I have faith that God has put me here to help you. To be with you, to show you what love is." He swallowed hard. "How do you see me, Laurel?"

"What do you mean?" Her brow furrowed.

"You once told me you want me to have more, that I deserve more."

She shrugged. "Yes, you do deserve more. I can't be ... I don't think I can be normal."

"Who wants normal?" he grinned as she shook her head.

"I want something more for you."

"Why?" He squeezed her hands.

Her gaze focused on his, watching intently. "Because I love you. I want you to be happy."

"Will that change?"

"No, it's not like that." She frowned. "I've not, this hasn't really happened to me before. I'm not taking it so lightly that I'll change my mind."

"Then you should know."

"Know what, Dev?" she sighed out his name, making him grin.

"We're both in this for good. Being in a relationship means you want more for your partner than you do for yourself. This is what it means to love. And when you do start to think about how God fits into that, it's much better. He helps you give that love even if you're hurt or frustrated. He fills the void and gives us the ability to love."

She leaned forward and kissed him, her fingers running across his cheek.

"What was that for?" he murmured, his thumb grazing across her bottom lip.

"I don't know." She shrugged. "I just ... I think you've got other things in mind and I..."

Dev chuckled. "Other things?" he sighed. "I'm not going to push you here. I've known you for, what? Three months? And in that time, you've dealt with more than anyone should. It's not like I've even decided I'm ready to jump to the next step." His fingers moved around hers, settling on her ring finger. Glancing down, he sighed.

"What are you doing?" she whispered.

"Just thinking." He smiled.

Wrapping her arms around his neck, she leaned into him as he pulled her in close, her sitting in his lap. There'd been few times they were this close. With all the time they'd spent together, he did what he could to keep above board. Besides, it was much too easy to get wrapped up in her, want more from her being so close.

"You've got something on your mind."

"A lot is on my mind." He chuckled and glanced down.

"Then tell me."

His jaw clenched a moment.

"Dev?"

Sighing, he let her go as she sat up in front of him, resting her hands against his chest as she watched him from just inches away.

"What do you want in this life?"

"What?" His eyebrow cocked as heat filled his face. "Why are you asking?"

She shrugged. "You ask me questions like that all the time. Tara asked me a while back, and I didn't really have an answer. I don't think I've ever wanted more because, I just figured it wouldn't happen."

"And now?"

"Happiness." Her bright eyes found his.

"I want that for you too." His heart pounded. "I think I can help you with that."

A small smile appeared on her lips, and he pulled her in for a slow kiss.

"Laurel?" He pushed the hair from her face, trailing a finger down her jaw. "Do you want to get married someday?"

She took a deep breath. "I don't think I would be very good at it," she whispered, a sheen covering her eyes.

"Why not?"

"I mean, I would want to, but I—" tears trailed down her cheeks. "Dev? I want you to be happy too."

Wrapping her up in a hug, he smiled. "You make me happy. In my whole life, I've never even considered marrying anyone, and in this short time with you, I'm thinking it sounds like a great idea."

"Me?" She sat back, wiping her face with wide eyes. "But I'm a mess."

"Not a mess. A work in progress. We all are. I'm not going to be perfect either. I think you've already seen that." He gave her a wink. Wrapping his arms around her waist, he studied her features in the firelight. "I love you, Laurel. I've never said that to anyone else, not like this. I told you that God put me here to find you. I think He put me here for another reason."

She swallowed hard, her fingers running across his collarbone, her eyes avoiding his.

"You're who He wanted me to meet, to fall in love with. I know you think this is all about you, but it's not. I need you much more than I realized. You've shown me what it means to genuinely love someone. How to care about others, what sacrifice really means. You ask me what I want, and I want you. Every day, all the time, forever."

Her body trembled in his arms and he finally caught her gaze.

"Would it be okay if someday I asked you to marry me?"

Her jaw clenched as her eyes bounced around his face. "You sure about that, Hollister?"

"Yeah, even if you do call me Hollister." He narrowed his eyes, letting a smirk out, then kissed her, finding himself ready for a future with this amazing woman.

EPILOGUE

"Laurel? You ready?"

Laurel sighed at Dev's voice echoing through the door.

"Can you tell him I need just a minute?" she muttered.

"Of course." Tara grinned and gave her wink. "By the way, his friend Bruce is single, right?"

She nodded and let out a chuckle. "Thanks," she whispered.

"Any time."

Tara took off out the door, and Laurel gripped her hands together, trying to ease her nerves. There would be only about ten people at the wedding, but she was already on a border-line panic attack.

Jesus, please give me some comfort and grace here.

Cracking the door, she saw Dev's back as he talked with Chuck.

"Dev?"

He turned and hurried over to her. "You okay?"

"I just ... I just ..."

"Just breathe." He pushed the door open and wrapped her up.

Burrowing into his neck, her arms slid around his waist, and she closed her eyes.

"Tara said you needed a minute."

"I'm not sure I can do this."

"You want me to bring the pastor in here?"

She smiled and shook her head.

After a few moments of silence, he kissed her cheek.

"Then we need to get out there and get married. Soon," he mumbled.

Leaning back, heat crept up her cheeks as he stared down at her.

"I ... I can't believe ..." he trailed off as a smile filled his face. "You look amazing. More than amazing," he muttered.

"Chuck was going to walk me out, and I guess ..." she didn't finish as he leaned down and kissed her gently.

"Then let's get moving. Because I want to finish that kiss later," he whispered.

"You sure about this, Hollister?"

"Never been more sure about anything in my life, soon-to-be Mrs. Hollister."

She edged a smile as her nerves eased off. "Then let's go."

Dev kissed her again, then with a groan, stepped through the door. He led her over to Chuck who eagerly waited at the doors of the sanctuary.

"See you in a bit," he whispered and kissed her head.

Taking a deep breath, she closed her eyes and took a few breaths.

"You've got a good man, Laurel."

"Yeah, I think so." She looked up at Chuck with a grin.

As the music started, the doors opened, and Dev's bright face took her breath. God saved Dev just for her. In all her life, she never had anyone want her more than Dev Hollister.

That peace washed over her soul as she let out a prayer.

Thank you for saving me when I finally believed in You, Jesus. Thank you for being there and giving me everything I could ever want on this earth.

COMING SOON FROM CINDY BONDS:

Book One of the Tactical Response Team (TRT)

Coming November 16, 2021 from Scrivenings Press.

scrivenings.link/tacticalresponseteam

Bexley Bowers has lost everything during her 30 years on earth. Struggling to find her path, she's targeted and kidnapped by a crazed terrorist.

Evan Mitchell retired from the Navy only to find himself back at work, clinging to his job with the Tactical Response Team. He meets Bexley while on assignment, and a strange tug on his emotions leaves him scrambling. Bexley is too stubborn and too beautiful. He'll never be able to get her out of his mind—especially now that he's her protection.

When Bexley finds herself in trouble once more, can Evan and his team arrive in time?

Fighting the clock and their pride, Evan and Bexley must decide which is more important—their egos or their future.

———————

Sneak Peek at the Tactical Response Team series book covers ...

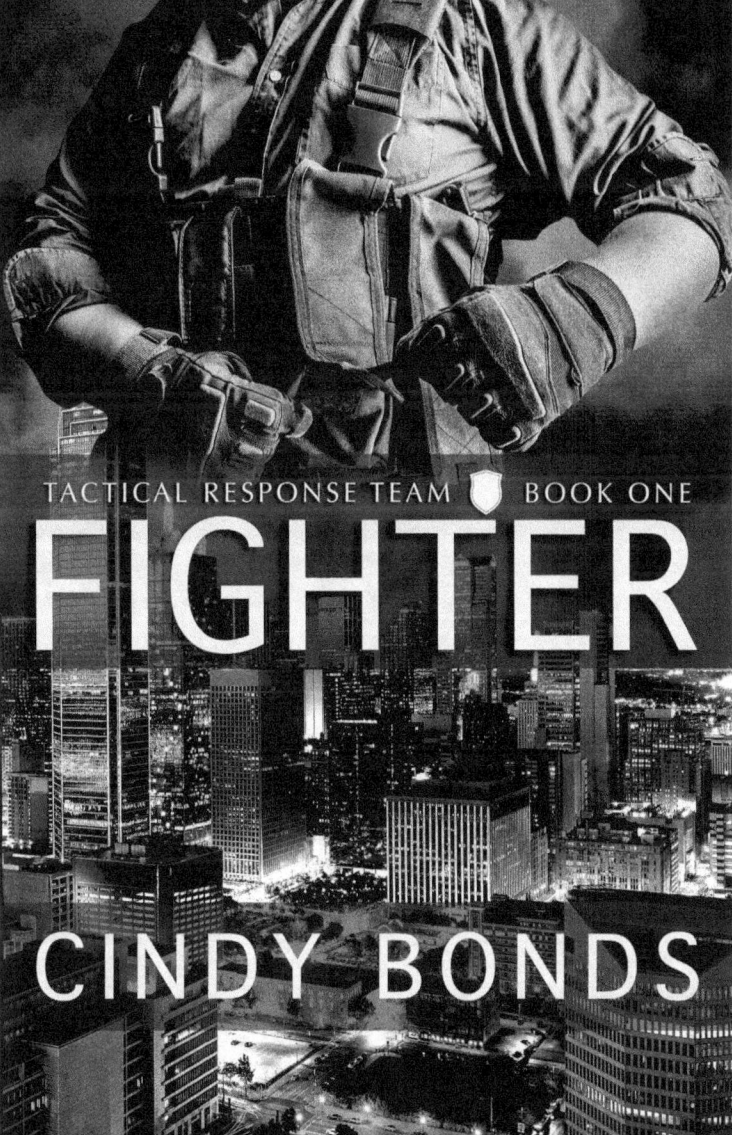

TACTICAL RESPONSE TEAM BOOK ONE

FIGHTER

CINDY BONDS

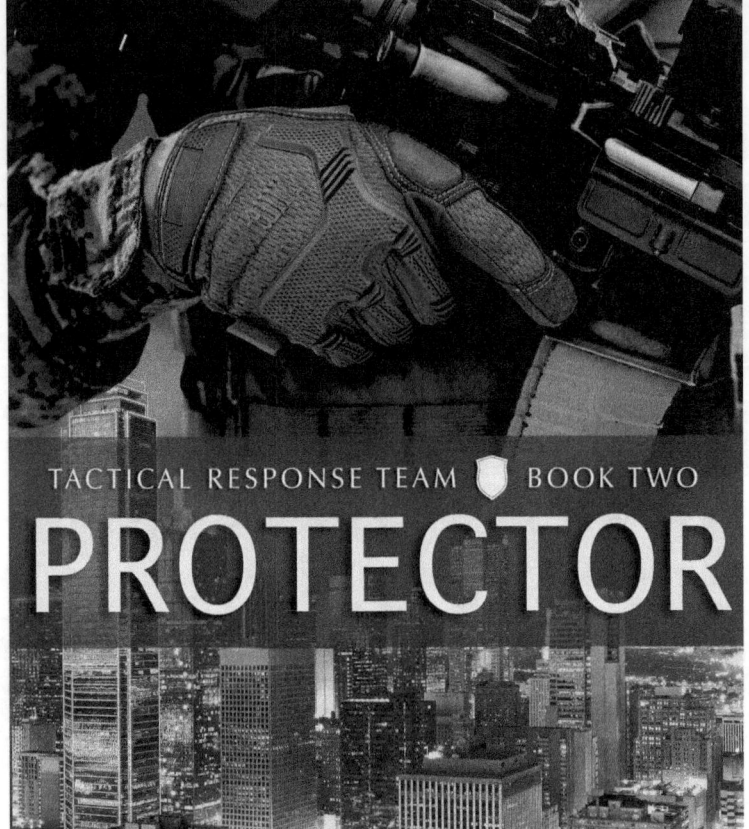

TACTICAL RESPONSE TEAM 🛡 BOOK TWO

PROTECTOR

CINDY BONDS

TACTICAL RESPONSE TEAM ⬥ BOOK THREE

SURVIVOR

CINDY BONDS

FIGHTER — PROLOGUE

"So, what'd they do to get asylum?"

Lieutenant Evan Mitchell frowned at Sergeant Rogers. "Not our concern. We just follow orders, Sergeant."

"Yes, sir."

Glancing at the trio walking ahead of him, he'd wondered the same thing.

The couple had a woman with them. She had to be older from the way she held her head, appearing unfazed by the danger they were in. A younger woman would be terrified to see men with guns raid their compound and escort them out of town.

But she seemed unaffected. Covered in a burka, only her eyes showed in the dim light. Big and piercing, they looked more determined than afraid.

Whoever they were, the U.S. government deemed them worthy enough for a SEAL team escort to American soil. They'd executed the entry without a hitch. If they could just get to the exfil without trouble ...

As they approached the helipad, Evan turned. That overwhelming feeling that had saved him and his team in the past told him they needed cover. *Now.*

A glint on the hillside three clicks away caught his attention. "Down! Everyone down!"

The tremendous wave threw him backward. His body slammed into a Humvee, knocking the wind from his lungs. Burned-out remnants of an assault vehicle, now in flames, sat in front of him. The smell of sulfur stifled his breath.

"Lieutenant!"

Evan gulped in air. "Protect the bird! Get them out of here!"

Small arms fire erupted. He righted himself and rushed to the defensive. Straining to see through blurred vision, he fired on the insurgents. The sound of another shell whistled through the air.

"Down!"

His team took cover just as the blast shook the ground. The roar of rotor blades drowned out the shouts and gunfire. Evan dove behind a vehicle and sprayed suppressive fire while the helicopter lifted and banked away.

"Sir? Where's the evac?"

"They'll be here! Stay at your position!"

The small arms fire ceased as the helicopter disappeared into the darkness. Evan steadied himself from his position and sucked in a deep breath, still shaky from the blast's impact.

"Sir?" A hand grabbed his arm.

Spots appeared. A wave of dizziness sent Evan to his knees.

The echoing sound of Rogers' voice rolled through his head as his world collapsed and went dark.

ABOUT THE AUTHOR

Cindy lives with her husband Garrett in rural Arkansas. They have two children, Conner and Kenzie, and are surrounded by farmland and cattle. With a full-time job, a part-time job and being a mom, carving time for her writing has become an art!

Cindy is a past semifinalist in the American Christian Fiction Writers (ACFW) Genesis award contest with her novel, *Hostage*.

She enjoys writing strong female characters and has a heart for military stories. Her creative streak a mile wide, she dabbles in photography, scrapbooking and anything else that lets her creativity loose!

ALSO BY CINDY BONDS

Hostage

Her confidence shot, Agent Macy Packer desperately wants to go back to her regular life, before she was taken hostage. To forget the pain, the fear and forget the man that helped her through all of it, then disappeared.

Kane Bledsoe is finally healed, his scars serving as a reminder of his time in captivity. But all he can think about is the blue-eyed woman that saved him. She had saved them all and left him with a burning hope.

A chance meeting and an attack prove Macy is still in danger. Kane pushes himself into the investigation, doing what he can to provide protection.

The enemy is clear, he wants Macy.

Kane will have to decide just how far he's willing to go to protect her. Can he sacrifice himself when the time comes?

scrivenings.link/hostage

———————————

MORE ROMANTIC SUSPENSE FROM SCRIVENINGS PRESS

Death of an Imposter

Trouble in Pleasant Valley

Book Two

Rookie detective Bernadette Santos has her first murder case. Will her desire for justice end up breaking her heart? Or worse—get her killed!

Her first week on the job and rookie detective Bernadette Santos has been given the murder of a prominent citizen to solve. But when her victim turns out to be an imposter, her straight forward case takes a nasty turn. One that involves the attractive Dr. Daniel O'Leary, a visitor to Pleasant Valley and a man harboring secrets.

When Dr. O'Leary becomes a target of violence himself, Detective Santos has two mysteries to unravel. Are they related? And how far can she trust the good doctor? Her heart tugs her one way while her mind pulls her another. She must discover the solutions before it's too late!

scrivenings.link/deathofanimposter

Deadly Guardian

Trouble in Pleasant Valley - Book One

When the men she dated begin dying, Madison Long must convince the police of her innocence and help them determine who has taken on the role of her guardian before he kills the only man she ever truly loved, Detective Nate Zuberi.

Madison Long, a high school chemistry teacher, looks forward to a relaxing summer break. Instead, she suffers through a nightmare of threats, terror, and death. When she finds a man murdered she once dated, Detective Nate Zuberi is assigned to the case, and in the midst of chaos, attraction blossoms into love.

Together, she and Nate search for her deadly guardian before he decides the only way to truly save her from what he considers a hurtful relationship is to kill her—and her policeman boyfriend as well.

scrivenings.link/deadlyguardian

Rescued Hearts

Mary Wade Kimball's soft spot for animals leads to a hostage situation when she spots a briar-entangled kitten in front of an abandoned house. Beaten, bound, and gagged, Mary Wade loses hope for escape.

Discovering the kidnapped woman ratchets the complications for undercover agent Brett Davis. Weighing the difference of ruining his three months' investigation against the woman's safety, Brett forsakes his mission and helps her escape the bent-on-revenge brutes following behind. When Mary Wade's safety is threatened once more, Brett rescues her again. This time, her personal safety isn't the only thing in jeopardy. Her heart is endangered as well.

scrivenings.link/rescuedhearts

Stay up-to-date on your favorite books and authors with our free e-newsletters.

ScriveningsPress.com